PRAISE FOR HERE IN ...

**LEGACY LANE**

You know that Robin Lee Hatcher is going to transport you to a new world with her gentle, emotionally charged writing style. Legacy Lane is another example of her enchanting voice... The second in this series, Veterans Way, comes out in 2005. I know I am anxiously awaiting it!— **Round Table Reviews**

Robin Lee Hatcher's books are much anticipated and justly so. Her characters are real, the plots interesting, and always, the story warms the readers heart. Legacy Lane is exactly the kind of book we expect from her. Warm, witty, sweet, and heartwarming, this first book in the Hart's Crossing series stokes our fires of anticipation for book number two! — **The Road to Romance**

**VETERANS WAY**

Robin Lee Hatcher has a way of touching the heart and mind. Her tender stories of love and faith go a long way in soothing the soul and the senses. And can't we all benefit from that from time to time? — **Once Upon a Romance**

In this second installment of Hart's Crossing, Hatcher writes a heartwarming story of unexpected love in the senior years. In Stephanie, the reader feels like they're visiting a favorite aunt. Great characterization is always one of this author's strong points. (4 Stars – Compelling, Page Turner) — **Romantic Times Bookclub Magazine**

## DIAMOND PLACE

This is a simple, sweet romance penned with Hatcher's customary knack for invoking emotions. It's the type of book that makes the reader want to live in a place such as Hart's Crossing, and they can do that with this endearing story. ~ **RT Book Reviews**

## SWEET DREAMS DRIVE

I really don't care much for novellas…not much bang for your buck. But I have to say that I adore the Hart's Crossing series by Robin Lee Hatcher…and each story is adorable. — **Deliciously Clean Reads**

This final novella in the Hart's Crossing series is as heartwarming as the first book was. Hatcher evoked some long forgotten emotions. Emotions from when I was like Patti—young and newly married and stressed out with the new baby. Patti and Al dance a hormonal waltz, until a purchase Patti makes brings it all to the surface. Poignant and endearing, Sweet Dreams Drive is highly recommended. — **Novel Reviews**

# HERE IN HART'S CROSSING
## FOUR CHARMING SMALL TOWN NOVELLAS

ROBIN LEE HATCHER

*Here in Hart's Crossing* Copyright © 2018 by RobinSong, Inc.
*Legacy Lane* © 2004
*Veterans Way* © 2005
*Diamond Place* © 2006
*Sweet Dreams Drive* © 2007
First RobinSong Inc. ebook editions, 2018

This is a work of fiction. Names, characters, places, and incidents are either the product of the author's imagination or are used fictitiously. Any resemblance to actual events, locales, organizations, or persons living or dead is entirely coincidental and beyond the intent of either the author or publisher.

All rights reserved. No part of this publication may be reproduced, stored in a retrieval system, or transmitted in any form or by any means—electronic, mechanical, photocopy, recording, or any other—except for brief quotations in printed reviews, without the prior permission of the publisher.

# LEGACY LANE

HART'S CROSSING #1

## CHAPTER 1

May 2005

*A*ngie Hunter stared out the tiny window of the Bombardier turboprop, keeping a death grip on the armrests as the plane bounced and dropped in the turbulent air above the snowy-white mountain range.

Oh, how she hated flying in a tin can. Give her a first class seat in a jumbo jet any day. Not that she'd had other options when she made her flight reservations. Only regional airlines flew into the airport nearest her destination, and those airlines used small planes like this one.

Maybe she should have driven from California to Idaho. It might have been nice to have her own automobile for the next eight weeks, and the trip could have been made in an easy two days.

"Don't be silly, dear," her mother, Francine Hunter, had said when they talked last week. "I have a perfectly good car, and I won't be driving anywhere for quite some time."

*I must be out of my mind.*

In the seventeen years since Angie left Idaho, she'd returned infrequently and never stayed longer than three nights at a stretch. While earning her degree, she'd taken summer jobs near the university. Part-time employees didn't get vacations, so the occasional long weekend was all she could manage back then. As an adult, she'd had the demands of her job as a reason to rush back to the city.

"I'll go stark raving mad before this is over," she whispered to her faint reflection in the window. "What have I let myself in for?"

The whine of the engines changed as the plane began its approach. Angie felt her stomach tighten.

The flight attendant, a perky twenty-something blonde in maroon Bermuda shorts and a white blouse, began her landing announcements: Fasten seat belts. Make sure seats are in fully upright position. Turn off electronic devices. Stow all luggage. No smoking until in a designated smoking area in the terminal. No mobile phones until cabin door opens. Enjoy your stay. Thanks for flying today.

With the rough air seemingly behind them, Angie loosened her grip on the armrests. The flight attendant made a final pass down the aisle. She smiled at Angie when she reached her row.

*Sure, you can smile, Miss Perk. You'll be flying out again in another hour or so. I'm stuck here for the next two months!*

Angie drew in a deep breath and released it slowly. She should be ashamed. After all, her mother needed her. Eight weeks wasn't going to kill her.

*And it's not like I have a lot to hurry back to.*

She winced at the thought.

Ten minutes later the plane touched down, quickly slowed, and taxied toward the terminal. Angie glanced out the window. The terminal was a single-story building; there were no Jetways. The passengers of this plane would descend the narrow steps built into the cabin door, then walk across the tarmac. Thankfully, it wasn't raining.

As the plane braked to a halt, the clicking of opening seat belts filled the cabin even before the seat belt sign dimmed. Angie reached for her purse and carry-on bag beneath the seat in front of her. When she stood, she cracked her head against the overhead compartment.

Oh, how she hated these small commuter planes.

Oh, how she hated everything about her life at the moment.

∼

STANDING BETWEEN JOHN GUNN ON HER LEFT AND TERRI AND Lyssa Sampson on her right, Francine Hunter raised up on tiptoes. Her heart raced in anticipation of that first glimpse of her daughter. Francine was almost glad she was scheduled to have knee surgery. Otherwise, who knew when Angie would have found time to return to Hart's Crossing. Angie's job at her big city newspaper was important and demanding; she hadn't taken a vacation in over five years. Or was it more than six? And a serious boyfriend hadn't been in the picture for Well, too long, as far as Francine was concerned.

"There she is!" Terri—Angie's friend since kindergarten —exclaimed.

Angie walked toward them, looking like a model in one of those glossy fashion magazines. She wore a sky blue blouse tucked into a pair of skinny jeans that fit her long, slender legs like a glove. Her thick, dark hair fell loose to her shoulders, where it flipped up on the ends.

"Hi, Mom," Angie said as soon as she'd cleared the security area.

Francine kissed her daughter's cheeks, first one side, then the other. "It's so good to see you, dear. How was your flight?"

"Don't ask." Angie turned toward Terri. "I didn't expect to see you here."

"Are you kidding?" Terri replied. "I couldn't miss your homecoming."

Softly, Angie said, "It's not a homecoming, Terri. Just a visit. Just until Mom's back on her feet."

There were volumes of meaning behind those simple words that Francine wasn't meant to hear but did.

*O God*, she prayed, *help us find a way back to one another. Help Angie find her way to you. Make these weeks she's here with me be a new beginning for us.*

Terri glanced at the child beside her. "Angie, you remember Lyssa."

"You're kidding!" Angie's eyes widened in surprise, and she shook her head. "This can't be your daughter. She wasn't this tall the last time I saw her."

"Kids grow a lot in four years, Ang. Lyssa was five last time you breezed through town. Now she's nine." Terri softened her not-so-subtle rebuke by adding, "We miss you when we don't see you. E-mails and phone calls just aren't enough."

Francine decided now would be a good time to interrupt. "Angie, you haven't met our church's new pastor, John Gunn. Pastor, this is my daughter, Angie."

"A pleasure to meet you, Angie. Your mother has told me a lot about you."

"All good, I hope." Angie smiled politely as she shook the pastor's proffered hand. "It's nice to meet you, too."

"I offered to drive your mother down here in my SUV," John said. "She wasn't sure how much luggage you'd have and was afraid it wouldn't fit into her trunk."

"I didn't bring a lot."

Francine touched her daughter's forearm. "Well, let's go get what you did bring, shall we?" She didn't want to say so, but she needed to get off her leg. Her bad knee was throbbing something fierce.

"Ang," Terri said, "why don't you and Pastor John get your luggage while Lyssa and I take your mom to the car."

"Sure. That's fine with me."

John handed the keys to his vehicle to Terri before walking with Angie toward the baggage claim area.

"You hold on to me, Mrs. Hunter." Terri tucked Francine's hand into the crook of her arm. "We'll get you to the car and off that leg."

"Thank you, dear. I didn't want to make a fuss and spoil Angie's arrival, but I am hurting a bit." Gratefully, she leaned into Terri and allowed herself to be helped outside.

∽

Their destination was about an hour's drive from the airport, but the time passed quickly, aided by Terri's efforts to catch Angie up on all the latest news of the folks of Hart's Crossing. As owner-operator of Terri's Tangles Beauty Salon, she was in a good position to know, perhaps even better than Bill Palmer, the editor of the local weekly newspaper, the *Mountain View Press*.

Headed toward the rugged mountain range to the north, they drove through farmland that had been reclaimed from the high desert country of southern Idaho. An abundance of horses and cows grazed in pastures turned emerald green by irrigation. Tall poplars shaded old farmhouses and barns that had been bleached over the years by the relentless summer sun.

At last, John Gunn slowed his Ford Expedition as the two-lane highway topped a rise, then spilled into Hart's Crossing's Main Street. Of course, the heart of downtown was all of three blocks long. Blink and you'd miss it.

Several people sat on benches outside the Over the Rainbow Diner, licking ice cream cones and enjoying the mild spring evening. Two women pushing strollers gazed through the window of Yvonne's Gifts and Boutique. The Apollo Movie Theater's marquee flickered and sputtered, as if it couldn't decide whether to stay on or off; Angie noticed the film they would show this Friday and Saturday was at least a decade old.

A typical Monday evening in Hart's Crossing where there was nothing much to do.

"It looks the same as ever," she said softly.

John Gunn chuckled. "You'd be surprised. I think you'll find lots of changes, thanks to our mayor and the city council."

His comment irritated Angie. She was the one who'd grown up in this town, not him. She certainly knew better than he did if things were different or the same. Glancing at the driver, she said, "Well, *you're* new. I know that much."

If he thought her rude, he didn't let on. "Indeed. Relatively so, anyway."

Rather than say something she would regret later, Angie looked out the passenger window again, staring through the glass as they followed the familiar route from the center of town to her mother's home.

*Eight weeks. I can survive anything for eight weeks.*

## CHAPTER 2

Angie panicked when she saw sunlight filtering through the curtains. She'd overslept. She'd be late for work.

She tossed aside the bed coverings and sat up. Only when her feet touched the plush, Barbie-pink throw rug did she remember she was in her girlhood bedroom. She also remembered she no longer had a job to be late for. She'd quit last week. Packed up all her personal belongings in a cardboard box and stormed out of the building in a snit.

With a groan, she pressed the heels of her hands against her eyes. What a mess! How could everything have gone so wrong so fast?

Angie had given the *Bay City Times* 150 percent from her first day on the job. She'd routinely put in sixty, seventy, eighty hour work weeks. She hadn't taken a day off or called in sick in years. Social life? Forget it. She had none. She couldn't remember the name of her last boyfriend. She'd eaten, slept, and breathed the newspaper. But she'd been willing to sacrifice anything and everything, especially after she'd been promised Mr. Stattner's position at the paper when he retired as city editor.

Well, not promised but given reason to believe. It was what she'd worked toward for more than a decade.

Last week, she'd been passed over by management. They'd given the position to Brad Wentworth—that was the last straw. When Brad "The Jerk" Wentworth was made city editor over her, she was outta there.

Brad actually had the nerve to call and ask her to reconsider. "Come in tomorrow and let's talk, Angie. Don't throw away your career over this. There'll be other openings down the road."

"I can't," she'd told him. "My mother is scheduled for surgery, and I'm flying to Idaho on Monday to be with her while she recovers."

Of course, she hadn't *planned* to come back to Hart's Crossing. Not at first. What she'd really meant to do was hire a nurse for the duration of her mother's convalescence. But losing that promotion had changed everything, and now here she was.

Angie stood and reached for her robe. If she wasn't mistaken, the scent of coffee brewing was wafting through her bedroom door. She padded down the stairs on bare feet in search of her morning dose of caffeine.

Angie found her mother seated at the kitchen table, reading the latest edition of the *Mountain View Press*. "Morning, Mom," she mumbled, making a beeline for the mug tree beside the coffeepot.

"Good morning, dear. I didn't expect you to be up this early. Would you like me to make you some breakfast?"

"No, thanks. I rarely eat this early."

"Not good for you, you know." Her mother folded the paper and set it on the table. "As hard as you work and as many hours as you put in at that office every day, you need to start off the day right."

"Well, I'm not putting in a lot of hours at the office now." Angie turned, leaned her backside against the counter, and took her first sip. "Mmm. What's your secret? You've always made the best coffee. You could charge over four bucks a cup for this where I live."

"Thank you, dear, but there's really no secret to it. I just follow the directions on the coffeemaker." Her mother smiled and released a happy-sounding sigh. "Oh, it's so good to have you home again."

*Home again*

Angie let her gaze roam around the kitchen. It hadn't changed much through the years. It was still painted bright yellow, and as always, there were white and yellow curtains at the window over the sink, although the pattern was different from what she remembered. The Formica table with its chrome legs and the matching chairs with their plastic-covered seats and backs, straight out of the fifties, were like old friends. The mixer and mixing bowl on the counter were the same ones her mother had used when Angie was growing up. So were the canisters and the Princess wall phone.

Francine Hunter didn't throw away much.

Unlike her daughter, who was a card-carrying member of the use and discard generation.

*Or I was until last week. That could all change if I don't find the right job at the right salary.*

But that was unlikely. Angie had an excellent work history and all the right qualifications. She would probably find a new job before she'd even used up her accumulated vacation days. All she needed to do while she was here in Hart's Crossing was search the Internet for openings and send out resumes.

"Is there anything special you'd like to do today?" her mother asked, drawing Angie from her thoughts.

"Not particularly." The day stretched before her like an eternity. When was the last time she'd had nothing scheduled in her day planner? She wasn't much good at being idle. Actually, she wasn't much good at relaxing. Period.

"Why don't you call Terri and see if the two of you can go to lunch? She takes Mondays and Tuesdays off from the salon, and Lyssa will be in school. You should enjoy yourself for a couple of days before my surgery. After that, you'll have your hands full."

Angie swept the hair back from her face with one hand. "Yeah, maybe I'll do that. Are you sure you don't mind?"

"Of course not, dear. I'll have your company for the next eight weeks." She smiled again. "And I'm so thankful to the Lord for that."

Angie nodded as she turned to pour herself another cup of coffee. She'd learned it was better to remain silent when her mother started talking about God.

∽

Lord, Francine prayed as she stared at her daughter's back, *please break down that wall. It's been up between us for much too long.*

Francine's memories of Angie's early childhood years were happy ones. Her husband, Ned, had been an insurance salesman. An excellent one, too. He'd loved what he did, loved helping people plan for secure futures. Francine had been a stay-at-home mom, leading Brownies and driving her daughter to piano lessons and dance lessons and baking cookies for the baked food drives. They'd taken a two-week family vacation every summer. One year it was to the Pacific coast, another year to the Atlantic. They'd seen Mount Rushmore and Niagara Falls and Bryce Canyon and the mighty Mississippi River from one end to the other.

Ned had died in a car accident when Angie was twelve. The years that immediately followed had been hard for mother and daughter. Not financially, for Ned had provided well for his loved ones, a fine example of a man practicing what he preached. But emotionally, they'd walked a difficult path, dealing with grief combined with the normal stresses that came with a girl's teenage years.

Then, at the age of forty-four, Francine Hunter had fallen in love with Jesus, and it had changed her forever. The Hunters had been a churchgoing family, like most folks in Hart's Crossing, but Francine had suddenly discovered Jesus wasn't merely an example for her to live by, that the words in the Bible weren't just good stories. Jesus was real and he was alive and he loved her. Loved her so much he not only died for her but rose for her.

Once Francine had "seen the light" for herself, she'd tried to make her daughter see it, too. She'd preached at her and prayed over her and tried to fix her in countless ways—the majority of them wrong ways. She'd pushed and shoved and offended. She'd cajoled and lectured. Her heart had been right, but her actions had been all wrong.

And in her zeal for Jesus, she'd driven her daughter away, first from the church and then from Francine herself.

*Oh Lord, make her hungry for you. I don't care how. Just make her hungry.*

∼

THE HOMES IN THE HUNTER NEIGHBORHOOD HAD BEEN BUILT IN the early 1900s. Most of them were two stories with front porches—some screened-in, some open-air—but each house had a distinct personality all its own. The front yards were small patches of green, cut short by the sidewalk, a sidewalk rippled in places by the roots of the large maple trees that lined both sides of the street.

As Angie walked toward town later that morning, she remembered the many times she'd ridden her bicycle along this tree-shaded thoroughfare or skated down this sidewalk, trying her best to avoid the cracks and breaks in the cement. Terri

Sampson—her last name had been Moser then—had lived across the street, and she and Angie had been inseparable. They'd had camp outs and slumber parties. They'd gone swimming together and ridden horses together and, as crazy teenagers, skipped school together. And they'd pulled more pranks on unsuspecting family members and friends than either of them could count.

Angie smiled at the memories.

"Angie Hunter? Is that you?"

She halted and looked toward the street. A white Jeep had stopped, and the driver, an attractive woman with short brown hair, leaned out the window, grinning broadly. She looked familiar but

"It's Cathy Lambert, used to be Cathy Foster."

"Cathy Foster?" Angie echoed. "Good grief. I don't believe it." She walked toward the Jeep. "How long has it been?"

"Since high school graduation. Why don't you come to the class reunions?"

Angie shrugged but ignored the question. "Are you visiting your folks?"

"No, my husband and I live here now." Cathy cut the engine, obviously unconcerned about interrupting traffic by parking in the middle of the street.

"You moved back to Hart's Crossing? But I heard you were living in the east somewhere. Boston, wasn't it?"

"No, Philadelphia. That's where my husband is from. But with our kids getting older, I convinced Clay to give my hometown a try. It's a better environment for raising a family."

Angie supposed she should know Cathy had children. Her mother had probably told her when each one was born.

"So what finally brought you for a visit, Angie?"

"Mom's having surgery. I'm going to look after her for a couple of months."

"A couple months? But that's wonderful. Clay and I will have you over for a barbecue. I'd love for you to meet him and the kids. Cait's a young woman at fifteen and Cassidy just turned thirteen. I told Cory he doesn't get to grow up as fast as his sisters have."

Clay. Cait. Cassidy. Cory. Angie's head was swimming. "And how old is Cory?"

"Seven, and he's all boy." Cathy glanced at her wristwatch. "Oh no. I'm going to be late for my next appointment. Gotta run." She started the Jeep. "I'll give you a call at your mom's."

Angie stepped back, and Cathy drove away, waving out the window as she went.

∽

"CATHY AND HER HUSBAND ARE DENTISTS," TERRI TOLD ANGIE as they settled into a booth at the Over the Rainbow Diner. "But you knew that, right? When they moved to Hart's Crossing, they built a new office right next to the medical clinic. Sawtooth Dentistry." She laughed. "They named it after the mountain range, but I still think it sounds funny."

"She's the last person I thought would move back to Hart's Crossing."

"No, Ang. You're the last person anybody'd think that of." Terri leaned forward, her smile fading. "But I'd love to see it happen. How about it? Aren't you ready to give up that crazy career of yours and settle down? Get married and have a family like the rest of us?"

"It's tough to get married if I can't find the right guy."

"Have you been looking?"

Angie raised an eyebrow. "Have you?"

Terri simply smiled again. "You bet I'm looking."

"After what Vic did to you, I wouldn't think you'd ever want—"

Terri touched the back of Angie's hand, then shook her head.

"Sorry," Angie said softly.

"Remember that old Osmond tune, 'One Bad Apple'? Well, it's true, Ang. One bad apple doesn't spoil the whole bunch. Vic was Vic. He cheated on me, and it hurt when he left us." Terri gave her head another slow shake. "It hurts even more that he hasn't made any effort to contact Lyssa in over six years." She leaned toward Angie. "But the Lord's looking out for us. I hope I can find the right guy, the one God means for me to marry. One day, I hope Prince Charming will ride into town and sweep me off my feet." She grinned. "There. I said it. I'm a romantic. Go on and make fun of me."

Angie didn't feel like making fun of her friend. In fact, she felt somewhat envious of Terri's hopes for the future, although she wouldn't admit it aloud. Thankfully, Nancy Raney arrived, putting an end to their conversation.

"How are you girls?" Nancy slipped an order pad and pen from the pocket of her pastel-striped apron. Then to Angie, she said, "Real nice to see you back in town."

"Thanks, Nancy."

"You two know what you want?"

"I'll have a cheeseburger," Terri answered. "With fries and a Diet Coke."

"Sounds good." Angie knew she'd regret it next time she got on the scales. But hey, she didn't have a job—or a man—to stay thin for. "Make mine the same, with a slice of lemon in the Diet Coke."

"Gotcha. I'll bring your drinks right out." Nancy turned and headed for the kitchen.

"So," Terri said, "how will that paper survive without you for the next eight weeks?"

Angie shredded the edge of her paper napkin. "They'll have to do it for longer than that." She glanced up. "I quit last week."

Terri's eyes widened. "You quit?"

"Yeah."

"Your mom didn't say a word."

"Mom doesn't know. I haven't told her. She thinks I'm using up some of my vacation." Angie shrugged. "It's sort of the truth. I am drawing my vacation pay. I had a lot of time saved up."

"Wow. I don't know what to say. I'm shocked."

"Me, too. I haven't been unemployed since I was a teenager."

"Well, at least now you can stay in Hart's Crossing a little longer. Take some time to relax a bit. Hey, maybe you could stay for good."

"Stay?" Angie leaned her back against the upholstered booth. "And do what? What would I do around here for employment?"

"I don't know. Get a job reporting for the *Press*. Write that novel you used to talk about all the time. Flip burgers at the drive-in if you had to."

"Very funny."

Terri's voice softened. "I wasn't trying to be funny. Give it some thought, will you? You belong here. I don't think you've been truly happy since the day you moved away."

## CHAPTER 3

*"I don't think you've been truly happy since the day you moved away."*

What an absurd thing for Terri to say. Angie had been very happy since leaving Hart's Crossing. She'd gone to college. She'd excelled in her career. She'd experienced exciting things and seen exciting places during the years she'd worked as a foreign correspondent, and she loved absolutely everything about big city living.

Okay, maybe not the traffic during commute hours, but everything else.

Well, maybe not *everything* else, but almost.

"At least I could get a skinny vanilla latte whenever I wanted one," she muttered the next morning as she stared at the coffeemaker, impatiently waiting for the brewing cycle to end.

"What was that, dear?"

"Nothing, Mom. Just talking to myself."

Francine Hunter chuckled. "You're much too young for that habit."

"Not really."

"Perhaps it's the writer in you. You've always had a creative spirit. Always had so much going on inside that head of yours. You're like your father in that regard, and he used to talk to himself all the time."

"Did he?" Angie filled two ceramic mugs with coffee and carried them to the table, setting one in front of her mother. "There you go."

"Thanks, dear." Her mother added a spoonful of sugar and stirred it. "What's on your agenda for the day?"

"I'm not sure. I guess I'll do some work on the Internet if you don't mind me tying up the phone line for a while." She tapped a fingernail against the tabletop. "Maybe I should order cable service."

"Heavens, no!" Her mother shot her a horrified look. "There's nothing worth watching on the channels we have now. Why pay for more worthless shows?"

"I meant cable Internet service. It won't tie up the phone line when I'm on the computer, and it's about twenty times faster than most dial-ups."

"Fast. Faster. Fastest. Everybody's in such a hurry these days." Francine took a sip of coffee. After a moment she said, "How difficult it must be for today's generation to obey the Scripture that says, 'Be still, and know that I am God.' Nobody seems to know how to be still anymore. Everyone's so busy. What's the term that means a person's trying to do about six things at once?"

"I think you mean multitasking."

"Yes, that's it. Multitasking. It's a dreadful word, isn't it?"

Angie opened her mouth to disagree, then closed it again. Maybe her mother was right. Maybe it was a dreadful word. Just because she'd spent the past seventeen years multitasking every part of her life didn't mean it was a good thing.

"I don't think you've been truly happy since the day you moved away."

"Dear," Francine said, interrupting Angie's thoughts, "you do whatever you wish about the cable thing. I'm sure you'll need to check in with your office occasionally, and if cable or whatever will help you, you should have it. I don't want your stay with me to be an inconvenience to you."

Angie couldn't put it off any longer. This was the perfect opportunity to tell her mother that she was unemployed. "Mom, I—"

She was saved by the proverbial bell. This one, the front doorbell.

"I wonder who that could be this early in the day." Francine rose from her chair. "Excuse me while I see."

As she sipped her coffee, Angie wondered why she was reluctant to tell her mother she'd quit her job. For that matter, why was she reluctant to share much of anything about her life?

"When did we stop talking?" she whispered. Then she shook her head. "When did *I* stop talking?" Before she could seek an answer to those questions, her mother returned, followed by their visitor.

"Look who's come to see you, Angie."

Peeking around Francine's back, Till Hart grinned, the smile deepening the creases in her wizened face. "Land sakes alive. Aren't you a sight for sore eyes?"

Till Hart, petite and spry at seventy-five years old, was the never-married granddaughter of the town's founding father. She was the sort of person who'd never known a stranger, especially not in Hart's Crossing. She, in turn, was beloved by everyone who knew her.

"Miss Hart." Angie got to her feet. She was about to offer her hand, but before she could, Till stepped forward and embraced her.

"It's been too long since you were home." After a second tight squeeze—the woman was surprisingly strong for one so slight in stature and advanced in years—Till released her and stepped back, searching Angie's face with her gaze. "Too long." She lowered her voice. "Your mother misses you, you know. Use this time well. We can never get yesterday back. Take it from someone who's wasted a yesterday or two."

Angie felt a sting of guilt.

Francine stepped toward the kitchen counter. "Till, would you like some coffee?"

"No, thank you, Frani. I'm out for my morning constitutional, and I mustn't stay. I just wanted to say hello to your daughter while I was in the neighborhood." She patted Angie's shoulder. "You come see me, and we'll have ourselves a nice chat." As sweetly spoken as the words were, they seemed more command than invitation.

"I will, Miss Hart."

"Good. Well, I'm off." She flicked a hand in the air, half-wave, half-salute, then turned and headed for the front door, calling behind her, "Don't forget your promise, Angie. You come see me." Seconds later, the front door closed behind her.

Francine chuckled as she settled onto her chair once again. "I swear, Till's a force of nature. She'll never change."

Angie was strangely comforted by her mother's comment. She didn't want Miss Hart to change. Then she realized she was equally as comforted by the belief that her mother would never change either.

How surprising.

~

TERRI MARKED OFF ANOTHER DAY ON THE LIST. "THAT TAKES CARE of three weeks of meals for the Hunters," she told Anne Gunn. "One more week should do it."

Anne, the pastor's wife, arched an eyebrow as she leaned back in her chair. "How much food do you think two women will eat? You may be overplanning a bit."

"Hmm. Maybe you're right. As thin as Angie is, she won't eat much, and Francine isn't likely to have a large appetite right after surgery. Maybe I should start over, plan for meals to be delivered every other day."

Anne nodded. "I think so."

Terri ripped off the yellow sheet of paper from the pad and drew a new grid. Then she began rearranging the names and dates.

"I'm looking forward to meeting Angie at church on Sunday. I've heard a lot about her from her mother since we came to Hart's Crossing." Anne turned her glass of iced tea in a circle between her fingers. "John said she and Francine will drive down to Twin Falls Sunday afternoon so they can be at the hospital early Monday morning."

"I wouldn't count on Angie being in church, Anne."

"Why not?"

Terri looked at the pastor's wife. "She says religion isn't for her." Seeing the questions in Anne's eyes, she gave a little shrug and set down her pen. "Lots of reasons, I suppose. Mostly, she's too busy for God. She's very self-sufficient and likes to be in control. Besides, she's always thought her mom went off the deep end when we were in high school. Francine *was* a changed woman after she accepted Christ."

"As we all are. Or at least we're supposed to be."

"Yes." Terri nodded, remembering the moment she gave her heart to the Lord and how the whole world seemed to change in an instant. "But Francine … Well, she was determined her daughter would see the light. She sort of hit Angie over the head with the gospel on a regular basis."

"Ah."

"A year or so later, Angie left home for college. By then, she'd closed her mind to anything her mom said about her faith. It's created a tension between them ever since." She picked up her pen again. "I keep praying Angie will come to understand that

Christianity isn't about a religion but about a relationship with Jesus. The same way I did." She smiled. "No doubt she thinks I went off the deep end, too."

Anne Gunn returned the smile. "No doubt."

∽

WHILE ANGIE WAS AT THE MARKET, BUYING A FEW GROCERY AND sundry items, Francine climbed the stairs slowly, carrying a stack of folded towels in her arms. After placing them in the linen closet in the upstairs bathroom, she went to Angie's bedroom, pausing in the open doorway. The room was tidy, the bed made, the desk and dresser tops free of clutter. In truth, there was little evidence anyone was staying in the room except for the suitcases tucked underneath the bed, peeking from beneath the pink and white gingham bed skirt.

Of course, her daughter's room hadn't always been this neat. Angie had been a typical teenager in most regards. Posters on the walls. Loud music blaring from her stereo or boom box or whatever the kids had called them in those days. Clothes scattered on the floor, despite Francine's relentless nagging.

She sighed as her thoughts drifted back through time, back before Angie's teenage years, back to when Francine's husband was still living and their daughter was carefree. They'd been a happy family, signs of affection displayed frequently and for all to see. And Angie had been such a delightful child.

Things had begun to change with Angie following Ned's death, but Francine didn't know how much of what went on had been the norm for teenagers and how much had been in reaction to losing her dad.

*Thank you, Lord, for the years of love Angie and I shared with her father. Now please help Angie catch a glimpse of you in these weeks she's at home with me.*

She turned away from the bedroom and started down the stairs, holding onto the handrail as she went.

*And Lord, if it wouldn't be asking too much, I would so love to see her happily married and providing me a grandchild or two.*

## CHAPTER 4

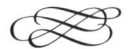

On Thursday, Angie phoned in the order for a cable Internet connection. The installer would come out the next morning to do the wiring, she was told. This surprised her. She'd expected to have to wait a week or more.

Excited by the prospect of being able to start her job hunt earlier than anticipated, she set up her laptop and portable printer on the desk in her bedroom, the one she'd used in high school. Oh, the things that old desk had seen. Many a night she'd opened her diary and poured out her dreams onto its pages, writing in bold, bright colors. She'd written about places she wanted to visit and things she wanted to accomplish. She'd even written about the sort of man she would one day marry.

She shook her head. Now *there* was a pipe dream. All the good men had been taken long before she started looking. She'd wanted to be established in her career before she contemplated marriage, but then...

Feeling suddenly restless, she grabbed her purse from the top of her dresser and left the bedroom. She found her mother dozing in the easy chair in the living room. Not wanting to wake her, she turned to leave.

"What is it, dear?" Francine asked softly.

"Sorry, Mom. Didn't mean to disturb you."

"You didn't. I was only resting my eyes. Did you need something?"

"No. I'm going into town to buy some printer paper. Do you want me to pick anything up?"

Francine shook her head as her eyes drifted closed again. "No, thank you, dear." She drew a deep breath and let it out. "I put the car keys on the rack beside the back door."

"I think I'll walk. I need the exercise."

"Whatever you like, dear."

Angie realized suddenly that her mother looked her age. Not old, exactly, but aging. Unlike the sixty-something women of Angie's acquaintance who had their faces lifted and peeled on a regular basis, Francine Hunter looked natural. Normal. Comfortable in her own skin.

*Peaceful.*

Angie felt an odd tug at her heart. For a moment, she was tempted to explore the feeling, to see what had caused it and what it might mean. But she didn't. Introspection and self-analyzing were for people who had little else to do with their time. Angie was a woman of action, always busy. Always.

She quickly left the house, almost as if pursued.

Angie's trip to the drugstore—the most likely place in town to find the office supplies she wanted—took her past the elementary school, the Big Burger Drive-In, the Elk's Lodge, Suds Bar and Grill, Tin Pan Alley Bowling Lanes, Smith's Market, Hart's Crossing Community Church, Shepherd of the Valley Lutheran Church, White Cloud Medical Clinic, Sawtooth Dentistry, and both the junior and senior high schools. Angie managed to make it all that way without anyone stopping to say how good it was to see her back in town.

Her luck didn't last once she was inside Main Street Drug.

She turned a corner into an aisle and ran right into Bill Palmer. Literally.

"Whoa!" he said as he grabbed her shoulders to steady her. A moment later, his brown eyes widened. "Angie?"

"Hello, Bill." She took a step back. "How are you?"

"I'm great." He looked her up and down, his gaze not discourteous but definitely intense. "No need to ask how you're doing. You look fabulous."

A flush warmed her cheeks. "Thanks."

As a freshman in high school, Angie'd had a bad crush on Bill Palmer, the handsome senior class president. From afar, of course. He hadn't known she existed.

"So you're here to look after your mom while she's recuperating. The surgery's next Monday, right?"

"Yes." *I guess nothing's ever private in a place like Hart's Crossing.* She didn't know the half of it.

"I heard Brad Wentworth got the city editor position at the *Bay City Times.*"

Angie felt the color drain from her face. "How did you know that?"

"It's a small world. E-mails zip across the country in seconds. Editors talk."

She released a soft groan.

"Yeah. That's how I feel about Wentworth. I've met him several times over the years, and I think he's kind of a ... Well, he's sort of a—"

"Jerk," she finished for him.

Bill laughed so loud everyone in the store turned their heads. "Exactly the word I was looking for," he said when he brought his mirth under control and could speak again. Then he lowered his voice. "Do you think you'll be able to work with him, feeling the way you do?"

"No." She drew a deep breath. "I quit before coming here."

This was information Bill hadn't gleaned through his editorial network. His surprised expression told her so. She found some satisfaction in that, at least.

He recovered quickly enough. "Ever think of working for a small town paper?" His mouth curved into a grin. "I could put you to work at the *Press*."

Funny. Working for a small town newspaper like the *Mountain View Press* was the absolute last thing Angie had ever wanted to do. But right then she couldn't for the life of her remember why.

∽

BILL PALMER LOOKED INTO ANGIE'S GOLD-FLECKED HAZEL EYES and suspected he was a goner. It wasn't as if he'd never looked into them before. He'd grown up in this town with Angie, had seen her at community functions while they were still in school, and had run into her on her infrequent visits to see her mother after she'd left home. But suddenly, standing there in aisle four of Main Street Drug, Bill *really* saw her.

For one moment, he thought he detected a glimmer of interest in her eyes, but then she told him she had to hurry back home. Something about lots of work awaiting her. Then she grabbed a ream of paper off a nearby shelf, said good-bye, and hurried away.

*Wow! What do you think of that?*

Bill's closest friends knew he was a romantic, and in a town the size of Hart's Crossing, he doubted there was anyone who didn't know he'd like to marry and have kids of his own. But even more than that, he wanted to marry the right woman. He wanted a marriage that was blessed by God. So he'd waited.

Something in his heart told him his waiting might be over.

∽

Terri Sampson stood in front of the mirror and stared at her reflection as she swept her curly red hair off her neck. As summer approached, it was tempting to cut it short. But she wouldn't. Short hair made her resemble a wire brush that had gone to rust.

The bell over the salon door jingled, and Terri released her hair and turned, thinking her next appointment had arrived early. But it was Bill Palmer.

"Hey," she said in greeting.

"Hey, yourself."

After Terri's husband left her and their divorce was final—more than five years ago now—mutual friends had encouraged the never-married Bill to ask Terri out. Of course she'd said yes when he finally did. After all, Bill was funny and thoughtful, not to mention handsome. What woman wouldn't want to go out with him? But they'd both known on the first date that romance wasn't in their future. However, they'd found the next best thing—a close friendship.

"How's the beauty business?" he asked.

"Beautiful. How's the word business?"

"Wordy."

Bill made his way to the back room and returned a short while later with an open pop can in hand.

"Help yourself," Terri said, grinning.

He took a swig. "Don't mind if I do. Thanks."

Terri sat in the styling chair and gave it a shove with one foot, spinning it around one time.

"Slow day?" Bill perched on the edge of the dryer chair, forearms resting on his thighs.

"A little. I've got about thirty minutes until my next appointment. You?"

"Finished my last article an hour ago." He took another drink of soda. "Guess who I ran into over at the drugstore earlier today? Angie Hunter."

Terri cocked an eyebrow.

"Has she always been this pretty? Or have I been comatose for the past two decades?"

*Bill and Angie? Hmm.* What could be more perfect than to have her two favorite people in the world find love with each other? Except that Angie hated Hart's Crossing and Bill loved it. And besides, Bill had a strong Christian faith and Angie ... Well, Angie didn't.

"Did you know she quit her job at the *Bay City Times*?" Bill asked.

"Yes. She told me."

"I hinted she might want to come to work for me at the *Press*. I'd be happy to give her a column or let her cover the news."

"Bill, that isn't likely to happen. Angie's never wanted to move back to a small town."

"People's wants can change."

"They can." She wondered if she should say anything more. No, she decided. This was definitely something she shouldn't interfere in, friend or no.

∽

ANGIE HAD EXPECTED, WHEN SHE FINALLY TOLD HER MOTHER about quitting her job, that Francine would pressure her to stay in Hart's Crossing longer than the agreed-upon eight weeks. She'd also expected, in one way or another, to hear an "I told you so."

Instead, her mother said, "Well, dear, I'll ask God to give you a job that you'll love, one that will bring you pleasure, even more than the old one did."

"Do you really think God cares what sort of job I have?" She'd meant it to be one of her usual flip responses, the sort she used whenever her mother brought up her religious beliefs.

Oddly enough, it didn't sound or feel flip when it came out of her mouth.

Francine turned from the stove, where she was frying chicken in a large skillet. "Oh, Angie. He cares infinitely more than you could imagine."

"It seems to me he's got lots more serious things to worry about. Wars and famine, for instance."

Her mother set the lid on the frying pan, then joined Angie at the table. Her expression was earnest and tender. "Honey, God knows everything about you. He created you to be just who you are, with all of your unique talents and abilities. He knows the very number of hairs on your head. Of course he cares about the job you'll have next. He wants to use you in it. He wants you to fulfill your purpose in life."

Angie felt something heavy pressing upon her lungs. "You believe that, don't you?"

"Yes, I do believe that. He loves you. He loves you so much he sent his Son to die for you."

"Greater love hath no man," Angie whispered, repeating aloud the words she remembered from her childhood Sunday school class.

Her mother reached across the tabletop and took hold of Angie's hand. "Yes." There were tears brimming in her eyes.

Angie withdrew her hand and rose from the chair. "You know how I feel about organized religion, Mom. It isn't relevant today. And how could any person know which religion is true, if one even is? There are so many to choose from."

"When you meet the living Lord, you'll know what's true."

If only Angie could believe like that

But no. No, she couldn't. Wouldn't. Religion wasn't for her. It wasn't. Her life as a journalist was all about facts and irrefutable proof. How could a person prove God?

With a shake of her head, Angie turned and left the kitchen.

## CHAPTER 5

As promised, the installer from the cable company arrived before nine on Friday morning. The guy was short, cute, young—maybe twenty-five—and had spiky platinum blond hair and startling blue eyes.

"So you're why Mrs. Hunter's finally getting cable installed," he said to Angie as she led the way to her upstairs bedroom. "Never thought I'd see the day there'd be cable in your mom's house." When she glanced over her shoulder, he chuckled. "You don't remember me, do you, Angie?"

"Sorry. No."

"I'm Eric Bedford."

The name didn't ring a bell.

"You know the summer you lifeguarded at the pool?" As he spoke, he set down the toolbox he carried and opened the lid. "I was always splashing you and pretending to drown." He grinned. "Angie Pangie."

"Good grief. You're one of *those* bratty runts?"

"Ouch!" His grin didn't fade. "I remember you calling us that. We deserved it, too."

35

Angie sat on the edge of her bed. "What a summer. You and your gang of friends made my job unbearable."

"Well, we did our best." Eric pointed toward the desk, where the laptop was in plain sight. "I take it this is where you want the connection."

"Please."

"The order says you're only getting Internet service. You want me to wire for cable TV while I'm at it, just in case? Won't cost any extra."

"Sure. Go ahead."

He set to work. "So how long are you back for?"

"A couple of months." Strange, that didn't sound as bad as it had a few days ago. "My mom's having surgery on Monday, and I'm going to look after her while she's recuperating."

"Nothing serious, I hope."

"Her knee."

"Ah." He moved the desk away from the wall and leaned down behind it.

Angie rose from the bed. "I'll leave you to your work."

"Any dogs in the backyard?" Eric asked before she reached the bedroom door.

"No."

"Okay. Thanks."

Angie went downstairs to the kitchen, where she poured herself another cup of coffee, then she sat at the table, her thoughts drifting to the summer she was seventeen. There weren't many job opportunities for teenagers in a town the size of Hart's Crossing. Not then, and she supposed not now. She and Terri had considered themselves lucky to get jobs as lifeguards at the public swimming pool.

But Eric and his friends ...

She smiled to herself. Maybe it hadn't been so bad. Those boys had flirted with the female lifeguards in the obnoxious ways only young boys could.

She remembered the hot summer sun baking the concrete, and the glare reflecting off the water's surface. She remembered the noise of kids at play, splashing and yelling and laughing. She remembered the mothers with their babies, and toddlers in the shallow end of the pool, and the teenage boys, darkly bronzed, showing off for the girls on the high dive.

Simpler times. A time when all her dreams had still seemed possible.

*"I don't think you've been truly happy since the day you moved away."*

Was Terri right? Angie wondered. Had true happiness escaped her? She'd been successful in her profession—or at least, had thought she was—but what about other parts of her life? Who were her friends, people she could call and ask to go with her to a movie or a concert or a play? What, as Terri had asked her when they talked last night, did she do for fun?

*I like to run.*

Running was one of the ways Angie kept fit so she would have enough energy for the long hours she put in at the newspaper. Besides, running gave her time to think about the articles she was working on.

But did running bring her happiness? Did it make her any friends?

*Why is it the only real friend I have is in my hometown and not the city where I live?*

A frown furrowed her brow.

*Terri seems happy. Am I?*

Angie's best friend had so little in terms of career success and financial security. Terri's deadbeat ex-husband had taken off with another woman and left her to raise their daughter alone. All she had was an ancient car, a small home with a medium-sized mortgage, and her beauty salon. And yet … and yet Terri was happy.

Angie pictured her friend in her mind. She remembered the

way Terri smiled as she ran her hand over Lyssa's strawberry blond hair, a look of motherly pride and unquestionable joy in her eyes.

Terri was more than happy, Angie realized. Terri was content.

A wave of restlessness washed over her. Maybe she needed to go for a run now. She couldn't say she cared for the direction her thoughts had taken her. Not at all.

∽

THE THIMBLEBERRY QUILTING CLUB HAD BEEN IN EXISTENCE FOR more than thirty years, and Francine had been a member almost from the beginning. She never missed the weekly meetings if she could help it. She loved to quilt, of course, but mostly she enjoyed the time of fellowship with the other women. Most of the quilts these women made went to people in homeless shelters and other places of need. Francine hoped having something beautiful—as well as warm—to wrap up in at night would bring someone a moment of pleasure in a time of hardship.

She looked up from her needlework to trail her gaze around the long table. There were six of them present today. Francine had invited Angie to join them, but her daughter had declined while rolling her eyes, as if to say, "You've got to be kidding."

Till Hart sat at her left, wire-rimmed reading glasses perched on the end of her nose. She was easily the most skilled of the all the quilters in the Thimbleberry Quilting Club. Not only were her fingers surprisingly agile for a woman her age, but her mind was equally nimble. She could carry on a detailed discussion on any number of topics and never miss a stitch.

Next to Till was Steph Watson. Last summer, Steph had lost her husband of more than fifty years; she'd had a rough spell of it. Francine remembered only too well what that first year of widowhood was like—but Steph seemed to be doing better now.

In the chair beside Steph was the youngest Thimbleberry, Patti Bedford. A newlywed of six weeks, Patti glowed with marital bliss. To hear her talk, her husband, Al, was perfection personified.

*Ah, young love. I remember what that's like, too.*

To Patti's left sat Mary Benrey, the secretary at Hart's Crossing Community Church. Mary, God bless her, was all thumbs with a needle and thread, but she remained determined to one day make beautiful quilts, and so she never gave up trying. She had the patience of a saint, even with herself.

Next to Mary was Ethel Jacobsen, the pharmacist who owned Main Street Drug. Ethel, a no-nonsense type, was frustrated beyond words over Mary Benrey's ineptitude with quilting. Patience was most definitely not Ethel's forte. So why she always chose to sit next to Mary was a mystery to Francine. Maybe she liked to be frustrated.

Turning her gaze to the quilting piece in her hand, Francine said a silent prayer of thanks to God for each woman in the group.

"Frani," Till said, breaking into her thoughts, "is Angie planning to stay at a motel near the hospital during your recovery or is she going to return to Hart's Crossing each night?"

"She hasn't decided. I don't think she's thrilled with the thought of driving my old Buick back and forth every day, but she isn't keen on staying at a motel either."

Mary said, "Well, there'll be plenty of others coming down to see you when you're ready for visitors. We could bring her if she wanted."

Francine knew her daughter was too independent for such an arrangement. Angie liked to be in control. Angie *needed* to be in control.

*Why is that, Lord? What is it that drives her need to control every detail of her life? And why is she so alone?*

An ache for her daughter overwhelmed Francine, and her vision suddenly blurred. She was thankful the others were too busy with their sewing to notice her tears.

*Oh Father, Angie needs you more than she needs control. How can I help her see that?*

## CHAPTER 6

Saturday morning was cool and blustery, but the Little Leaguers were troupers. They all showed up for their regularly scheduled games with the visiting teams.

"Strike 'em out, Lyssa!" Terri shouted from her place on the sidelines.

Her daughter didn't seem to hear. Lyssa stared hard at the batter as she tugged on the brim of her baseball cap. She drew her arms in close to her chest, preparing for the pitch. Then she delivered a fastball. The batter swung and missed.

"Way to go, Lyssa!" Terri jumped from her lawn chair, whistling through her teeth.

"Terri Sampson, that sound could shatter glass."

Terri turned to see Angie, a blanket draped over her arms, step up beside her chair. "You came!"

"Yes," Angie grumbled, "but I don't know how you talked me into it. It's *cold* out here."

"Pansy." Terri grinned as she returned her attention to the pitcher's mound. "Shh. Lyssa's getting ready to pitch again."

The windup.

The pitch.

Strike three.

End of inning.

Terri whistled and shouted and made a general idiot of herself.

"I never knew you liked baseball this much," Angie said when they were finally seated, Terri in her lawn chair, Angie on her blanket.

"I never used to. But I like whatever Lyssa likes, and she loves baseball. Her dream is to play in the Little League World Series."

"That's a big dream."

Terri nodded. "Yeah. Don't I know it."

"Aren't you afraid she'll be hurt if she doesn't make it?"

"Oh, sure. No mother wants her child to be disappointed. But life is often hard. I wouldn't do Lyssa any favor by trying to protect her from it. And everybody should have dreams for their future." Terri looked at Angie. "As long as Lyssa learns to trust Jesus and wants what he wants more than anything else, she'll be okay. Besides, God's willing and able to take every hurt and turn it to good in her life if she follows him."

Angie stared at Terri for several moments, then gazed toward the ball field.

Terri didn't intrude on her friend's silence. She suspected there was a great deal going on inside that pretty head.

~

WHAT WAS WITH ALL THIS GOD TALK? ANGIE WONDERED. FIRST her mother, now Terri. The things they said and the way they said it made their faith seem more than a religious crutch for old ladies and little children. Their faith seemed intimate and personal.

Worse yet, listening to them made her feel as if they had

something she didn't have—which was ridiculous. Angie had more money in her savings, checking, and 401k accounts than her parents had made in their lifetime. She had a college degree and a resume that spelled success. Her monthly mortgage payment was probably more than Terri made in two months in her salon. Angie might not be rich, but she certainly was able to afford the things she wanted. Even now—when she was unemployed—she was far better off than most folks in Hart's Crossing.

And yet...

A shout went up from the crowd. Angie looked to her left to see Terri hopping up and down, waving her arms and screaming. A quick glance at the ball field explained why. Lyssa had hit a home run.

Oh, the joy on that little girl's face as she rounded the bases and ran toward home plate. In that moment, Angie envied Terri more than she could express.

~

THE HART'S CROSSING CAVALIERS—ALONG WITH THEIR PARENTS, grandparents, friends, and supporters—jammed the tables and booths of the diner on Main Street to celebrate their victory over their long-standing rival, the Rebel Creek Warriors. The noise level was almost deafening, and Angie wondered how she could gracefully escape without hurting Terri's or Lyssa's feelings.

"Mind if I join you?" a deep male voice asked.

Angie barely had a chance to see who was standing in the aisle before Bill Palmer slid into the booth beside her.

"Quite the game." He leaned across the table toward Lyssa. "Congratulations, champ. Anything you want to say to your fans for the next edition of the paper?"

Grinning, the girl answered, "I'm real proud of the Cavaliers.

They played their hearts out today, and the whole team made this win happen. I'm real proud to be one of 'em."

Bill's gaze moved to Terri. "Have you been coaching her on what to say to the press?"

"No." Terri draped an arm around Lyssa's shoulders and gave her a hug. "But she watches ESPN. She knows how the sports stars reply in those after-game interviews."

Bill looked at Angie again. His brown eyes seemed enormous, sitting as close as he was, and his smile was completely disarming. "I'll bet Little League baseball wasn't something you covered for your paper."

"No. Never."

Bill frowned as he touched his right earlobe. "It's noisy in here."

Angie nodded.

"Did you want to order anything?"

She shook her head.

"Want to get out of here?"

She hesitated an instant before nodding again.

Bill looked across the table at Terri. "Mind if I steal her?"

"No. It's okay. We're going to go soon anyway." To Angie, Terri said, "I'll see you tomorrow."

Bill slipped from the booth and held out a hand to help Angie do the same. Her heart pattered like a silly schoolgirl's as she accepted it.

It took them several minutes to make their way to the door, what with all the back-slapping and self-congratulating and high-fiving over the day's win over the Warriors. Angie also noticed a few curious looks, warning her that she and Bill would be the subject of gossip and speculation before morning.

The silence outside the diner was most welcome after the clamor inside. Angie and Bill stopped on the sidewalk and drew in deep breaths in unison. Realizing what they'd done, they both laughed.

"I'm getting too old for that kind of racket," Bill said.

"You're not old." Nobody *old* looked like Bill Palmer, Angie thought. "Not even close."

"I'm knocking on forty's door. Remember what we thought of that age when we were twenty?"

"Forty isn't old."

"I hope not." He motioned with his hand to indicate they should start walking. "There's still a few things I'd like to do before I'm officially over the hill."

"Like what?"

"Get married and have a family, for one. Travel abroad. I've always wanted to go to Ireland. And I'd like to try my hand at writing the great American novel."

Angie smiled. "I toyed with the idea of writing a novel once."

"What stopped you?"

"Never enough time." She shrugged. "Too busy with a real job, I guess. You know how it is."

"Used to, but I'm learning the importance of focusing my life better. While there's lots of good things I can do, not all of them are part of God's plan for me. I'm trying to discern what those plans are."

More God talk. It seemed she couldn't escape it. Not even from Bill.

Dave Coble, the chief of police, drove toward them on Main Street in his white car with the HCPD seal on the doors. As he passed them, he leaned close to the open window. "Some victory, wasn't it?"

"Sure was," Bill called back.

All this fuss over a kids' baseball game. It boggled the mind. But it was a good opportunity to change the subject.

"Speaking of real jobs, Bill, you haven't heard of any openings for a city editor, have you?"

He gave her a long look before asking, "In a hurry to leave us already?"

"Not a hurry, actually." She had butterflies in her stomach again. "I promised Mom I'd stay with her for the next eight weeks. She should be well on her way to full recovery by the end of that time, and it would be nice to know where I'll be living when I leave. After all, I'll need to sell my house and ship my furniture somewhere."

"Hmm. Eight weeks." His smile came slowly. "Who knows what could happen in eight weeks?"

Her mouth went dry, and those butterflies in her stomach turned into stampeding elephants.

"Who knows?" she echoed in a whisper—completely forgetting what they'd been talking about.

## CHAPTER 7

There was something unnerving about seeing her mother in a hospital bed.

Watching as a nurse checked the IV in Francine's arm, Angie realized she couldn't recall a time in her life when her mother had been sick, beyond the occasional cold. Francine Hunter had always enjoyed a robust good health, but now she looked vulnerable, even frail.

"Knock, knock." John Gunn poked his head into the room. "Are you receiving visitors this morning?"

Francine's smile revealed genuine gladness. "Oh, Pastor John. Do come in. I didn't expect to see you today. You didn't have to drive all the way down here."

"I know, but I wanted to. I thought you might like prayer before they take you to surgery." He glanced toward the chair in the corner where Angie sat. "Good to see you again."

Angie nodded as she rose to her feet. "And you." She was grateful he hadn't mentioned her absence from church yesterday. She'd already felt her mother's disappointment over it.

John walked to the side of the hospital bed. He patted the

back of Francine's right hand, where it lay atop the thin white blanket. "Are you feeling anxious, my friend?"

"A little."

"Remember what the Scriptures tell us, Francine. Jesus healed the sick and fulfilled the word of the Lord through Isaiah, who said, 'He took our sicknesses and removed our diseases.'"

Angie's mother visibly relaxed.

"Let's pray, shall we?" John looked at Angie again. "Care to join us?"

Even as she was about to shake her head in refusal, Angie stepped toward the opposite side of the hospital bed. She did her best not to look surprised by her own actions as she took hold of her mother's left hand.

The pastor's voice was gentle as he prayed, and yet there was something powerful—and mysterious—in the words he spoke. Angie felt them wash over, through, and around her. They shook her in an odd yet comforting way.

"Amen," John said at last, and Angie's mother echoed with a softer, "Amen."

Before Angie could form the word, a nurse announced from the doorway, "We're ready for you now, Mrs. Hunter."

Angie opened her eyes and met her mother's gaze. "I'll be right here when you get back." She bent down and kissed her on the forehead. "I I love you, Mom."

"I love you, too, dear. Don't worry about a thing." Her expression was serene. "The Lord holds me in the palm of his hand."

Angie stepped backward, out of the way of the orderlies. A minute or so later, she felt a lump forming in her throat as her mother was wheeled from the room. She wished she'd said she loved her one more time.

"If you'll come with me." The nurse glanced between Angie and the pastor. "I'll show you where the waiting room is."

## LEGACY LANE

~

SNAIL-LIKE, THE MINUTE HAND INCHED ITS WAY WITH AGONIZING slowness around the large, white-faced clock in the waiting area. The *tick-tick-tick* of the sweep second hand pounded in Angie's head like a sledgehammer.

Right around the moment Angie thought she might start screaming, Anne Gunn and Terri arrived. Anne went to sit beside her husband. Terri sat down next to Angie.

"Thanks for coming," Angie whispered.

Terri gave her an understanding nod as she took hold of her hand and squeezed gently.

"It seems like it's taking forever."

"I know. But she's going to be fine." Terri brushed some loose strands of hair away from Angie's face, the same way Angie had seen her do with Lyssa. "If your mother follows the doctor's orders and takes care of herself the way she's supposed to, this new knee will allow her to do things she hasn't been able to do in a long while. And she'll be able to do them without the constant pain."

Angie felt a stab of shame, realizing she had no idea what her mother hadn't been able to do because of pain. Why hadn't she asked? If not when she'd first heard her mother needed surgery, at least since she'd arrived in Idaho.

Unfortunately, she knew the answer to those questions. Prior to returning to Hart's Crossing for this temporary stay, she'd been too busy with her career to think of anyone else. Since her arrival, she'd been too busy wondering what her next job would be.

*Me, me, me. My, my, my. Have I always been this self-absorbed?*

"Angie?"

Pulled from her unpleasant thoughts, she looked at Terri.

"Did you get to talk with your mother's surgeon this morning?"

Angie shook her head. "The nurse said he'd see me afterward." She glanced toward the waiting room doorway, then back at Terri. "I should have insisted on a consultation with him last week. I should have asked him a lot of questions."

"Don't worry. Your mom says he's by far the best knee surgeon in the area."

Angie was tempted to ask if that was a good enough recommendation. It wasn't as if this were a big city where a person had hundreds of qualified surgeons to choose from. Maybe she should have insisted her mother come to California for a consultation and surgery. Why hadn't she thought of that before?

"Harry Raney had knee surgery two or three years ago," Terri continued, "and he said it gave him a whole new lease on life."

"Harry's a good twenty years younger than Mom."

"Speak of the dickens, look who's here. Harry and Nancy. And they've brought Bill and Miss Hart with them."

Angie was both surprised and comforted by the presence of the newcomers. She'd expected to be alone in the waiting room this morning, and instead she was surrounded by people who knew and loved her mother.

Nancy Raney sent a little wave in Angie's direction as she and her husband went to sit near the Gunns.

"Is Frani still in surgery?" Till asked as she approached Angie.

"Yes. I thought I would have heard something by now but—"

"Don't worry that pretty head of yours." The older woman patted Angie's cheek. "Our church's prayer chain has been storming the gates of heaven on your mother's behalf for weeks and especially this morning."

"Thanks." Angie's emotions rose in her chest and made her voice sound strange in her own ears.

"Here, Miss Hart." Terri indicated the chair on her left. "Sit beside me."

"I think I'll do just that. Then you can tell me all about the game on Saturday. I'm so sorry I missed it. I hear Lyssa was the hero of the day."

Angie watched Till Hart settle next to Terri, then turned to look toward the entrance again, just in case the doctor had come while she was distracted. Instead, she found Bill Palmer standing before her.

"How are you doing?" he asked tenderly.

"Okay." She felt the threat of tears. "I didn't know you'd be here."

He gave a little shrug, accompanied by an apologetic grin. "It was a slow news day."

A week ago, she would have said every day was a slow news day in Hart's Crossing. But now ... now she appreciated the thoughtfulness of his sacrifice. Even a small town paper made demands on an editor.

She wondered who among the people she knew in California would do the same for her if she were having surgery? Who would gather to sit in the waiting room the way these people had gathered to wait for news of her mother? Not a soul she could think of.

"Miss Hunter?"

"Yes?" Angie was on her feet as soon as she heard the authoritative, no-nonsense voice, knowing instantly it had to be Dr. Nesbitt, her mother's orthopedic surgeon. He stood in the waiting room doorway—a man in his fifties with a square jaw and close-cropped dark hair—still wearing his hospital scrubs. She hurried across the room.

Before she could open her mouth to ask her first question, he answered it. "Everything went well. No surprises. Your mother is in recovery now."

"When can I see her?"

Dr. Nesbitt gave her a half smile. "The nurse will come for you as soon as your mother's alert and ready for visitors." After a brief pause, he proceeded to explain a little more about the procedure, how long her mother was expected to remain in the hospital, and then what Angie should expect once her mother's rehabilitation began. When he was finished, he asked, "Now, do you have any questions for me?"

Angie shook her head. "I don't think so. I think you told me everything I wanted to know."

"Good." He shook her hand. "Don't worry. It shouldn't be long before the nurse comes for you."

As Dr. Nesbitt walked away, Angie wondered if his definition of *long* was the same as hers.

Terri came to stand beside her. "I told you everything would be fine."

"Yeah. You did." She felt almost giddy with relief as she turned toward the others in the waiting room. "Mom's okay. The surgery went fine."

"Wonderful," Till Hart said.

"Thank the Lord," John Gunn added.

Everyone smiled, and Angie felt their love for her mother spill over onto her.

## CHAPTER 8

For the entire week Angie's mother was in the hospital, a stream of daily visitors made the drive down from Hart's Crossing to Twin Falls. In no time at all, cards, flowers, and balloons filled Francine's room, so many gifts that she soon shared them with others in the hospital. Whenever her mother was taken to physical therapy or for some test or another, there was someone from Hart's Crossing ready to accompany Angie to the cafeteria for a bite to eat or another cup of coffee. And there was always someone ready to tell another story about the Frani they knew and loved.

"Your mother was the most popular girl at Hart's Crossing High. Cutest thing you ever did see. I had a terrible crush on her my senior year. But once she met your father, she had eyes for nobody but Ned. Oh, those two were something, I'll tell you. And could they ever cut a rug. Once the music started, they never left the dance floor, those two."

"Remember the time Frani and Till took on the city council over the gazebo in the park? It's almost as old as the town itself, and it was a shambles. Everybody expected it to be torn down, if it didn't fall down on its own first. But Frani and Till were like dogs with a bone. They wouldn't let the members of the council rest until those repairs were made. Now it's one of the finest landmarks in our town, and I make a point to thank them every Fourth of July when we're all down there celebrating."

"Your mother has the most tender heart of any woman I know. Did you know she's been taking fresh-baked cookies to that women and children's shelter in the next county for more than a decade? Rain or shine, every week she drives over there. She reads to the little ones and comforts those women. She gives them advice when they want it, and she sits quietly with those who don't. Francine has a gift straight from God himself."

"I haven't known your mother many years, Angie, but as her pastor, I'd say Proverbs 31 would be a good description of her. 'She is clothed with strength and dignity, and she laughs with no fear of the future. When she speaks, her words are wise, and kindness is the rule when she gives instructions.'"

"Remember when we were kids, Ang, and your mom set up that tent in your backyard so the neighborhood girls could have a camp out? She was trying to get that center post in the right spot, and the whole thing collapsed on her. We were laughing so hard we were rolling on the ground and never lifted a finger to help her. I thought for sure she'd be spittin' mad by the time she got untangled from all that canvas. My mom sure would've been, but yours just laughed along with us. She's always been a good sport."

So many stories, all told with love. So many reminders of moments Angie had forgotten or had never known at all.

∽

As dusk settled on Hart's Crossing, Angie sat on the front porch in her mother's favorite wooden rocker, wrapped in a bulky sweater, with a soft lap blanket covering her legs and a mug of hot herbal tea held between her hands. The evening air was cool but inviting, scented with the green of newly mown lawns and the purple of lilac bushes in bloom. She was thankful for the quiet of the neighborhood after the busyness of the day and the stress of the previous week.

It was good to be home.

*Home.*

She allowed the idea to settle over her, accepting it as truth.

It *was* good to be home.

Angie closed her eyes as she took a sip of tea. Her mother had been discharged from the hospital earlier in the day, and now she was asleep in her bed, surrounded by some of her favorite things, including her well-used Bible, an overflowing bookcase, a collection of spoons from various vacation spots she'd visited in her lifetime, and the many photos of her husband, daughter, and friends that decorated the walls, dresser, and night stand.

Angie pictured her own oversized bedroom back in California. The walls were blank except for a large painting by an up-and-coming Bay area artist that hung over a decorative fireplace. No photos cluttered any surface. No bookcase; Angie rarely had time to read for pleasure. Certainly no collection of spoons.

How sterile, she thought. If a stranger were to walk into her house, what would they discover that would tell them anything personal about Angie Hunter?

Nothing, she feared, except for her dress size.

She thought of all the visitors who had come to see her mother in the hospital. All of those people knew Francine so well. They knew her past and they knew her heart. They were connected in countless ways.

*And who am I connected to?*

No one, really. At least, not in California. If she never went back, no one would miss her. She'd been replaced at the newspaper. Her colleagues were only that, her colleagues. They ate the occasional lunch together. They chatted at company Christmas parties. But Angie never let any of them into her personal life—because she didn't have one. She was too focused on getting ahead, too determined to prove her value to the paper, too set on moving up one more rung on the ladder of success. She'd used her money to acquire a large house where she never entertained and a fancy car that never went anywhere except work. She had the best of everything and yet …

Angie opened her eyes, surprised to discover the dark of night had arrived while she was lost in thought. She set the mug of cooling tea on the floor, shoved the blanket from her lap, stood, and walked to the edge of the porch. Placing her hands on the railing, she turned her face toward the sky.

*When did I lose myself?*

For some inexplicable reason—at least, inexplicable to her—she recalled going to the movies with her mother to see the Cecil B. DeMille classic, *The Ten Commandments*. She'd been no more than twelve when the film came to play at the Apollo, but she remembered scenes from the movie as if she'd watched it yesterday. She remembered Moses on top of that mountain, the wind swirling about him, and she recalled the voice of God proclaiming, "Thou shalt have no other gods before me."

A breeze stirred the trees, dancing through the leafy branches. It whispered a question in Angie's heart: *What other gods have you put before him?*

Suddenly chilled, she turned and went inside.

## CHAPTER 9

*E*njoying the pleasant warmth of a beautiful late spring day, Francine reclined on a lounge on the back patio, her face turned toward the afternoon sun, her eyes closed. The pain in her knee was noticeably less today, nearly three weeks post surgery. Still, she was impatient with the recovery process, even though the physical therapist said she was right on schedule.

"Mom," Angie called from the back doorway, "can I get you anything?"

"No, thank you, dear." She turned her head on the cushion until she could see her daughter. "I'm fine for now."

"Would you like some company then?" Angie stepped outside.

"I'd love it." Francine motioned toward the patio chair next to her.

Angie walked over and sank onto the padded seat. "What a beautiful day."

"Indeed."

"Miss Hart called. She said to tell you she'll drop by around three."

Francine chuckled as she looked at her daughter. "If Till brings another covered dish, I won't be able to fit into any of my nice clothes. I'll be on a diet for the next six months if I'm not careful."

"Too true. I know I've gained a few pounds since you got out of the hospital, and there's enough food in your refrigerator to feed us both for another month or two."

Francine didn't think a few extra pounds would hurt Angie in the least, but she kept that opinion to herself.

Angie patted her stomach. "I need to start running again. I talk about it, but I never do it. I don't know why. I've always been faithful with my exercises. I think I'm getting lazy."

*Lazy* wasn't a word she would use to describe her daughter. Angie had worked diligently, taking care of Francine's every need, driving her to physical therapy appointments and cleaning the house and running errands and welcoming the daily round of visitors. And she'd done it all without complaint.

But the best times were when, like now, Angie came to sit with her. Oh, how blessed Francine was by these precious moments of companionship with her daughter. How she had ached for them through the years. How she would miss them after Angie went away again.

*O Lord, forgive me. I don't mean to feel sorry for myself. You've given us these weeks together. Let me rejoice in them while they're here.*

"Mom?"

"Hmm?"

"When I was a little girl, we pretty much always went to church, didn't we? You and Daddy and me."

Francine tried not to look surprised by the question. "Yes, we did. We rarely missed a Sunday. Why do you ask?"

"Well I was wondering something." Angie's gaze was fastened on some point beyond the treetops. "You've always believed in God. Right?"

Francine's pulse fluttered rapidly, like the wings of a hummingbird as it hovers near a feeder. "Yes, I've always believed in him."

"Then what changed about your beliefs when I was in high school?"

Francine had longed for this moment, but now that it had come, she feared she wouldn't be able to find the right words. The Bible said to always be ready to explain her Christian hope, but she felt anything but ready. What if she said the wrong thing? What if she made matters worse? She and her daughter had been estranged for so long. What if she couldn't find the right words?

*No one can come to me, unless the Father who sent me draws him.*

Francine felt herself grow calm. It wasn't her job to convince, arm-twist, or out-debate. She was simply supposed to be ready and willing to explain her hope. Hers and hers alone.

～

IT WAS THE PINNACLE OF INSANITY TO ASK HER MOTHER SUCH A question. Angie couldn't imagine what had possessed her to do it.

No. That wasn't true. She did know. Ever since that night on the porch, more than a week ago, when she'd remembered the line from that old movie, those same words had continued to repeat in her head: *"Thou shalt have no other gods before me."*

Worse still, her own subsequent question had repeated as well: *What other gods have you put before him?*

She tried to ignore the voice, those words, but they persisted all the same.

Perhaps if she were in her own environment, in her own place, she could have sorted it through, could have figured out why this seemed to trouble her so. But here in Hart's Crossing, in her mother's home, with people coming and going all the time, laughing and joking and sharing memories, bringing gifts and trays of food…

Well, it was hard to think, that's all.

"Angie," her mother said softly, ending the lengthy silence, "I believed *in* God always. From the time I was a child, I believed. But I somehow missed the part about him believing in me."

Angie looked at her mother. "I don't know what that means."

"I didn't either until I started reading my Bible. That's when God's truths began to open up to me. That's when I began to realize God wanted to be personal in my life. He wasn't way up in heaven, watching me muddle through. He was with me, and he spoke to me every day as I read from his Word."

"Every religion has its own book, Mom."

"Christianity is much more than a religion, darling, although even many who call themselves Christians fail to understand that. I did for many years." She shook her head slowly. "And the Bible is much more than a mere book. It's holy because it was written by a living God. It has the power to change people, the same way it changed me." She spoke in a quiet voice, and the strength of her belief was almost hypnotic.

Angie resisted, saying, "It's just a book written by a bunch of men thousands of years ago."

"Is it?" Her mother's eyes narrowed slightly. "Angie, you've been a journalist for many years. You deal in facts. You know how to dig for truth. Why don't you investigate to see if what I say is true? God isn't afraid of our reasoning, and he isn't surprised by our questions or our doubts. He gave you your intellect. So why don't you use it?"

That was a challenge Angie hadn't expected her mother to make, and her reply was even more unexpected. "Maybe I will."

## CHAPTER 10

"Shoo!" Till Hart crossed her wiry, age-wrinkled arms over her chest and stared at Angie with the determination of a drill sergeant. "Get out, young lady, and don't come back for the rest of the day. We'll see to your mother."

"But—"

"You know better than to argue with your elders. Shoo, I said."

Angie looked from Till to Steph Watson to the three other members of the Thimbleberry Quilting Club who stood in her mother's living room, sewing baskets in hand.

Till's hand alighted on Angie's arm, and her voice softened when she spoke again. "Go on, now. You haven't had a day to yourself in nearly a month. We promise we won't let Frani do anything she shouldn't."

Angie glanced toward her mother.

"I'll be fine, dear. Go and enjoy yourself."

"If you're sure."

"I'm sure."

As Angie turned toward the stairs, Till said, "And remember. Don't come back until supper time."

Fifteen minutes later—wearing a baseball cap, a pair of comfortable Levis, a pale green T-shirt, and her white athletic shoes—Angie walked toward town, breathing in the sweet midmorning air. It felt good to get out for a while. She hadn't realized how much she'd missed having some alone time, and she was glad Till Hart had insisted. Not that she'd minded these weeks of caring for her mother. It had actually been an unexpected blessing. She'd felt as if she were coming to know her mother in a new—and better—way.

"Good morning, Angie," a woman called from a driveway. "How's your mother today?"

Recognizing Liz Rue, the woman who owned Tattered Pages Bookstore, she answered, "She's doing well, Mrs. Rue."

"Tell her I'll be by to see her again soon. I received a shipment of new novels yesterday, and I know she'll want to read some of them while she's laid up. I'll bring by a few and let her choose."

"I'll tell her. Thanks."

Was there anybody in town who didn't know and care about her mother?

When she walked past the elementary school a short while later, Angie remembered that today was the last day of the school year.

*Lyssa must be excited. More time for baseball.*

She smiled, remembering summers in Hart's Crossing when she was a kid. Long, warm days of fun. Bike rides and swimming and camping and horseback riding. It seemed to her that she'd had access to most of the back doors in town. If her mother wasn't near, someone else's mother was. What a carefree existence.

She wondered how Terri managed, a self-employed single mom with a deadbeat ex and no close living relatives for backup support. Was there some sort of daycare program in Hart's Crossing? Or did Lyssa have to go into the salon with her mother during the summer months? It couldn't be easy for Terri, juggling so many things while raising a daughter alone.

In contrast, all Angie had to think about was herself. She used to believe hers was the perfect life. But lately, she wasn't so sure.

"Hey, stranger."

She slowed her steps at the sound of Bill Palmer's voice. She glanced quickly at Terri's Tangles Beauty Salon, her original destination, then almost without a conscious decision, headed across the street to where Bill stood.

"How's your mom?"

"Doing well."

"Glad to hear it. Sorry I haven't been by to see her this week. I had to go out of town for a few days. But I plan to drop by tomorrow after church, if that's all right."

"We'll be there."

"Hey, if you'd like, I could come by before church and take you both with me."

Surprisingly, Angie was tempted to say yes. "Sorry. Mom doesn't think she can manage being out that much just yet. And you know my mother. If she was able, she'd be there in a flash. She doesn't like to miss church."

"I know. I'm the same way. Best day of the week, in my humble opinion."

Again she was tempted to respond, this time to tell Bill about the books she was reading. Research, she called it. She'd taken up her mother's challenge to investigate the Bible and its accuracy. Of course, she should have been using that time to look for a new job, but employment hadn't seemed such a pressing concern lately.

As if knowing her thoughts, Bill asked, "How's the job hunt going?"

Angie shrugged.

"Care to see *my* office?" He tipped his head toward the door to the newspaper.

"Sure." She smiled, pleased by the invitation. "I'd love to."

He moved toward the door, opened it, and motioned her through. "Beauty before age."

What was it about Bill Palmer that made her so prone to blushing? Angie looked at the floor instead of him as she stepped inside.

The front office of the *Mountain View Press* was a cluttered hodgepodge of desks, bookcases, file cabinets, and heaven only knew what else that was hidden beneath stacks of papers and files. It smelled of dust, ink, and old newsprint.

Ambrosia.

"I know where everything is, too," Bill declared with a chuckle. "There's a method in my chaos."

Angie laughed with him. "Of course there is."

"Here. Let me clear off a chair for you."

In short order, Angie was seated on the opposite side of Bill's desk. She expected him to turn on his computer or check his voice mail. He did neither. Instead, he locked his hands behind his head and leaned back in his chair.

"So," he said, "besides taking care of your mom and looking for work, what are you doing with yourself? This is the first time I've seen you in town since your mom came home."

"I'm only here because of Miss Hart. She and the Thimbleberry bunch ran me out of the house. They think I've been too cooped up and need some sun and exercise."

"Ah."

She glanced around the newspaper office again. "They were right."

"Care to take a drive with me into the country?"

*Thump-thump.* She wondered if he heard her pulse jump. *Thump-thump.*

"I'm working on an article about Kris Hickman. Remember her?"

"*Crazy* Kris?"

Bill gave her an amused look. "Yeah. That's what they called her in high school."

Embarrassed by her outburst—it wasn't the kindest of nicknames—Angie decided against asking what sort of story he might want to write about Kris. After all, the *Mountain View Press* was a family-friendly weekly newspaper, and there wasn't anything family-friendly about Kris Hickman. At least not the girl Angie remembered. Kris had been a wild-living, rough-talking teenager who drank, smoked, and popped pills. A year older than Angie, Kris had dropped out in her junior year and ridden off to parts unknown on the back of her boyfriend's Harley.

Angie remembered the worry *that* had caused the parents in Hart's Crossing, afraid their own children might be unduly influenced.

Once again, Bill seemed to read her mind. "It's a freelance piece for a magazine, and this is just the sort of story they love."

"What sort is that?"

"Come on and see for yourself. We'll only be gone a couple of hours or so, and I promise you'll find the time it takes worthwhile." He leaned forward, and there was a hint of a challenge in his brown eyes. "Maybe you'll want to write the story yourself."

*Thump-thump.* "Okay." *Thump-thump.*

⁓

BILL HAD TO ADMIT THAT HE LOVED THE PINK-PEACH COLOR THAT infused Angie's cheeks as she looked at him. Maybe it was male pride rearing its ugly head, but he suspected Angie hadn't blushed much in recent years. He rather liked the idea that he was the one who'd made her do it.

"I should call Mom and let her know where I'm going. I wouldn't want her to worry."

"Good idea." Bill pointed toward the desk on the opposite wall. "You can use that phone while I gather my notes and recorder."

He watched her rise from the chair, turn, and walk across the room. She looked cute in that baseball cap, T-shirt, and Levis. He'd take that outfit hands down over some pinstriped business suit.

Man, he had it bad. He'd fallen for her. There was no denying it.

~

Francine hung up the telephone and turned her head to find five pairs of eyes watching her.

"That was Angie. She's going somewhere with Bill. Something about a story he's working on."

"Hmm." Till resumed her sewing. "Bill and Angie. That would give her a good reason to stay in Hart's Crossing."

Francine felt a flutter of hope. She didn't know a finer person than Bill Palmer. When she'd prayed for a husband for her daughter, she'd always asked God to send a mature Christian man who exemplified godly values. That certainly described Bill.

Still, her hope was mixed with concern. Angie had begun asking questions about God. She was spiritually hungry. Francine didn't want her daughter's blossoming desire for truth to take a backseat to romance.

Francine sent up a quick prayer, asking God to put a shield around Angie at the same time he was opening the eyes of her heart.

## CHAPTER 11

Bill Palmer drove a 1965 red Ford Mustang convertible, the sort of car people in California would kill to own. Bill's had belonged to his father, who'd purchased it new when he was fresh out of college, and both father and son had kept it in superb condition.

With her ponytailed hair whipping her cheeks, Angie stared at the majestic mountains to the north as the Mustang—top down—sped along the deserted country road. Bill didn't try to engage her in conversation; he seemed content to let her lose herself in thought.

Except she wasn't thinking about anything. She was simply enjoying *being*. Being with Bill. Being in this convertible, sun on her face, wind in her hair. Being away from the hustle and bustle of life. No to-do list to check. No appointments to keep. No stress or worries.

After about fifteen minutes, Bill slowed the car and turned onto a single-lane gravel road. It wound into the foothills, dead-ending when it reached an old, weather-beaten, two-story house surrounded by a corral, a barn, and other outbuildings in various stages of disrepair. Two black-and-white border collies rose from the porch and barked a warning before racing out to circle the Mustang, heads slung low. They didn't look particularly ferocious, but Angie made no move to open her door, just in case.

"Lady. Prince. Get back here."

Angie looked toward the house again. A rail-thin woman with pixie-short brown hair, wearing a faded plaid shirt and denim coveralls, stood in the front doorway of the house, her face shadowed by the porch roof. She held a toddler in the crook of one arm, balancing the child on her hip.

"Is that Kris?" Angie asked. The girl she remembered had been on the chunky side, and her hair had been long, reaching all the way to her waist.

"Yes, that's her." Bill opened the driver side door as he waved toward Kris. "Hope you don't mind," he called as he stood. "I brought a friend with me."

"Don't mind a bit." Kris moved to stand on the edge of the porch.

As Angie got out of the car, two things registered in her mind. First, two young girls—perhaps three and four years of age—had come out of the house to stand near Kris, each gripping one of her pant legs. Second, the right side of Kris's face bore an angry scar that pulled at the corners of her eye and mouth.

Bill met Angie at the front of the car and took hold of her arm. "This is Angie Hunter, Francine's daughter. Maybe you remember her from Hart's Crossing High." They walked together toward the foot of the porch steps.

"Well, I'll be." Kris's grin was lopsided due to the scar, but it was genuine. "It's good to see you again, Angie. I hear your mother's recovery is going well. Give her my best, will you?"

"Of course."

"Come on up and have a seat on the porch." Kris touched the head of the older of the two girls. "Ginger, can you and

Lily play with your dolls while Aunt Kris visits with her guests?"

Ginger nodded but didn't budge.

Kris looked at Bill. "Would you mind taking the baby while I get the girls settled?"

"Glad to." He released Angie's arm, then handed her the steno pad and pen he'd carried in his other hand. "Come here, Tommy," he said as he climbed the three steps.

The toddler grinned and nearly sprang from Kris's arms to Bill's. It was obvious this wasn't Bill's first visit to the Hickman place.

While Bill, little Tommy in arms, and Angie sat on two straight-backed chairs, Kris and the girls disappeared inside. Minutes later, they were back, Kris carrying a blanket along with several dolls and stuffed animals. She spread the blanket on the floor near a third chair and soon had Ginger and Lily seated in the center of the blanket, playing with their toys.

"Sorry," she said. "They're still pretty shy around strangers. A whole lot better now than they were six months ago, though." Softly, she added, "Thank God."

Those two words on the lips of the "crazy Kris" of Angie's memory would have sounded totally different than the way they sounded now.

"Can I get either of you something to drink? I made some sun tea yesterday."

"I'm fine," Angie answered.

"So am I," Bill echoed.

"If you're sure." Kris sat on her chair.

Bill shifted Tommy to his left thigh. "We're sure." He glanced at Angie. "You mind taking notes since I'm holding the little guy?"

She shook her head, rather glad for something to do. Otherwise, she was afraid she would stare too long at Kris's scar.

Bill reached into his shirt pocket and withdrew his tiny

recorder before saying, "Kris, why don't you tell us your story in your own words? We'll save any questions until the end." He set the recorder near his interview subject and turned it on.

"Okay." Kris glanced down at the two small girls, then turned her head to gaze toward the rolling landscape. "I guess if I say I was a wild kid, it wouldn't surprise either one of you."

*No,* Angie thought, *it wouldn't.*

"I was using drugs and drinking pretty heavy by the time I was a sophomore. I was way more than my mom could handle, that's for sure. She was a widow by then. Trying to raise me right and take care of this place by herself was too much. When she tried to discipline me, I fought back. I was a real hellion." She took a deep breath and let it out. "Finally I took off with my boyfriend, Grant. He was both my lover and my supplier, and I needed him for both reasons. Over the next couple of years, we traveled all around the country. Wherever the wind blew us, that's where we ended up."

Kris's tale was not unlike the stories of countless other women trapped in the drug and alcohol culture. The poverty. The homeless, vagabond existence. The verbal and physical abuse that came in waves. And eventually, abandonment by the man she thought she loved. A succession of other men followed, complete with reckless, meaningless sex and an increasing need for a chemical high.

"When the car accident happened—" she touched the scar on her cheek—"I was so wasted I didn't remember a thing. Still don't. I came to in a hospital in Richmond, Virginia, and they told me the driver, the man I was with, was killed in the crash." There were tears in her eyes, but she blinked them away before they could fall. "The sorry thing is, I didn't even know his name. Had no idea where he picked me up or how long we were together. Days? Weeks? Months? Truth was, I didn't even know I was in Richmond until later on. So I laid there in that hospital bed, knowing I was never going to be pretty again, that I was always going to have a scarred face. I understood the mess I made of my life, and I saw what I'd become, and I wished God would strike me dead right then and there." Her smile, when it came, was nothing less than angelic, despite its lopsidedness. "Instead, he gave me a glimpse of heaven. It was like the walls of that hospital room slid open, like automatic doors at a department store, and Jesus was standing there, saying, 'Look what I have for you, Beloved, if you follow me.'"

Angie was transfixed by both the expression on Kris's face and by her words. She forgot about the steno pad and her note taking. She almost forgot to breathe.

"So I followed him," Kris finished softly, "and there hasn't been a day since that he hasn't made me glad for it."

Kris continued with her story, telling of the many months of her recovery, both from the accident and from her addictions. She told of the woman from a local church who took Kris into her home and nourished her with love.

"It took me over a year to work up the courage to call home. I hadn't talked to Mom since I ran away at sixteen, and I was afraid she wouldn't be able to forgive me. Finally I realized I had to call, whether she forgave me or not. I had to tell her how sorry I was for what I did to her, for the way I disrespected her. Only I was too late. Mom had passed away about the same time as my accident, and I never even knew it." Her voice lowered, and the tears returned to her eyes. This time she allowed them to fall. "I never got to tell her how sorry I was for what I put her through. People think there'll be plenty of time to make amends with those we love, but that isn't always true."

Kris fell silent, but Angie knew there was more to come. The evidence of that was sitting on Bill's lap as well as playing with dolls on a blanket next to Kris's chair.

"It took a while for me to work through the pain and confusion I felt. And all the guilt. I carried around a load of it for a long time before I laid it at the foot of the cross like Jesus tells us to. And then he sent these little ones into my life to love and to love me in return."

"You're not really their aunt," Angie said, suddenly remembering Kris was an only child, same as she was.

Kris stroked Ginger's hair. "No, I'm not. That's just what the kids call me. I became friends with Susan, their mom, in a Bible study we were in together, and later I took care of her when she was dying of cancer. She had no other family to see to her, and she wasn't married to their father. Besides, he took off when she got pregnant with Tommy, and nobody knew where he was. After they found her cancer, the doctors wanted her to have an abortion, said it would improve her chances of surviving longer, but she wouldn't do it. Susan said she wouldn't take his life to save her own. She went home to be with the Lord when Tommy was about five months old. Long enough for her to take care of arrangements for her children to stay with me. After we buried Susan, the kids and I moved back here, to the house Mom left me in her will. It's a miracle, really, the way God's provided for us all."

A miracle? Wouldn't a miracle have been for Susan to live instead of die of cancer? Wouldn't a miracle have been if Kris hadn't been scarred in that accident or had never run away from home in the first place?

As if Kris heard Angie's thoughts, she said, "I didn't have anybody. They didn't have anybody. But together, we make a family. That's God's miracle. All things work together for good for those who love God and are called according to his purpose."

Angie was incredulous. "You're saying you think this all worked out for the best?"

"For the best?" Kris shook her head slowly. "No, I'm not saying that. Lots of bad, hard things happen to people, and plenty of it isn't the best. The best won't happen until this world is free of sin, once and for all, and God's will is done on earth the same way it is in heaven. But for now, he takes what the devil means for harm against us, and he turns it into something beautiful in the lives of those who trust Jesus. That's what he's promised in his Word." Kris leaned forward in her chair, her gaze so filled with peace it pierced Angie's soul. "That's how much the Lord loves us."

The old Angie—the one who'd arrived in Idaho on that small plane thirty-one days before—would have scoffed outright. She would have accused Kris Hickman of sermonizing or, at the very least, being simpleminded. But today, seeing something in this woman's eyes, hearing it in her voice, she neither scoffed nor accused. She listened, and she tried to understand. She wanted very much to understand where that sort of peace came from

Because she knew she didn't have it.

CHAPTER 12

Angie tossed and turned on her bed that night, unable to fall asleep, unable to shake the voice in her head and the memory of Kris Hickman and those three children, unable to ignore the peace she'd read in Kris's eyes, despite the painful nature of her story.

"I was way more than my mom could handle. So I laid there in that hospital bed, knowing I was never going to be pretty again. Jesus was standing there, saying, 'Look what I have for you, Beloved, if you follow me.' So I followed him. I never got to tell her how sorry I was for what I put her through. People think there'll be plenty of time to make amends with those we love, but that isn't always true. It's a miracle, really, the way God's provided for us all. He takes what the devil means for harm against us, and he turns it into something beautiful. That's how much the Lord loves us."

"That's how much the Lord loves us."

"That's how much the Lord loves us."

At 3:00 A.M., Angie gave up and got out of bed.

Tucking one leg beneath her bottom, she sat on her desk chair, opened her laptop, and turned it on, determined she would seriously begin her job search. Surely that would help cure whatever ailed her. Getting back to the real world was what she needed. Getting back to the hustle and bustle of the newspaper business.

Only instead of clicking the Internet link on her desktop, she opened her word processing program. She sat there a while, staring at the cursor blinking on the screen, and then she typed: Kris Hickman is an unlikely heroine in a very different kind of love story.

It wasn't a bad lead. Maybe not the best, but not bad either. And it didn't matter one way or the other since she had no intention of writing the article. It was an interesting story but had nothing to do with her. Maybe she simply needed to jot down a few things in order to clear it from her head.

*"I never got to tell her how sorry I was for what I put her through. People think there'll be plenty of time to make amends with those we love, but that isn't always true."*

Perhaps those were the words that troubled Angie most of all. What if something far worse than knee problems had affected her mother? What if she'd died without Angie seeing her again? She'd neglected her mother for so long. Oh, she'd made those occasional visits and had called on a semi-regular basis, and her day planner had helped her remember to send flowers on Mother's Day and birthday gifts every February, items purchased in haste and without much thought for whether or not they were things her mother would want or need.

But what about the one thing that really mattered? What about giving of herself, of her time? No, that she hadn't done. But what was a career woman to do? Angie had to have a job, didn't she?

Of course, Bill had offered her employment at the *Press*. The pay couldn't be much, but if she sold her house in California, she would have a nice nest egg to see her through for a long spell. Despite her dire expectations, she hadn't found these weeks in Hart's Crossing onerous. Maybe she'd even enjoyed them.

She thought of Kris Hickman again and the strength of faith that had been revealed as she related her story. A strong faith shared by Angie's mother, Bill Palmer, and Terri Sampson, to name only a few of the people she knew. For the first time in her life, Angie wanted to know *why* they believed what they believed. Perhaps if she stayed in Hart's Crossing a while longer, she would find the answers to the questions that plagued her.

Angie swiveled her chair around 180 degrees, thinking that her life had been a good deal simpler when she wasn't so bent on self-analysis and spiritual discovery.

∽

FRANCINE AWAKENED TO THE SMELL AND SOUND OF BACON sizzling in a frying pan. Turning her head on the pillow, she looked at the red numbers on her digital clock. Six-forty. What on earth? Angie rarely ate breakfast, let alone this early in the morning.

Francine sat up and reached for her robe. A short while later, aided by her cane and moving slowly, she made her way out of her bedroom, down the hall, and into the kitchen. The table had been set with the bright yellow plates Francine favored. The clear-glass tumblers had been filled to the brim with grapefruit juice.

"My word," she said. "Are we expecting company?"

Standing at the stove, her back toward the kitchen entrance, Angie glanced over her shoulder. "Morning, Mom." She smiled at Francine as she pulled the skillet from the burner. "I thought I'd get a jump start on breakfast. Are you ready for your eggs? I can fry them now that you're up."

"Thank you, dear." Francine wasn't nearly as hungry as she

was curious. "Just one egg, though." She took her usual seat at the table.

"Okay." Angie removed the strips of bacon from the frying pan and placed them on paper towels to drain before taking the eggs out of the refrigerator. "I couldn't sleep last night, Mom. I was thinking a lot about the meeting Bill and I had with Kris Hickman."

Angie hadn't said much to her mother when she returned home the previous afternoon, and Francine had been careful not to press for details. She'd sensed Angie wasn't ready to talk. Now it appeared her daughter was ready to open up.

"I was thinking maybe I—" Angie stopped abruptly, pulled the skillet from the burner a second time, and turned toward Francine. "Mom, I love you."

A lump formed in Francine's throat. "I love you, too, dear."

"I . . . I need to tell you how sorry I am."

"Sorry? For what?"

Angie came to the table and sat down. "I love you, Mom, but I haven't shown it the way I should. I've been so stingy with my time. I've loved you when it was convenient for me and my schedule. That's a selfish, self-centered kind of love. All these years, you've never chastised me for my selfishness, even though it must have hurt you." Tears brimmed in her daughter's eyes. "I'm so sorry."

Francine took hold of one of Angie's hands and squeezed. "You're forgiven, my darling child. I've always understood how important your career is to you."

Angie shook her head, as if denying her mother's statement. "Last night I kept thinking of how Kris never got to tell her mom she was sorry, never got to spend time with her as an adult. She never got a second chance with her mom after she ran away from home. I don't want that to happen to us. I want to be close to you, Mom."

For a time, neither woman spoke. Neither was able. They sat

in silence, holding hands, and allowed forgiveness to flow between them. Finally, Angie sniffed, rose from her chair, and went to retrieve the box of tissues on the kitchen counter near the telephone. After wiping her own eyes and blowing her nose, she brought the box to the table so Francine could make use of the tissues, too.

Francine was still dabbing at the corners of her eyes when her daughter said, "Mom, I think maybe I'd like to stay in Hart's Crossing a while longer. What would you say to that?"

"Oh, honey. I'd love it more than anything. You know I would."

Angie sat down again. "I don't know for how long. But I ... Well, I need to figure out some things about myself. I need to change some of my priorities. I think I could do that better here, without the pressures of my career pulling me this way and that."

*Thank you, Jesus. Oh, thank you.*

"I thought I'd talk to Bill later this morning. He mentioned I could do some work for him at the *Press*. I doubt he could pay me much, but the money isn't an issue right now."

Francine had the almost irresistible urge to jump from her chair and shout "Hallelujah!" while dancing about the kitchen, bum leg or no. But she managed to maintain control of her emotions, pretending calm. "You do what you think is best, dear. You're welcome to stay with me for however long you wish."

"Okay, then." Angie grinned. "Guess I'll fix the rest of our breakfast now. I'm famished."

∽

ANGIE CHOSE TO WALK INTO TOWN LATER THAT MORNING. Sunlight filtered through the leafy tree branches to cast a latticework of light and shadows upon the sidewalk and street.

The buzz of lawnmowers came to her from several directions. Three boys, about the same age as Lyssa, rode their bikes past her, going in the opposite direction, and all of them said "Hey" as if they knew her.

*Hart's Crossing never changes.*

Just a month ago, she'd thought the same thing with derision. Now she was glad for it, even while knowing it wasn't entirely true. Her hometown had changed. People had moved away. Others had arrived to make this place their home. The high school had been remodeled. The Lamberts had built their dental clinic. Hart's Crossing Community Church had a new pastor in John Gunn, and Dr. Jeff Cavanaugh had taken over the practice of old Doc Burke when he'd retired.

But Angie could still count on the wisdom of Till Hart and the juicy hamburgers at the Over the Rainbow Diner and the folksy news included in the *Mountain View Press*. She knew kids would still ride their bikes down the middle of the street and the police chief would know most folks by name and neighbors would go to hospital waiting rooms to sit with family members, whether asked or not.

Maybe in the weeks and months to come, however many that might be, she could add to her list of things that had and had not changed about Hart's Crossing.

And about herself.

Seeing the "open" sign in the door of Terri's Tangles Beauty Salon, she stopped there first. She found her friend seated in her salon chair, sipping a cup of coffee.

"Hi, Terri," Angie said as bells tinkled overhead.

"Well, hey. Didn't expect to see you this morning. What's up?"

"Not much."

Terri's eyes narrowed. "Then why do you look like the cat that swallowed the canary?"

"Do I?" Angie sat in a blue hard-plastic chair. "Maybe it's because I'm happy."

"Why? What's happened?"

"Maybe it's none of your business." She tried to sound irritated but failed.

"Everything's my business. I'm a hair stylist. People tell me as much as any therapist or bartender might hear." She wiggled her fingers in a spill-the-beans fashion.

Angie pushed her hair away from her face as she turned her head to look out the window. Across the street was the Hart's Crossing Municipal Building and the city park with its white gazebo near the river.

"Ang?"

Without looking at Terri, she said, "You know how lots of towns put speed bumps on certain streets when they can't get traffic to slow down the way they're supposed to?"

"Yeah."

"Well, I feel like somebody installed a giant speed bump in my life this spring." Angie turned toward her friend again. "I'm going to slow down and take a look at the neighborhood I'm passing through. Maybe I'll discover I like it more than I thought I would."

Terri leaned forward in her chair. "And that means what, exactly?"

"It means I'm not in such a hurry to return to the rat race. It means I want to figure out what matters in this world. It means I want to spend more time with my mom so we can get to know each other again. It means I want to see more of you and Lyssa, too." *And more of Bill Palmer*, she thought, but she couldn't bring herself to speak those words aloud just yet.

"It means you're going to stay in Hart's Crossing!" Terri squealed as she jumped up from her chair.

Angie grinned. "Yeah, that's what it means. At least for now."

## CHAPTER 13

Long after darkness blanketed Hart's Crossing, long after the lights in the homes in the Hunter neighborhood winked out, long after her mother retired for the night, Angie sat in one of the rockers on the front porch. She watched the twinkling stars overhead and thought how they didn't seem as bright in the city.

What was it her mother used to say? *God's in his heaven. All's right with the world.*

Tonight, Angie could believe it.

Only she didn't think he was just in his heaven. It seemed the more Angie looked around, and the more she was with her mother and Terri and Bill and Kris and Till and others, the more she thought it was possible God was here on earth, too.

"Am I right?" she whispered. "Are you here?"

It might be nice if he would answer her in the same way he spoke to Moses in *The Ten Commandments*. Then there would be no shred of doubt. But he didn't. If God listened to her soft inquiry, he didn't give her an audible reply.

Maybe he wanted her to figure it out for herself, the slow way. Maybe this was another speed bump in the road of her life.

What was it she'd read in the past few days? That it was impossible to please God without faith, and that faith was the confident assurance that what was hoped for was going to happen.

Faith in the unseen, in the hoped for. A huge request for someone with Angie's penchant for fact gathering, for trusting only in the seen and the proven. Huge but maybe not impossible. She had a legacy of faith and love—from her mother and from her friends in Hart's Crossing—to help her find the way.

"Who knows?" she said, still staring at the heavens. "Maybe you'll even see me in church tomorrow. Now wouldn't that shock the good folks of my hometown?"

Smiling in amusement, Angie rose from the rocker and went inside.

# VETERANS WAY

HART'S CROSSING #2

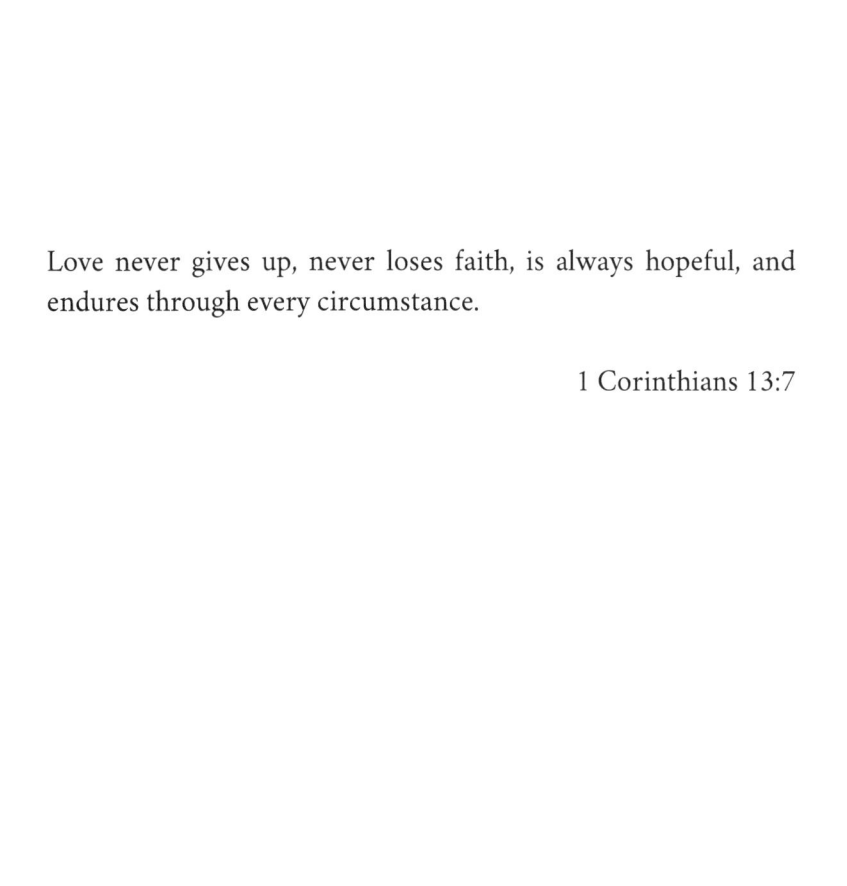

Love never gives up, never loses faith, is always hopeful, and endures through every circumstance.

1 Corinthians 13:7

# PROLOGUE

August 14, 1945

Stephanie would never forget the jubilation that raced through Hart's Crossing, Idaho, at the end of World War II. People danced in the streets and blew horns and whooped and hollered and set off fireworks. As a nine-year-old, she couldn't quite grasp the significance of everything her parents and other adults said about V-J Day, but she understood something wonderful had happened.

So did ten-year-old Jimmy.

Maybe that's why he gave Stephanie her first boy-girl kiss right there outside the Apollo Movie Theater on that warm August night. The kiss might not have been as dramatic as the photograph she would see later on the cover of *Life* magazine, the one of that sailor bending a nurse over his arm and kissing her on the lips. But that didn't stop Stephanie's heart from racing, and it didn't stop her from deciding, right then and there, that she was going to marry Jimmy Scott when she grew up.

# CHAPTER 1

September 21, 2005

Stephanie Watson loved autumn, especially the warm and hazy butter-yellow days of Indian summer.

For what seemed the first time since her husband Chuck's death last year, she took pleasure in the beauty of her surroundings as she walked along the street toward town. The leaves on the trees that lined the thoroughfare were turning yellow, gold, orange, and red, and flowerbeds wore a spectacular coat of riotous colors.

Why, she wondered, did nature's palette seem more vibrant in autumn?

Next year, she would plant chrysanthemums along the front of her house. And asters. She was partial to asters. She hadn't gardened this year. Last spring, the idea of watering and weeding all summer long seemed far more than she could manage. But next year? Yes, next year she would be ready.

Her widowed friends had told her things would get better, that even though she continued to miss her husband of fifty years, time would dull the pain. She didn't believe them at first.

She didn't believe them for a long while. But it seemed they were right. The pain in her heart was less, and the memories in her mind were sweeter.

Stephanie was thankful to God for that.

Bells chimed overhead as she opened the door to Terri's Tangles Beauty Salon. Terri Sampson glanced over her shoulder, her hands busy with blow-dryer and brush as she finished styling Till Hart's silver-gray hair.

"Please tell me you're early, Steph." Terri's gaze darted to the clock on the wall.

"I am. It's such a beautiful day I hated to stay indoors another minute. So I decided to walk over." Stephanie met Till's gaze in the mirror. "Good morning, Till. How are you?"

"I'm dandy, thanks. And you?"

"I'm good, too."

Till and Stephanie had known each other since they were girls, living their entire lives in this sleepy little town on the plains of southern Idaho. The two women had many things in common, many of the same beliefs, likes and dislikes. However, while Till, the granddaughter of the town's founder, had never married, Stephanie had been married nearly all of her life.

Memories of Chuck flashed in her mind, and she felt a bittersweet warmth in her chest. How she missed him, his wry sense of humor, the gentle touch of his hand beneath her elbow as they crossed the street, his grumpy complaints as he searched for his ever-misplaced eyeglasses.

Terri turned off the blow-dryer, bringing a sudden silence to the beauty shop.

After a moment, Till said, "Steph, you'll never guess who's returned to Hart's Crossing to live." She didn't wait for an answer. "James Scott. Can you imagine? After all of these years, he's decided to move back to Idaho." Till looked at Terri. "You know the big blue house on Horizon Street?"

"The Patterson house?"

"That's the one. Only the Pattersons didn't own it. It's belonged to the Scott family since it was built back in the late thirties. The Pattersons rented it for twenty years."

Stephanie sat on one of the chairs attached to a hair dryer. "I didn't know the Scotts still owned that house. I thought it was sold after Mrs. Scott went to live in Seattle with James and his wife."

"No." Till shook her head. "Betty Frazier has been managing it for them for at least a decade. She was chomping at the bit to sell it, too. It would have brought her realty firm a very nice commission. I can tell you, she *never* expected James to return to live in it. Who would? Not after fifty years."

"Fifty-two years," Stephanie corrected. "He was eighteen when he went into the army."

Till leaned toward Terri and, in a stage whisper, said, "Steph and James were sweet on each other when they were kids. Everyone except his mother called him Jimmy back then. My, oh my. What a handsome fellow he was."

Terri's eyes widened with interest. "Is that right, Steph? You had a boyfriend before Mr. Watson? I can't picture that"

"After fifty years with Chuck, it's hard for me to imagine it either." Stephanie smiled. "But it's true. Jimmy Scott was my first love."

Terri sat on the second dryer chair. "Tell me more. You know there's no keeping secrets in a hair salon."

Stephanie allowed memories to drift through her mind—sweet, innocent, misty. Goodness, who was that girl and when had she become the white-haired woman she saw in the mirror today? It seemed only yesterday that Jimmy Scott kissed her outside the Apollo Movie Theater. But yesterday was actually sixty years ago.

"Well?" Terri prompted.

"I was his best friend when we were in elementary school, and when I was nine, I decided I was going to marry him. That was the night he gave me my first kiss." She laughed softly. "We dated all through high school, and by then everyone else expected us to get married, too."

"So what happened? Why didn't you marry him?"

"For one thing, he never asked me. He meant to, I think, but he never did. After he went into the army, we corresponded, but then I met Chuck and he stole my heart."

"And you had to write Mr. Scott a Dear John letter?" Terri looked from Stephanie to Till and back again. "How awful for him."

Stephanie shook her head. "Actually, he'd met someone, too. It all turned out for the best. If he hadn't gone away, I might not have married Chuck, and James might not have married Martha. They were together almost as many years as Chuck and I."

"James lost his wife about three years ago," Till told Terri as she rose from the styling chair, patting her hair with her right hand. "To cancer. I heard she was ill for a long time before passing. Must have been terribly hard on him and their children, losing her that way."

As difficult as losing Chuck was for Stephanie, she was thankful her husband hadn't suffered. He'd enjoyed good health right up to the end. On the day he died, he'd played a round of golf, come home, sat in his easy chair, and slipped into the presence of Jesus.

Till stepped toward the cash register. "What's the damage, Terri?"

"Fifteen today, Miss Hart."

"You need to raise your prices, young lady." Till placed two bills on the counter, a twenty and a five. "A worker is worthy of her wage, you know." She gave a farewell wave to Stephanie, and then left the salon.

"Just give me a minute to sweep up, Steph, and then we'll get you started."

"No hurry. Take your time."

Time was one thing Stephanie had plenty of these days.

～

JAMES SCOTT STOOD IN THE LIVING ROOM OF HIS BOYHOOD HOME, wondering if he was as crazy as his children thought. Why would a man in his right mind leave the city where he'd lived and worked for more than forty-five years to return to a small town like Hart's Crossing? That's what his son and eldest daughter had asked several times over the past few weeks. James had a hard time giving Kurt or Jenna an answer, mainly because he wasn't sure himself.

James and his wife, Martha, had loved living in Washington State. They'd owned a lovely home in Bremerton, purchased long before Seattle area housing prices shot through the roof. All three of their children—Kurt, Jenna, and Paula—had been raised in that four-bedroom home, and it was there Martha had breathed her last one windy March morning more than three years before.

Maybe if his kids and grandkids lived in the Pacific Northwest, James would have remained in Bremerton. But Kurt and his family had settled in Pennsylvania after a series of job-related moves; Jenna lived in England with her husband of five years; and Paula, a divorced mom of two, had a home in Florida. Visits to Washington were few and far between for all of them. James understood. They had busy lives of their own.

"But Hart's Crossing, Dad?" Jenna had made it sound like the end of the world. "You haven't been back there since Grandma Scott moved in with you and Mom. I was still a teenager, for Pete's sake. Why not move into a nice retirement community? There's got to be some good ones in your area. That way you can still be near your friends."

"I have a few friends in Idaho, too," he'd answered her.

"Besides, the cost of living is less there, and I own that house free and clear."

"Dad, you're not having money problems, are you?"

That comment had irritated him. Did she think he was in his dotage? "No, Jenna. I'm not. But thanks for asking."

His daughter might live halfway around the globe, but James had been able to imagine the exasperated expression on her face at the end of that phone call.

Well, it was done now. His kids would have to accept his decision, like it or not.

The doorbell rang. James was glad for the interruption. He needed to stop woolgathering and resume his unpacking. He pulled open the door and discovered a woman on the stoop. "Yes?"

"Jimmy Scott, it really is you. I heard you were back, but I needed to come see for myself."

No one had called him Jimmy in decades.

"Have I changed so much?" she asked, a twinkle appearing in her faded blue eyes.

James pushed open the screen door, peering more closely at the woman. About his age, she had a cap of curly white hair and a pleasantly round face with plenty of lines etched around her eyes and mouth. She looked familiar but he couldn't quite ...

Then she smiled.

"Steph!"

"In the flesh."

He motioned her inside. "How are you?"

"I'm well, James. And you?"

"Good. I'm good." He went to the sofa and cleared away some of the clutter to make room for her. "Have a seat. I'd offer you a cup of coffee, but the coffeemaker isn't unpacked yet. How 'bout a glass of water?"

"I don't need a thing, thanks. I'm fine." She settled onto the couch. "I can't stay but a moment anyway."

James moved a box off his recliner and sat, too.

"I should apologize for barging in this way. But when Till told me this morning that you moved back after all these years, I just had to stop by to say hello. It's such a surprise. Such a nice surprise."

"My kids think I've lost my mind, returning to a rural town in Idaho when I could live anywhere else in the country."

She laughed. "Most adult children *would* think that insane. Tell me about your children and grandchildren."

James was happy to oblige. "My oldest, Kurt, lives in Pennsylvania. He and his wife have three kids, a boy and two girls. Kurt's in the computer business, but don't ask me what he does. I know just enough to send and receive email and surf the Internet a bit."

He didn't add that his son was always sending him new software to try out and that his failure to use them was a great disappointment for Kurt.

"My middle daughter, Jenna, and her husband live overseas. In England. He works for the U.S. government over there. They've been married about five years. No children yet, but they're still hoping it will happen."

*Hope* was a mild word for what his daughter felt. Jenna ached for a baby. But at forty-one, she heard her biological clock like the *bong* of Big Ben, and her childlessness had left her angry at God.

"My youngest, Paula, got divorced last year. She's a school teacher living in Florida with her two daughters."

James wasn't sorry his philandering ex-son-in-law was out of the picture, but his heart broke whenever he spoke to Paula and heard the lingering sadness in her voice. He wished he could make it better.

Stephanie put her hands together in front of her chin, almost a clap but not quite. "Five grandchildren. How wonderful for you."

"What about your family?"

"My daughter, Miranda, has made me a grandmother of two, Isabella and Foster. They live right here in Hart's Crossing, so I'm quite spoiled." Her smile was gentle as she added, "It must be hard for you, having your family living so far away. Is that one of the reasons you came back to Hart's Crossing?"

"Mostly. Or maybe I'm trying to recapture a bit of my youth." He shrugged. "But I think there were just too many memories in Bremerton to stay."

Stephanie's smile faded. "I know what you mean."

James saw the sorrow that mirrored his own. "Of course you do. I heard about Chuck's passing. I'm sorry for your loss. The few times I met him, he seemed like a real nice guy."

"He was. Salt of the earth." She rose from the sofa, the sparkle gone from her eyes. "I've taken up enough of your time. I should be getting on home."

"I'm glad you stopped by." He followed her to the door. "I'm sure we'll see each other again."

She smiled. A bit halfhearted but still a smile. "In a town this size, I can guarantee it."

James watched her descend the porch steps, then closed the door and returned to work. At the rate he was going, he wouldn't find that coffeepot for another week.

∽

"You set eternity in our hearts, Lord," Stephanie said softly as she walked toward home. "So no matter how long people live, no matter how old they are, it always feels wrong when death comes to someone we love."

She thought of James, leaving his home in Washington after all these years because there were too many memories of his departed wife. Would Stephanie do the same if her daughter and family weren't here in Hart's Crossing? Would she run away if she could?

And yet, James hadn't looked like a man who was running away. Yes, there had been a note of sadness in his voice when he'd mentioned the memories, but there had also been strength of purpose in his gaze. He hadn't doubted his decision to return to Hart's Crossing. Not a bit.

But wasn't that always true of James? Even as a teenager, he'd seemed to know with unshakeable assurance where he was to go and what he was to do. It was that certainty that had taken him away from Hart's Crossing, changing the course of both their lives.

Stephanie wondered what would change next, now that he'd returned.

## CHAPTER 2

September was one of Stephanie Watson's two months to hostess the weekly meeting of the Thimbleberry Quilting Club. She loved having these women in her home. It made the old place feel lived in and less lonely. Most of the time, she rattled around in it like a bean in a baby's rattle.

Chuck and Stephanie's only child, Miranda, lived with her husband and two teenagers on the opposite side of Hart's Crossing—no more than two miles away—in one of the new subdivisions that had sprung up in the last few years. Miranda tried to stop by to see her mother on a regular basis, but with a job in the mayor's office and a busy family to care for, it wasn't easy.

Till Hart removed her wire-rimmed glasses and set them on the arm of her chair. "Oh, dear. My eyes do get tired these days." She shook her head. "Getting old is such a bother."

"Isn't that the truth," Francine Hunter said with an emphatic nod.

Stephanie couldn't agree more. Every year went by faster than the one before. It was enough to make an old woman dizzy. Still, if it weren't for her tired joints and miscellaneous aches and pains, she wouldn't believe she was sixty-nine. In her mind, she was no more than twenty-five or twenty-six, the same age as the club's youngest member, Patti Bedford.

"What do you think, Frani?" Ethel Jacobsen asked. "Should we start working on a wedding quilt for Angie? Hasn't Bill Palmer popped the question yet?"

Five pairs of eyes turned toward Francine, but she shook her head, disappointing them all.

"That man's besotted with your daughter," Mary Benrey, the secretary at Hart's Crossing Community Church, said to Francine. "Why on earth is he dragging his feet?"

"Well, at first he was waiting for her to become a Christian. Now that that's happened, I think he's waiting because he's afraid she'll bolt back to California if he moves too fast. She's always been so independent. Bill's taking no chances on spooking her."

Stephanie's thoughts drifted to the autumn she first met Chuck Watson. Jimmy Scott had been gone for four months, an eternity when a girl is seventeen and all her friends have dates on Friday nights.

She and her best friend, Wilma Milburn, were sitting in the booth closest to the door at the Over the Rainbow Diner when Owen Watson came in, accompanied by a tall, good-looking boy Stephanie hadn't seen before. Owen stopped when he saw them.

"Hi, Steph. Wilma. Meet my cousin, Chuck. He's gonna be staying with us for the next year. Chuck, this is Steph and Wilma."

Chuck Watson—broad-shouldered, golden-haired, blue-eyed—smiled at Stephanie. "A pleasure to meet you."

Unlike Bill with Angie, Chuck didn't waste any time. He asked Stephanie out that same night. When she said no because of Jimmy, he didn't give up. He pursued her relentlessly. Little gifts. Flowers.

Phone calls. He wore her down with his persistence. And one day, she just couldn't say no again. After their first date, falling in love with Chuck was inevitable. They were engaged by the New Year, and their wedding was the day after her high school graduation.

Chuck's one year in Hart's Crossing with his aunt, uncle, and cousins turned into a lifetime with Stephanie. Fifty years. How blessed she'd been to be his wife.

"Did you know Mr. Scott, Frani, before he moved away?" Patti Bedford asked, catching Stephanie's attention and drawing her thoughts back to the present.

"Not really. I was only eleven when he left Hart's Crossing to go off to war. Nothing mattered to me back then but playing with my favorite dolls and trying to escape practicing the piano when my mother told me to."

All the women laughed.

"He must have been a real heartthrob when he was younger." Patti took several careful stitches before adding, "He reminds me of Sean Connery. Don't you think so? Very distinguished with that white hair and close-trimmed beard."

Stephanie frowned. She didn't think James resembled the movie star at all. He looked like James. Sure, his hair was silver and thinning instead of black and thick, but he was still just an older version of the boy she'd known so long ago. Handsome, yes. But Sean Connery? She didn't see it.

"Well …" Till set her reading glasses onto the bridge of her nose. "One thing's for sure. His return has given folks something new to talk about."

～

James slid into a booth at the Over the Rainbow Diner and took a menu—one sheet of gold-colored paper encased in a plastic sleeve—from the rack beneath the window. After several days of his own rather pathetic cooking, he was ready for a meal prepared by someone else.

"Hello."

He looked up at the waitress as she set a tall glass of water on the table. An attractive woman in her early forties, she wore a white apron over a red and white striped dress that was straight out of the diner's heyday. The uniform went well with the retro decor.

"You must be Mr. Scott."

James raised an eyebrow.

She laughed. "There aren't that many strangers in town who fit your description." She held out a hand in welcome. "I'm Nancy Raney. My husband, Harry, and I own the diner."

"It looks great in here." He shook her hand. "Reminds me of when I was a boy."

"Thanks. It was pretty run down when we bought the place fifteen years ago. It took a lot of remodeling before we could reopen." She motioned with her arm, as if inviting him to inspect the interior a second time. "We tried hard to recapture the way it looked in some of the photos that folks like Miss Hart had in their albums. Photos and the memory of some who lived here in the 1940s and '50s."

"Old-timers, you mean?" He chuckled.

She pretended to be horrified. "I'd never call Miss Hart an old-timer." The twinkle in her eyes gave her jest away.

"Smart girl." He glanced again at the menu. "I'll take the Scarecrow burger with a chocolate shake. Well done on the burger."

"Coming right up, Mr. Scott."

After Nancy walked away, James dropped the menu in the rack and turned his gaze out the window. Across the street was the Apollo Movie Theater. He'd noticed on the day he arrived that, like this restaurant, it appeared to have been restored, at least on the exterior. The marquee announced that one of the summer's top action films would be playing over the weekend. Maybe he'd go see it tomorrow.

The door to the diner opened, and the sound of women's voices drew his gaze away from the window.

"Well, look who's here," Till Hart said as she and Stephanie neared his booth. "James, were your ears burning? We talked about you at our quilting club meeting this morning."

Out of habit, he started to rise.

Till waved him down. "Land sakes. Don't get up for us."

"Would you care to join me for lunch?"

Till glanced at her companion, then said, "We'd love to," and slid onto the seat across from him. Stephanie sat beside her.

"Are you feeling more settled?" Till asked.

James took two menus from the rack and handed them to the women. "Yes. Although, to be honest, it's a bit strange. The house is familiar from my boyhood, and my furniture is familiar from my house in Bremerton. But the two together?" He shrugged. "They seem an odd combination."

"I can imagine they would." Stephanie gave him a warm smile.

It occurred to James that she was as pretty today as she'd been when he kissed her on V-J Day. Granted, it was a different kind of pretty. Her face was softly wrinkled, and the freckles that had sprinkled her nose as a girl were gone. Her hair was white instead of the golden blond shade of her youth, and she wore it short and curly rather than long and straight, the way he remembered it. But the style flattered her. The one thing that hadn't changed was that smile. He'd always been partial to Stephanie's smile.

Nancy arrived at the table with two more water glasses. "Hello, ladies. Joining Mr. Scott for lunch today?"

"That we are." Till pointed at the menu without having looked at it. "I'd like the Emerald City salad, please, with the dressing on the side."

"Anything to drink?"

"Water's fine, thank you."

"And you, Mrs. Watson?"

"I'll have the same, Nancy. Thanks."

More people entered the diner. A farmer in overalls and work boots. A businessman in slacks and short-sleeved shirt, sans coat and tie. Two young mothers with several toddlers in tow.

"So tell me, James," Till said. "I'm sure you're sick of the question, but I want to know. What brought you back to Hart's Crossing?"

She was right. He was sick of that question. Sick of trying to come up with an answer that sounded logical—or at least humorous. This time he didn't choose his words carefully. He just spoke from his heart.

"Till, I've been asking God what I'm supposed to do with the rest of my life ever since I retired two years ago. When the Pattersons moved out of Mother's house, it seemed like the answer to my prayers." His gaze shifted to Stephanie. "I felt like the Lord said go, so here I am."

∼

His answer made Stephanie smile. She liked knowing that James was the kind of man who sought God's guidance.

Nancy approached their booth, carrying a large brown tray above her shoulder with one hand. In the blink of an eye, she placed the two salads, hamburger platter, and milkshake on the table. "Enjoy your lunch. Let me know if you need anything else." Then she was off to wait on other customers.

Stephanie picked up her fork. "The Scarecrow is my favorite burger," she told James. "I love fried onions."

"I hope it's as good as it used to be. I'll try not to breathe on you when I'm finished." He punctuated the comment with a wink and a grin.

*For goodness sake.* Stephanie caught her breath. *Patti's right.* James did bear more than a passing resemblance to Sean Connery.

# CHAPTER 3

**From:** "Kurt Scott" <kurtscott@fiberpipe.net>
**Sent:** Saturday, September 24 8:16 AM
**To:** "James Scott" <jtscott@fiberpipe.net>
**Subject:** Online yet?

Hi, Dad. Just wondering if your computer is up and running. Haven't heard from you since you called to say you and the movers got to Hart's Crossing okay. Directory assistance didn't have a local number for you as of yesterday, so I tried your cell phone but couldn't get through. I didn't bother to leave a message. I figured you're busy.

I wish I could take some time off to help you move in, but it just isn't possible right now. Glad you understand. Don't overdo it and hurt yourself with all that unpacking. Ask for help or hire somebody if you need to.

The kids returned to school a month ago, and now everybody's going a different direction several nights a week. I remember how we always had family dinners together when I was a boy, and I'm wondering how you and Mom managed that.

It seems like half the time at my house, nobody's home at the dinner hour, let alone sitting down to eat together.

Give us a call or respond to this email when you can. Sure hope you're not regretting your decision to move.

Kurt

~

**From:** "James Scott" <jtscott@fiberpipe.net>
**Sent:** Saturday, September 24 10:32 AM
**To:** "Kurt & Neta" <kurtscott@fiberpipe.net>
**Subject:** Re: Online yet?

GOOD MORNING, KURT. MY TELEPHONE SERVICE WAS FINALLY UP and working as of 4:45 p.m. yesterday. My number is 208-555-4632. I set up my trusty computer in my boyhood bedroom, which is now serving as my office. This is the first time I've turned it on, so I'm glad to see it's working. The worst of the unpacking is done, and except for a few minor aches and pains (which could be my age more than anything else), I'm feeling fine. You don't have to worry about me. I still have a modicum of good sense in this head of mine.

I had lunch today with two old friends. I haven't seen either of them in more than twenty years. Even when your grandmother was still living in Hart's Crossing, our paths didn't cross much. As you might guess, we had a lot of catching up to do. We did a fair share of reminiscing about the "good old days."

I'd planned to go to a movie later today, but I was invited to see the local high school football team—the Hart's Crossing Hornets—play against one of its biggest rivals, the Sawtooth Pioneers. (They were rivals fifty years ago, too. Some things never change.) Since the weather is good, I thought I'd do that. Go, Hornets!

I'll call you soon.

Love, Dad

~

STEPHANIE WAS NOT A HUGE FAN OF FOOTBALL, BUT SHE *WAS* A huge fan of her grandson, Foster. This was his first at-home game as part of the senior varsity football team. There was no way she would miss seeing him play today, short of a blizzard in September. Judging by the clear blue sky overhead and the warm breeze rustling the trees in her front yard, she needn't fear snow.

When the doorbell rang a few minutes before noon, Stephanie grabbed her jacket, lap blanket, and purse on her way to answer it.

The door opened before she got there. "It's me, Grandma," Isabella called. "Are you ready?"

"I'm ready, dear." She received her seventeen-year-old granddaughter's quick hug and peck on the cheek. "Are your parents with you?"

"No. Mom had some work to do at the office. She said she'll meet us at the school before the game starts, but I wouldn't bet on it. You know how she forgets everything else when she's working." She gave a little shrug, as if denying the disappointment in her voice. "Dad's helping with the concessions, so he went early with Foster."

Stephanie and Isabella stepped onto the porch, and Stephanie pulled the front door closed behind her, pausing to be sure it was locked.

"I like your jogging suit, Grandma. That blue matches your eyes. Where'd you get it?"

"From the Coldwater Creek catalog."

They walked to the curb, where Isabella had parked her Subaru Outback.

"Dear," Stephanie said as she opened the passenger side door,

"I hope you don't mind, but I offered to pick up an old friend of mine. He's just returned to Hart's Crossing, and I invited him to come see Foster play."

"No trouble." Isabella slipped into the driver's seat. "Where does he live?"

"On Horizon Street."

"I can get there off of Pine, right?"

"Yes." Stephanie fastened her seat belt. "That would be the best route to take."

Isabella turned the key in the ignition, glanced over her left shoulder, then pulled away from the curb. A responsible driver—at least when her grandmother was in the car—she drove slowly through a neighborhood filled with large trees, green lawns, and two-story homes, most of them seventy or more years old.

"Who's this friend of yours, Grandma?"

"His name is James Scott. We went to school together when we were children."

"The name doesn't sound familiar. Do I know him?"

"No. James left Hart's Crossing a year before I married your grandfather."

Isabella cast her a surprised glance. "He's been gone *that* long? What made him come back here of all places?"

"He felt it's where God wants him."

Isabella didn't respond to that, and Stephanie didn't expect her to. She knew her granddaughter was going through a questioning phase, wondering as she began her senior year in high school what God wanted her to do with her future. She supposed Isabella would be surprised to learn the elderly also pray for God to show them what to do with their lives.

A few minutes later, they pulled to a stop near the curb in front of the house at 2240 Horizon Street.

As they stopped, Stephanie recalled another time when she'd sat in a car in front of the Scott home. It had been a sunny day, much like this one, only in the spring. Instead of a midsize Subaru, that car had been a 1948 Chevrolet Fleetmaster, better known as a "Woody." And unlike today, Stephanie hadn't been happy.

"You didn't have to join the army, Jimmy." She'd choked back tears. "What about college?"

"That's why I joined, Steph. It'll help pay for college when I get out. You know Mom can't afford to send me, and since I didn't get that football scholarship, this is the only way I can get to college."

"But what if you're sent to Korea?"

He'd put his arm around her shoulders. "I probably will be, but I'll be okay. I don't plan to get hurt." He'd given her a cocky grin.

Stephanie had wanted to hit him. "Nobody *plans* to get hurt, Jimmy. Sometimes it just happens. Sometimes soldiers die." Right then, she'd felt like she might die, too.

"Hey. You know me. I'm tough. And I've got to come back for my best girl, don't I?"

She'd let her tears fall then, crying her heart out, and Jimmy had held her close as he promised again and again that he would be okay.

He'd been right about that. James hadn't been injured in Korea. But neither had he return to Hart's Crossing for Stephanie. By the time he'd gotten out of the military, things had changed for them both.

Stephanie couldn't help thinking that life was made more interesting by the different twists and turns it took along the way.

The door to the screened-in porch opened, and James stepped into view. He waved at her, then came down the four steps and walked briskly toward the car.

Stephanie pressed the button to lower her window. "Hello, James. Isn't it a beautiful day?"

"It certainly is." He opened the rear door and folded himself into the compact area behind Stephanie.

"This is my granddaughter, Isabella. Isabella, this is Mr. Scott."

"Hey, Mr. Scott." Isabella put the car in gear.

"A pleasure to meet you, young lady. Thanks for the lift."

"Any time for a friend of my grandma."

∽

"Isabella looks like you," James told Stephanie half an hour later as they sat, side by side, on the metal bleachers, with stadium seats supporting their backs.

Stephanie's smile told him she was pleased by his observation.

"And she's got that same charisma you had at that age."

That comment made her blush.

"Does your grandson look like you, too?"

She laughed, a pretty sound. "Heavens, no. He's the spitting image of his father. Only taller. Very tall for a boy his age. He turned sixteen this month."

"What position does he play?"

"Halfback. No, wait. Maybe he's a fullback. Oh, dear. I can never keep those positions straight. I was never much on football."

"I remember." And he did. Back when they were in school, she only went to the games because he was on the team, and even then, she went reluctantly. Stephanie had much preferred the theater arts and music to sports.

The high school band struck up a rousing chorus of the school song as it marched into view. It wasn't a large band, but the kids played with enthusiasm. Right after the band came the visiting team. Across the field, the fans of the Pioneers gave shouts of encouragement.

The noise level shot up several decibels when the Hornets, wearing the school colors of black and gold, ran onto the field. Parents and students jumped to their feet, cheering and waving signs, flags, and banners. The Hart's Crossing cheerleaders jumped and flipped and shook their pom-poms.

"Which one is your grandson?" James shouted above the din.

Stephanie hesitated a moment, her gaze moving down the line of players who stood on the opposite side of the field. Then she pointed. "There he is. Number 32."

James squinted. His eyesight was good for a man his age, but the width of a football field made reading the numbers on the football jerseys a challenge. When he finally found the boy, he nodded. "You're right. He is a tall drink of water."

She beamed with a grandmother's pride, and James couldn't help thinking she was the prettiest woman in the stadium.

# CHAPTER 4

For more than two decades, James and Martha Scott had attended a thriving interdenominational church on the east side of Puget Sound. The last James heard, the membership had grown to well over three thousand.

Back when his wife's health began to fail and the long drive to church each Sunday became impossible, members of the congregation had come to them, bringing love, comfort, prayers, and meals. And they'd kept coming, through the long days, weeks, and months of her illness, through the many hospitalizations, through her death and the funeral, and through James's time of mourning.

Leaving that godly family was the most difficult part of his move from Washington.

As the congregation of Hart's Crossing Community Church sang the last stanza of "O for a Thousand Tongues to Sing," James couldn't help thinking what a contrast this much smaller body of believers was to his former church. Yet the same Spirit was unmistakably present here. What an awesome thing that was, to know, no matter where James went, the Lord was there before him.

While he missed the electric keyboard, guitars, drums, and contemporary music of his former church—a surprising admission, perhaps, for a man of his age—James found no fault with the sermon delivered by John Gunn. The pastor's teaching from the book of Romans was direct and passionate. James knew he'd be glad to hear this young man preach many a sermon.

He glanced at Stephanie, seated on his right. She looked lovely in that blue and white outfit of hers. Very becoming.

Till Hart had been the one who invited James to come to Hart's Crossing Community this morning. When he arrived at the church, he'd looked around the sanctuary for her but hadn't found her. Seeing Stephanie, it had seemed a natural choice to sit beside her.

And why shouldn't he feel that way? They were friends. Longtime friends.

After another hymn and a benediction, the service ended. The sanctuary grew noisy, people visiting with one another as they dispersed.

John Gunn strode to the end of the pew where James stood. "You must be Mr. Scott." He held out a hand of welcome.

"Guilty as charged."

"Miss Hart told us you might visit today. We hope you'll return."

"I will. It was a good service."

The pastor motioned to an attractive woman on the opposite side of the sanctuary. As she drew closer, he confirmed what James suspected. "This is my wife, Anne Gunn. Anne, I'd like you to meet James Scott. He grew up in Hart's Crossing but has lived in Washington for many years. Isn't that what I heard? Washington State."

"Yes, that's right. In the Seattle area."

Anne shook his hand as her husband had moments before. "Welcome, Mr. Scott."

"Thanks. It's good to be here."

They visited for a few minutes until James sensed Stephanie moving away from him toward the opposite end of the pew. As politely and quickly as he could, he brought the conversation with John and Anne Gunn to a close with a promise to return the next Sunday. Then he retrieved his well-worn Bible from the pew and followed after Stephanie.

He caught up with her outside. "Steph."

She turned toward him.

Until that moment, he hadn't known what he intended to say. "I was wondering if you might have lunch with me. We could drive up to the resort, if you'd like. It would be my way of thanking you for the delightful time I had yesterday at the game."

She hesitated a moment before she gave her head a slow shake. "I'm sorry, James. My lunch is already cooking in the crock-pot."

"Oh." He was surprised by the disappointment her refusal caused. "Well, another time then."

She touched his forearm with her fingertips before he could move away. "Perhaps you'd like to join me at my place. The food won't be as fancy as what the lodge at Timber Creek serves, but it's nutritious."

His disappointment was gone in a flash. "If you're sure I wouldn't be intruding."

"I wouldn't have asked if that were the case." Her smile was as light and lovely as the Indian summer day.

James's old ticker beat like a set of bongos. "Then I'll be glad to come. When should I be there?"

"You may come now, if you like."

He would like. He would like it a lot.

The pot roast and vegetables that simmered in the Crockpot would normally provide four meals for Stephanie. But men usually had bigger appetites, James included if that Scarecrow burger he'd devoured on Friday was any indication.

"Please make yourself at home," she told him as they entered her house. "I'll just be a few minutes."

She went into her bedroom and changed from her Sunday attire into a pink cotton blouse and a pair of comfortable denim slacks. A quick glance at the full length mirror told her she'd added a few pounds over the summer. She would have to do something about that. Why did weight maintenance become so difficult as one grew older?

Never mind. Diets were best begun on Mondays. This was Sunday, and she had a guest waiting for her in the living room.

Not just any guest either. An old friend, one who was feeling lonely after his return to his hometown. She'd seen the loneliness in his eyes when she declined his invitation to dine at the resort. That was why she'd asked him to join her here, one old friend helping another.

"Can I get you anything to drink?" she called to James on her way to the kitchen.

"No, thanks." He appeared in the doorway. "I'd like to help. Why don't I set the table?"

There was something special, something intimate, about his offer, and her heart fluttered in response. "Okay." She motioned toward the sideboard. "You'll find napkins and the silverware in there."

"I like the way you've decorated the kitchen. This pale shade of green is very restful on the eyes."

Stephanie laughed softly as she lifted the lid of the Crockpot.

"What?"

She glanced over her shoulder, meeting his gaze. "Oh, I just thought of how Chuck wouldn't have noticed if I'd painted the walls with red and white stripes. He could be terribly obtuse at times." Odd, the way some things that were irritating about a loved one when they were with you became the very things you missed the most after they were gone.

Unexpected tears stung her eyes, and she glanced away, not wanting James to see them.

There was tender understanding in his voice as he said, "We're two lucky people, you and I. We both had good, long marriages."

Stephanie wiped her eyes with the hem of her apron. "I don't believe in luck. Making a marriage last fifty years takes God's blessing, plenty of faith and love, and even more grit and determination." She turned and offered James a tremulous smile. "But you know that as well as I do."

He nodded. "Yes, I do."

James returned to his table-setting duties. Stephanie suspected he was giving her time to collect her emotions, and she was grateful.

A short while later, with their food on the table, James pulled out a chair for her.

"Thank you, James."

"My pleasure. And I'm the one who needs to say thanks. This is much nicer than eating by myself." He sat opposite her.

"Would you like to say the blessing?"

"I'd be honored." He bowed his head.

Stephanie listened to his prayer and, when he was done, echoed his amen. Eyes open again, she motioned toward the platter of food in the center of the small kitchen table. "Please. Help yourself."

As he did so, he said, "Pastor Gunn preached an excellent sermon this morning."

"He's a gifted teacher. We're fortunate to have him. Although I must admit I wasn't so sure when he first came to us. He's so young. Not yet forty."

James chuckled. "Amazing, isn't it? How forty became young.

Remember the sixties when it was 'don't trust anyone over thirty.' I'm thinking eighty looks pretty good these days."

She nodded. It was true. In her mind, she was young, still ready and able to conquer the world. Her body, however, was headed downhill fast. There were times when she caught a glimpse of her reflection in the mirror and wondered who it was. Not her, certainly.

"Steph, I'm curious about something. Do you ever regret not leaving Hart's Crossing?"

She pondered the question, testing her feelings. "No. Not really. I've always been happy here. There are drawbacks to small town life, of course, but there are advantages, too. We know our next-door neighbors, and we never have to fight rush-hour traffic. Chuck had a good job with the county highway district. They hired him in 1955, and he worked there until he retired. Not many people stay with the same company for that long these days."

"No, indeed."

"At least twice a year, Chuck took me to Boise or Salt Lake for the weekend so we could see a play or the opera. He called it my biannual culture fix. Once he took me to New York City for an entire week. We saw five Broadway shows. It was heaven."

"You always were passionate about the theater."

She felt a rush of pleasure that James remembered that about her.

"You were a good actress, too. I wouldn't have been surprised to learn you were a famous performer on Broadway or a movie star."

Stephanie laughed softly, denying his comment with a shake of her head, even though acting on Broadway had been her dream, once upon a time and long, long ago.

James's gaze was gentle, and although he didn't laugh aloud, she knew he enjoyed the shared memories as much as she did.

Then, ever so slowly, his smile faded. His eyes narrowed, and his brows drew together in concentration.

After a long silence, he said, "Sometimes I wonder what would've happened to us if I hadn't joined the army."

∼

STEPHANIE'S HEART SKIPPED A BEAT, FOR JAMES'S QUESTION mirrored her own thoughts, her own *guilty* thoughts. It seemed wrong for them to sit in this kitchen, in a home her husband had paid for, wondering what might have been between them if James hadn't left Hart's Crossing.

And still she wondered.

## CHAPTER 5

**From:** "James Scott" <jtscott@fiberpipe.net>
**Sent:** Wednesday, September 28 8:02 AM
**To:** "Jenna & Ray" <jscottengland@yahoo.com>
**Subject:** Greetings from Idaho

Hello, Jenna and Ray.

All is well here. You'll be pleased to know that I feel more settled in my new/old home. The boxes are dwindling away a few more each day. It's amazing how many things your mother and I accumulated over the years. I sold a lot in my garage sale but maybe not enough. Don't worry. I did keep everything you said you wanted, and those things are in boxes in my garage.

Jenna, I know you were worried about me moving to this small town after being gone for five decades, but I can assure you, I'm going to be quite happy. The slower pace of Hart's Crossing agrees with me. Many of the people I knew as a boy have either moved or passed away, but there are a few old friends who still live here. It's good to become reacquainted with them.

I attended a small community church on Sunday and feel certain it will become my church home. The pastor is a young man—in his late thirties, I think—and an excellent teacher. He's on fire for the Lord, which is something I want in a pastor. You know how important it is for your father to be planted in a good, Bible-believing church. I can do without a lot, but I can't do without that. Or I sure wouldn't want to do without it, at any rate.

After church, I dined at the home of one of those old friends I mentioned above. I was one grade ahead of Stephanie Watson when we were in school. (Her last name was Carlson then.) She's a lovely woman. You would like her. She was widowed last year. She and her husband were married even longer than your mother and I.

I've hired a neighbor boy to mow the yard every week, and come spring, I'm going to get the exterior of the house painted. I'm not too fond of the bright shade of blue that's on there now.

By the time you two come to visit me, I should have a guest room all ready for you. I hope that visit will be some time soon. I miss you.

Love, Dad

P.S. My new phone number is 208-555-4632. I haven't changed my cellular service yet, and I still don't have an answering machine hooked up. Best time to catch me at home is in the morning.

∼

**From:** "Jenna Scott-Kirkpatrick" <jscottengland@yahoo.com>
**Sent:** Wednesday, September 21 10:02 PM
**To:** "Dad" <jtscott@fiberpipe.net>
**Subject:** Glad all is well

Hi, Daddy. Your email was waiting for me when I got home from work. I'm glad to know you're doing okay. I still don't understand why you wanted to move to Idaho, but it sounds like, for now, you're glad that you did. Just remember, you can always go back to Washington. Nobody will blame you if you change your mind.

Ray and I are planning a holiday in Greece within the next twelve months. He isn't sure when he'll be able to take his vacation, so we have to be flexible. Who knows when we'll make it back to the States? You should get your passport in order and come see us.

I'm glad to know you're making friends, but please be careful when it comes to relationships with lonely widows. You're a handsome man who's financially well off. Some women would be eager to take advantage of you. Don't lose your head, Daddy.

I love you,
Jenna

∼

"Don't lose my head," James muttered, staring at the computer screen. "Women eager to take advantage of me. Of all the idiotic—" He cut himself off.

Why did Jenna insist on treating him like a half-wit? No, worse than that. Like a child. Imagine what Jenna would have written if she knew he and Stephanie were going to the movies tomorrow evening.

He took several long, calming breaths.

In his daughter's defense, Jenna had no way of knowing what a wonderful woman Stephanie was. But he still thought it best if he didn't mention his growing attraction for her in future emails to his children.

"What they don't know can't hurt them."

James glanced through the remainder of the email in the Inbox. Nothing from either Kurt or Paula, but there was the daily devotional from purposedrivenlife.com. He paused to read it, and his spirits lifted in response to the words on the screen. It was good to know, even at the ripe old age of seventy, that God still had a purpose for his life.

Speaking of purpose, he'd best get on with his day. He closed the email program and powered down the computer.

A short while later, he backed his late-model Buick LeSabre out of the garage and drove to Smith's Market. For a small grocery store, the selection of packaged items and fresh foods was reasonably good. James wasn't picky at any rate. One of the downsides of growing older was the diminished delight one had in eating good food. Martha had been a gourmet cook, so James knew something about fine dining. Those days were gone.

Well, he supposed the lessened enjoyment helped keep his weight down, so he should be grateful.

He pushed the shopping cart around the end of the aisle and stopped when he saw Stephanie placing a box of Grape-Nuts into the red shopping basket on her left arm.

Now here was something he could still enjoy, he thought. Just seeing her brought a smile to his heart.

*What* would *have happened between us if I hadn't joined the army?* The question had plagued him since Sunday. And now, as he looked at her in this grocery aisle, new questions joined the first. *Would we have gotten married? Would we have had kids together? Would we have been happy?*

She glanced up. "James." A pale blush pinkened her cheeks.

"Good morning, Steph."

They hadn't seen one another since he went to her home for dinner, although they'd spoken by telephone when he called to ask her to the movies. Now he was keenly aware of how much he'd wanted to see her again.

"Good morning," she replied. "Doing a bit of shopping, I see."

He glanced down at the items in his cart, then up again. "Nothing that'll taste as delicious as the meal we shared."

The color in her cheeks intensified. That was the moment he suspected she'd thought of him often this week, too.

*Will wonders never cease.*

Oh, Jenna wouldn't be happy about this development. She wouldn't be happy at all.

∽

THE APOLLO THEATER FIRST OPENED ITS DOORS IN MAY OF 1927. The premier attraction was *Don Juan* starring John Barrymore.

In the years that followed, the theater saw the townsfolk of Hart's Crossing through the Great Depression, through World War II, through the turbulent sixties, through good times and bad times and everything in between. In the eighties, the theater doors closed, and folks expected the building would be torn down. But then Dave Coble, the town's current chief of police, bought the theater and began a lengthy period of historical restoration and modern improvements.

The Apollo's grand reopening occurred in late 1995. *Toy Story* was the feature film that weekend. Some people in town saw the movie two and three times.

One of Stephanie's earliest memories was of coming to the Apollo with her parents, her father wearing a suit and fedora, her mother in a floral print dress, hat, and gloves. Stephanie couldn't have been more than four years old at the time, but she remembered sitting in the first row of the balcony. She could still recall the images of horses galloping across the screen.

Another of her memories closely associated with the Apollo was of her first kiss. It was *that* memory that replayed in her mind as she and James approached the ticket booth on Friday evening.

"I hope it's a good film," James said.

"It's supposed to be excellent. I read a review in *People* when I was at the hair salon."

Friday wasn't her usual day to have her hair done, but she couldn't go to the movies with James with it looking a fright. So the instant the ladies of the Thimbleberry Quilting Club departed through the front door of her home this morning, Stephanie had hurried out the back door, into her car, and off to Terri's Tangles to get a cut and style.

James purchased two senior citizen tickets from the bored-looking teenager seated in the booth. When he turned toward Stephanie, her gaze slid to his lips, and she wondered what it would be like to kiss James now that he was a mature man.

Oh, what a thought! She never should have agreed to come with James tonight. This felt too much like a date. Dating? At her age? How ridiculous.

An odd smile curved the corners of James's mouth, as if he'd read her mind and was amused by what he found there.

Oh, good grief. She felt as giddy as a schoolgirl. Whatever on earth was wrong with her? She wasn't the giddy sort.

Tell that to the butterflies in her stomach.

"Would you like something from the snack bar?" James asked. "I could get us each a drink, and we could share a box of popcorn."

"All right." She doubted she could eat a single bite. "I'll have a Diet Coke, please."

While James stood in line for their refreshments, Stephanie waited in the lobby near the entrance to the theater. She studied the various posters on the walls that advertised the movies coming to the Apollo in weeks to come. During the school year, the theater was only open on the weekends, Friday evening through the Sunday matinee. Most movies played for one weekend, the occasional blockbuster being the exception to that rule.

There weren't many people here tonight, which caused her to wonder about the review she'd read. Maybe the film wasn't good after all. But she supposed the high school kids came to the 9:00 show.

She turned her head and saw Liz Rue, owner of the Tattered Pages Bookstore, walking toward her. "Hi, Steph. I'm glad I ran into you. The book you ordered came in today. I meant to call you, but I kept getting interrupted."

"That's all right. I wasn't in any rush. I'll come into the bookstore tomorrow to get it."

"Say, would you like to sit with Ivan and me? It's no fun to go to the movies alone and we—"

James stepped to Stephanie's side, holding a cardboard tray with the two large drinks and a large popcorn in it. "Sorry that took so long."

Liz looked as if she were choking on her unfinished sentence.

"Liz, have you met James Scott? James, this is Liz Rue. She owns the bookstore on Main Street, across from the Good Buy Market."

James nodded his head to acknowledge the introduction. "Nice to meet you, Ms. Rue. I stopped in your store the other day. The Tattered Pages, right?"

"Yes." Liz's gaze moved from James to Steph to James again.

Was she surprised to see Stephanie out with a man? Or was it seeing her with this particular man—the one who bore a striking resemblance to one of *People*'s Sexiest Men Alive—that surprised her more? Whichever it was, Stephanie had a sinking feeling she and James were about to become grist for the rumor mill.

How embarrassing!

James said, "Steph, let's find our seats, shall we?" To Liz, he added, "Please excuse us, Ms. Rue. I don't like to miss the previews of coming attractions."

"Of course. Enjoy the show. Steph, don't forget to pick up that book."

"I won't."

Longing for the dim light of the theater to hide her flushed cheeks, Stephanie followed James. He motioned her into a row, and she sank onto the second seat off the aisle, wishing she could simply disappear.

As James handed her the Diet Coke, he leaned close and whispered, "I don't mind, you know."

She looked at him, but his eyes were hidden in shadows. "Mind what?"

"I don't mind if they gossip about us." He paused, and she could just make out his smile. "Not if what they're saying is true."

Slowly, hesitantly, he leaned over and pressed his lips against her right cheek.

## CHAPTER 6

Stephanie's dreams were filled with James and that gentle, sweet kiss he'd placed upon her cheek in the darkened movie theater. She awakened the next morning feeling gloriously, joyously alive.

Miranda arrived on her doorstep at 8:00 a.m.

"Well, this is a surprise."

Judging by her daughter's dour expression, something was troubling her, but Stephanie didn't ask what. She'd learned through the years that it was best to let Miranda open up on her own.

She motioned her daughter inside, then led the way into the kitchen. "I didn't expect to see you today. I thought Foster had an away game."

"He does. We'll leave town in a little bit. I came over while Vince packs the car."

"Coffee?"

Her daughter shook her head. "No, thanks."

Stephanie poured herself a cup.

"Mom, are you okay?" Miranda leaned her shoulder against the refrigerator.

"I'm fine." She turned from the coffeemaker. "Why do you ask?"

"I don't know. I just thought ... Well, maybe I haven't been paying enough attention to you lately. I know you must get lonely, with Dad gone."

Stephanie nodded. "Yes, sometimes I'm lonely. But it's all right. I know you all have busy lives. I remember what it was like when you were in high school and going several directions at once. And I wasn't juggling a job like you are. I don't expect you to be at my beck and call, dear."

Miranda worried her lower lip, a frown furrowing her brow.

"Oh my," Stephanie said softly, realizing at last the reason for her daughter's unexpected visit.

"What?"

"This is about my date with James last night, isn't it?"

"Your *date?*" Miranda straightened away from the refrigerator.

Ironic, wasn't it, to have her daughter objecting to that term. Stephanie had resisted it, too—up until the moment last night when James kissed her.

Quelling a smile, Stephanie said, "Isn't that what they still call it when a man and woman go out to the movies?" She carried her coffee to the kitchen table and sat down.

"Mom, this isn't like you."

"What isn't like me, honey?" She feigned ignorance. Or innocence. Or both.

Was it wicked to tease her daughter this way?

Miranda joined her at the table. "Isabella says that man is an old school friend of yours. I'm sorry I didn't meet him last weekend. I should have been at the game, but—"

"His name is James." Stephanie felt a warm glow just saying it. "James Scott."

"Whatever. James. Fine." Her daughter was getting more

distraught with every word. "But Mom, you don't know anything about him. He hasn't lived here in, what? Fifty years?"

She couldn't contain the smile a moment longer. "Fifty-two."

"You shouldn't rush into a relationship, Mom."

Her good humor began to fade. "I would hardly call going to a movie rushing into a relationship. And you're wrong about my not knowing anything about James. You'd be surprised by the number of subjects we've talked about in a short period of time. He's articulate and he's interesting and he's got a delightful sense of humor."

"But people in town are *talking*, Mom."

"Then let them talk." Stephanie squeezed her coffee cup between both hands. Last week, she'd felt guilty for enjoying his company. Last night, she'd been embarrassed when she realized others might gossip about her and James. But this morning, everything was different. "Unless I'm breaking the law or falling into sin, what I do is no one's business but mine."

"*Mo-o-o-om.*" Her daughter drew the word out in a wheedling tone.

"And it isn't *your* business either, dear."

Miranda drew back in surprise.

Trying to soften her rebuke, Stephanie said, "I'm a grown woman, Miranda. I know my own mind and heart." She took a sip of coffee, giving herself a moment to weigh her words. "I may be a senior citizen, but I don't have one foot in the grave. I have every intention of living as full a life as the Lord will allow in the time I have left on earth. Your grandmother lived to be ninety-two, and her mother lived to be ninety-five. If I inherited those same genes, I may have another twenty-five years in me." She learned forward. "How would you want me to spend those years?"

"I ... You ..." Miranda glanced at her wristwatch. "Oh, great. I've got to go." She rose. "We'll talk about this another time."

Stephanie gave her daughter a patient smile. "If you wish."

A few moments later, alone again, she released a deep sigh. Had she been unkind or unreasonable in what she said to Miranda? She hoped not.

*Lord, show me if I was in the wrong. She's my daughter and she cares about me. I don't want to hurt her.*

She sipped her cooling coffee.

*Is it wrong for me to feel such fondness for James? Is it wrong for me to want to be with him? Am I being a foolish old woman?*

Perhaps she was reading too much into that simple kiss. James hadn't held her hand during the movie or tried to kiss her again after he took her home. Perhaps they were friends and nothing more.

*Do I want it to be something more?*

"Yes," she whispered, her heart acknowledging the admission with its quickened beat. "Yes, I think I do."

THE SCOTT FAMILY PHOTOGRAPH ALBUM LAY OPEN ON THE COFFEE table. It was a thick book, lovingly assembled by Martha through the decades. The cover had changed several times, as had the type of binding. At first, it had been a simple affair. But after his wife took a scrapbooking class about a decade or so ago, the album had become a work of art, beautifully detailing the years of their marriage: James and Martha's wedding day, the births of each of their children, vacations at the shore, and countless firsts—first teeth, first steps, first days of school, first home, first brand-new, not-previously-owned automobile. Photographs of the children graduating from high school, then college. Photographs of the children's weddings. Photographs of the grandchildren.

James flipped slowly through the pages that chronicled

forty-seven years of his life. Sometimes he smiled. Once or twice he wiped away a tear. Always he remembered and was grateful.

When Martha died, James thought this album was complete, but of course, it wasn't. Nor should it be. Another chapter of the story was finished. That was all. Just a chapter. Not the book.

The two weeks since he'd arrived in Hart's Crossing had proved that.

And today he'd discovered something new: James Scott was in love. Unexpectedly, completely in love with Stephanie Carlson Watson, his childhood sweetheart. After a fifty-two-year detour, his heart had returned to that first, innocent love of his youth.

Who would have imagined that was possible? Not James. His marriage to Martha had been a happy one. They'd had their ups and downs, of course. He and Martha had been known to fight with passion. They'd made up the same way. But love—or lack of it—had never been an issue. He'd never been tempted to be unfaithful. Never.

He toyed with that thought a moment. Was he being unfaithful to Martha by falling in love with Stephanie?

No, his heart answered with confidence. He even thought Martha would be pleased, were it possible for her to look down from heaven and see him today, because she'd been one of the most unselfish, truly giving people James had ever known.

Somehow he doubted his children, especially Jenna, would see it that way.

He closed the album, then covered his face with his hands, his elbows resting on his thighs.

*Lord, I'm in love with Steph, and I want to spend what years I can with her. I've got the feeling that's why you brought me back to Hart's Crossing. So unless you show me otherwise, I'm going to ask her to marry me.*

He ran his fingers through his gray hair.

*And Lord, I haven't proposed to a girl since I was a G.I. I was just a kid. This time, I'm going to need your help and lots of it.*

CHAPTER 7

The first Sunday James visited Hart's Crossing Community Church, he'd come alone. He'd sat beside Stephanie because she was the first person he saw whom he knew. The next Sunday—the one following their night at the Apollo—he'd come alone but looked for her and only her.

This Sunday was a different story. He'd arranged to escort Stephanie to church, after which the two of them would drive to the resort located in the mountains north of Hart's Crossing. At the Timber Creek Lodge, they would enjoy a sumptuous dinner prepared by a French chef of some renown.

What happened after that would be up to Stephanie.

James had a hard time concentrating on the sermon, and even singing one of his favorite hymns, "Rock of Ages," didn't help the nerves twisting in his belly. He was mightily relieved to hear the benediction spoken. He hoped Stephanie wouldn't be prone to linger and visit.

She must have read his mind. While she was polite, nodding her head and saying good morning to this friend and that, she didn't allow anyone to delay their departure. In short order, they were seated in James's Buick and driving out of town.

Once they reached the highway and a cruising speed of fifty-five, James said, "I have some music CDs in the player. Instrumentals. No singing. Would you like to hear them?"

"That would be lovely."

He pushed a button, and the soft sounds of stringed instruments came through the speakers.

James cleared his throat, feeling the need for conversation. "I was hoping your daughter would be in church this morning. I've wanted to meet her."

"Miranda and her family attend the Baptist church over on Park Street. Didn't I tell you that?"

Maybe she had. They'd talked about many things—their children, their grandchildren, his career, her hobbies, the Bible, sports, people they knew as children in Hart's Crossing, and so much more.

"When Miranda got married, she wanted to establish a life separate from her father and me, and that included going to a different church. She feared that too many people would still think of her as Stephanie and Chuck's daughter rather than as an adult. She wanted to make her own traditions and not feel as if she was still tied to her mother's apron strings." She paused briefly, then added, "Not that she *was* tied to them. Miranda was always fiercely independent, even as a toddler."

"Sounds like my Jenna." James laughed softly. "The word *independent* doesn't begin to describe her. For a long time, her mother and I doubted she would give up her precious autonomy for a more traditional lifestyle of love and marriage. But when she was thirty-six, she met Ray, and she fell for him. Hard." *A lot like her dad at the age of seventy.* "They were married just a few months later."

"Love is a wonderful thing."

James glanced quickly to his right, then back at the road. "Yes."

"You and I were very blessed to find the partners we did."

"Yes."

"So few people have staying power these days." She sighed. "At the first sign of trouble, they're ready to pack their bags and look for someone else to make them happy. They forget that love is an act of will as well as an emotion."

Music floated on the air as both driver and passenger became lost in thought.

∼

AS THE BUICK FOLLOWED THE HIGHWAY INTO THE MOUNTAINS, twisting and weaving as it climbed to a higher elevation, the question James had asked at their first Sunday dinner replayed once again in Stephanie's mind.

*"Sometimes I wonder what would've happened to us if I hadn't joined the army."*

They would have married, Stephanie answered silently. They would have married and had children and grown old together. But God had taken them in different directions. God had given them different partners to love and cherish, and that had been good and right.

But now? Now here they were, without Martha, without Chuck, still alive and still wanting to love and be loved. Was it possible that what might have been could happen yet?

James *had* kissed her on that Friday night, after all. And in these past weeks, they'd talked and talked and talked, in person and by telephone. They'd taken long walks together. They'd sat on his porch in the warmth of the afternoon while he read poetry aloud from a book with worn covers. They'd cooked for each other, and they'd eaten together at the diner. And they'd talked and talked and talked.

But was she reading more into all of it than was there? He

hadn't attempted to kiss her again. Perhaps he was just lonely after moving away from all his friends in Washington, from the home where he'd raised his family. That kiss, after all, had been on her cheek rather than the lips.

Goodness. Was she being a foolish old woman?

Chuck had teased her unmercifully about her romantic imagination and her fondness for three-hanky movies and novels. Was that what she was doing now? Letting her romantic imagination run wild?

*Oh, dear.*

"Look at all of that new development!" James exclaimed.

Pulled from her anxious thoughts, Stephanie looked at James instead of out the window.

"I had no idea things had changed this much up here," he said. "Some of those homes are enormous. Who can afford mansions around here?"

"Californians. Movie stars." Now Stephanie turned to gaze at the passing terrain and the elegant homes built along Timber Creek. "Most of these are vacation homes. The owners come here to ski in the winter or ride horses in the summer."

"I had no idea."

Stephanie wondered if he would be equally surprised to learn how her feelings for him had changed. Would it frighten him to know that she might care for him as more than a friend? That she might be falling in love with him for the second time in her life?

*Oh, dear. Oh, dear.*

~

THE DINING ROOM AT THE TIMBER CREEK LODGE WAS LARGE with high ceilings and an enormous stone fireplace as its focal point. Plate glass windows faced the main chair lift, and in the winter, diners could watch skiers and snowboarders *shooshing* down the mountainside. But now, in early autumn, the mountains were free of snow. Instead of a blanket of white on the ground, the changing colors of the trees provided a visual smorgasbord of orange, yellow, and red.

Since this was the off-season for the resort, the dining room wasn't busy when James and Stephanie arrived shortly after 12:30. The hostess led them to a table for two near the window. Their eyes were protected from the bright October sunshine by a wide awning.

"How beautiful," Stephanie said as she sat on the chair James held for her.

He didn't take his eyes off her. "Very beautiful."

"Your server will be Brandilyn," the hostess said. She set the menus on the table. "She'll be right with you."

"Thank you." James sat on the chair opposite Stephanie.

She looked at him. "I haven't been here in years. Thank you for bringing me. I'd forgotten what a lovely place this is."

"You don't ski anymore?"

"At my age?"

"You're not too old to ski. I still go several times each winter."

"I haven't skied since high school. I never liked it much."

"You didn't?" He was genuinely surprised. "But you came up here with me a lot."

"You're right. I did." A soft smile curved her mouth. "I guess it was the company that made it fun."

Encouraged by her words, James decided he couldn't wait until after they'd eaten. He had to say what he felt or burst. "I've always enjoyed the pleasure of your company. You know that."

There was that attractive splash of pink in her cheeks again.

"Steph, I'd like—" He swallowed hard, took a quick breath, then began again. "I'd like to have the pleasure of your company for the rest of my days."

Her eyes widened.

*Lord, have I gone too fast? Did I make a mistake? Am I going to blow this?*

He drew another breath and hurried on. "If I were a young man with what seems like all the time in the world, I'd wait to tell you what I'm feeling and thinking. I'd wait until I was certain what your answer would be. But I'm no longer young. Neither of us are. We both understand how quickly life rushes by." He reached into his jacket pocket. "I love you, Steph Watson. I've lived long enough to understand what it is I'm feeling. I want to be with you for the rest of my life." He pushed the small box across the table. "I love you, and I'm asking you to do me the honor of becoming my wife."

"Oh, my," she whispered.

Was that a good *oh-my* or a bad *oh-my*?

She opened the lid of the small white box. "Oh, James. I—"

"It was my mother's ring. It'll probably need to be resized. And if you prefer to have a wedding ring you pick out yourself, we can—"

"It's a beautiful ring, James." She sniffed softly. "Beautiful."

"Steph, is there any chance you might—"

She looked up. "Yes."

*Yes, what?*

"Yes, I'll be your wife." She brushed away tears with her knuckles. "I love you, too."

He was afraid to believe she'd given the answer he wanted. "Are you sure? I mean, you don't need some time to pray about it?"

"I'm sure." She laughed through her tears. "I've been talking to the Lord about you for days."

His spirits rose to new heights. "My kids will think we're crazy. They'll think we're moving too fast."

"So will Miranda."

As if prompted by an unseen director, they leaned forward.

Their lips met above the center of the table. The kiss might have lasted longer if their waitress hadn't arrived, making a throat-clearing sound to get their attention.

Unabashed, James looked at the waitress and said, "Congratulate us, miss. This lovely woman has agreed to marry me."

CHAPTER 8

From: "James Scott" <jtscott@fiberpipe.net>
Sent: Monday, October 10 6:10 AM
To: "Kurt & Neta" <kurtscott@fiberpipe.net>; "Jenna & Ray" <jscottengland@yahoo.com>; "Paula" <carpoolmom@fiberpipe.net>
Subject: Glad tidings

Dear Kurt & Neta, Jenna & Ray, Paula, and all my beloved grandchildren,

I've got some important news to share, and I hope you'll rejoice with me. I've asked Stephanie Watson, a dear, dear friend from my boyhood, to be my wife, and she's agreed. I could not be happier than I am today. As you know, few men are fortunate to find one woman who will love and cherish them, for better or worse, richer or poorer, in sickness and in health—and *mean* it! I've been blessed to have it happen twice.

I know you'll think I'm rushing into this, but I assure you I haven't lost my faculties. Steph and I are mature enough to know our feelings, and we understand what marriage means, having both had long and loving marriages that ended with the deaths of our spouses.

I hope you'll also be reassured that we've prayed about this, before either of us knew what the other was feeling. I believe God brought me back to Hart's Crossing (at least partly) so that I might have this blessing in my latter years. I am truly a happy, happy man.

We haven't decided when the wedding will take place. By the end of October, we hope. Maybe early November. I know that isn't much time. Only a few weeks to plan. It would mean the world to have all of you present, but I'll understand if it isn't possible because of work and school. However, I'd be glad to check airline schedules and so forth, and I can cover some of the cost of the airfare if that will help get you here. Between Stephanie's home and my home, there is room for everybody, even if some would have to sleep on blow-up mattresses on the floor. Let me know if you can come.

I love you all,
Dad/Grandpa

~

**From:** "Jenna Scott-Kirkpatrick" <jscottengland@yahoo.com>
**Sent:** Monday, October 10 5:50 PM
**To:** "Dad" <jtscott@fiberpipe.net>; "Kurt Scott" <kurtscott@fiberpipe.net>; "Paula Scott" <carpoolmom@fiberpipe.net>
**Subject:** Re: Glad tidings

DADDY, YOU CAN'T BE SERIOUS ABOUT MARRYING THAT WOMAN this soon. You barely know her. Please, stop and consider what you are doing. I'm sure you'll discover this is just loneliness. You never should have moved. That's why you're having a crisis now.

I'll call you tomorrow. Please don't do anything rash in the meantime.

Love, Jenna

∾

**From:** "Kurt Scott" <kurtscott@fiberpipe.net>
**Sent:** Monday, October 10 6:22 PM
**To:** "James Scott" <jtscott@fiberpipe.net>; "Jenna Scott-Kirkpatrick" <jscottengland@yahoo.com>; "Paula Scott" <carpoolmom@fiberpipe.net>
**Subject:** Re: Glad tidings

HI, DAD. I DON'T KNOW WHAT TO SAY. ARE YOU SURE YOU KNOW what you're doing? Of course, Neta and I just want your happiness, but this seems mighty quick for somebody who always considered things from every angle before making a decision.

Kurt

∾

**From:** "Paula Scott" <carpoolmom@fiberpipe.net>
**Sent:** Monday, October 10 10:15 PM
**To:** "Dad" <jtscott@fiberpipe.net>; "Kurt" <kurtscott@fiberpipe.net>; "Jenna" <jscottengland@yahoo.com>
**Subject:** Re: Glad tidings

OH, DAD. I'M THRILLED FOR YOU. FORGET WHAT KURT AND Jenna said. You just go right ahead and be happy. When I get to work tomorrow, I'll tell my supervisor that I need a week off at the end of October or first of November. You just let me know the date as quick as you can. I'll try to use the frequent flyer miles I've saved up, but I may need some help with the tickets if there aren't any frequent flyer seats to be had. One way or the other, you can count on the girls and me being there to celebrate with you and your bride. I can hardly wait to meet Stephanie. I know we'll love her, because you wouldn't love her if she wasn't everything you say she is.

Love, Paula

∽

Stephanie knocked on Miranda's front door and waited for an answer. There was a part of her that wished her daughter and family were out for the evening. Lucky James. He'd sent his children an email to announce their engagement.

"I suppose I should call each one of them," he'd told her, "but with their various work schedules and Jenna living overseas, this seems the better way."

The door opened, revealing Miranda.

"Mom." She paused. "This is a surprise."

An unpleasant surprise, judging by Miranda's tone. It was obvious her daughter hadn't forgiven her for what she'd said during their last conversation.

"I was hoping we could talk," Stephanie said.

"Sure. Come on in. I was just finishing the supper dishes."

Miranda led the way into the kitchen. It was a large room with all the modern conveniences a person could imagine or wish for, designed for entertaining, although Miranda and Vince seldom entertained. For that matter, Miranda seldom cooked. She was the Schwan's deliveryman's best customer. Schwan's and Pizza Hut.

Oh, dear. She was being so critical of her daughter.

Miranda went to the dishwasher and continued loading it. Stephanie didn't wait for an invitation to sit on one of the kitchen chairs. It obviously wasn't going to come.

Sinking onto the seat cushion, Stephanie said, "I'm sorry if I hurt your feelings the other day. That wasn't my intent."

Another plate clattered into place on the lower rack.

"Miranda, I know you spoke out of concern for me."

"Yes, I did." Her daughter placed several glasses in the top rack.

Stephanie drew a deep breath, praying for courage. "I hope we'll be better able to handle what I have to tell you now."

Her daughter straightened. There was a look of dread in her eyes, as if she already suspected what her mother would say.

"James asked me to marry him, and I accepted."

"Mom!"

"I love him, Miranda. I want to be his wife."

"How can you say that?"

Stephanie rose from her chair. "Loving James doesn't mean I didn't love your father, or that I don't still love him. He was my husband for fifty years. Most of the memories of my past are tied to him." She lifted a hand in supplication. "But honey, James is my future. I want to make new memories with him."

Miranda dried her hands with a dishtowel. "Do you know how outrageous this is? He's lived in Hart's Crossing What? Three weeks? A month? And now you say you want to marry him. Mom, this isn't like you."

"Isn't it? Your father always said I was a hopeless romantic. I don't think he would be surprised or disappointed. He'd be glad for me."

"If there's nothing wrong with this guy—" Miranda waved her hands in the air. "—why haven't I met him yet?"

"It isn't as if I've been concealing him from you. I expected you two to meet the day of Foster's football game, but you never came."

"I got stuck at work. I told you that."

Stephanie pressed her lips together, swallowing the remark that the game was on a Saturday and nothing about her work in the mayor's office was so urgent it couldn't have waited a few hours. Besides, that wasn't what this visit to Miranda's was about.

Echoing Stephanie's thoughts, her daughter said, "That's beside the point. When *will* I meet him?"

*Never* seemed like a good answer. She and James could elope and go live on a deserted island somewhere in the South Pacific.

"Mom?"

It was difficult to tell from Miranda's tone if she was more angry or hurt. Stephanie didn't want her to be either.

"Come for supper tomorrow night. You, Vince, and the children. Shall we say 6:30?"

*And please, God, soften her heart between now and then.*

## CHAPTER 9

*E*arly on Tuesday morning, James answered a knock on his back door. He felt a flash of pleasure at seeing Stephanie on the stoop. Then he saw the sadness in her eyes.

"Miranda didn't take it well," she said softly.

He drew her into the kitchen and into his arms.

"I don't understand why she objects so strenuously." Her words were muffled against his shirt.

He patted her back. "Would it help if I spoke to her?"

"We'll find out tonight." She pulled back from his embrace. "I've invited Miranda and her family to come to supper to meet you." She grimaced. "You're to be the main course, I'm afraid."

James chuckled. "I think I'll rather enjoy that."

"Oh, James. Why couldn't she just be happy for me? This past year has been difficult enough, learning to be alone. I'd never been alone before, not ever. I went from my father's house to my husband's house. After Chuck died, I thought I would be alone for the remainder of my days." She touched his cheek with her fingertips, adding, "But now, there's you, and I want to be with you."

Silently, he led her to the chairs at the table. After they sat, he took hold of both her hands, squeezing gently.

Tears filled her eyes, then spilled over. "She's so angry. I don't understand why she's so angry."

"I've given this some thought, and my guess is she feels threatened by your love for me. She's afraid she might lose the memories of her father if you marry again. Maybe she's afraid she'll lose you, too." James wiped the tears from her cheeks with the pads of his thumbs. "Don't cry, love. It will work itself out." His smile was meant to encourage. "Our children didn't have much time to get used to the idea of us dating, and already we're engaged. Once they see us together, they'll know we're doing the right thing."

"I'm not so sure, James. Miranda's so adamantly against it."

"Let me show you something. Wait here." He rose from the chair and went to his office, where he printed a copy of his youngest daughter's email. Upon returning to the kitchen, he handed the slip of paper to Stephanie.

He waited to see her smile. He expected her to be glad that Paula planned to come for the wedding. But that wasn't the response he got.

"What did Kurt and Jenna say?" She met his gaze. "Did they react like Miranda?"

He shrugged. "Not angry. A little concerned is all. But they'll come around. So will Miranda."

"Maybe we shouldn't get married so soon." She pushed a stray curl back from her forehead. "Maybe we should wait awhile."

Wait? If any two people should understand that there was no guarantee of tomorrow, it was James and Stephanie. Both of them had lost their life partners too soon. Now they had a chance for happiness together. They'd prayed about this marriage, separately and together, and both believed it to be God's will. What was the purpose of waiting?

James took hold of Stephanie's hands for the second time. "Don't falter now, Steph. We love each other." He looked deep into her eyes, willing her to see everything he felt for her—the love, the desire, the delight. "Don't break this old man's heart." He kissed her, his lips lingering a long while before he drew back and whispered, "I couldn't bear to lose you now."

∽

STEPHANIE KNEW HER LOVE FOR JAMES WAS REAL. LOVE WASN'T A commodity that ran out or was used up over time. No, the more one loved, the more love one had to give. It multiplied as it was spent. Loving James didn't negate the love she'd had for Chuck. If anything, it made that love seem even more special. Because she'd been happy with her husband for fifty years, it made her want to taste that happiness again with James.

She wished her daughter understood that.

Stephanie stayed with James for another hour. Little by little, his quiet confidence helped calm her jangled nerves.

She left his house, feeling better than when she arrived, and drove toward Smith's Market to purchase the food for that night's supper. She wanted the gathering to be special. The menu would include grilled steaks, baked potatoes with all the fixings, and a nice tossed salad. Oh, and strawberry cheesecake. Cheesecake was Miranda's favorite dessert.

But instead of turning left onto Hart Street, she turned right and drove several blocks before she realized she'd gone the wrong direction. When she stopped the car, meaning to turn it around, she discovered she was in front of Francine's home.

Perhaps this hadn't been an accident, the result of wandering thoughts. Perhaps she'd been drawn here for a purpose.

It was no secret in Hart's Crossing that Francine and her daughter, Angie, had been estranged for many years. But since this past spring, their troubles had been resolved. The two of them were close again.

Hoping to gain some wisdom, Stephanie got out of the car and walked to the front of the Hunter home.

When the door opened, she was greeted by Francine's warm smile. "Steph. What a nice surprise."

"I hope I haven't come at a bad time. It's early, I know."

"Never too early for a visit with a friend," Francine answered. "Come in. Would you care for some coffee or tea?"

Stephanie shook her head. "No. I'm fine, thanks." She was anything but fine. Otherwise, she would be at the market, looking over the packages of steaks.

"Let's sit in the living room. We can enjoy the fall colors outside while we chat." After both had settled onto chairs, Francine leaned forward and patted Stephanie's knee. "What's troubling you, dear friend? You look like the world is atop your shoulders."

"It's about ... it's about James. We ... he and I ... James asked me to marry him."

Francine's face broke into an enormous grin. "Oh, Steph. That's wonderful! I take it you had the good sense to say yes."

She nodded.

Francine rose from her chair and embraced Stephanie. "I couldn't be happier for you. Have you shared the news with any of the other Thimbleberries?"

"No. Not yet."

"Well, we must do so at once. Oh, they'll all be delighted. This is such marvelous news. A wedding. I love weddings."

Stephanie touched Francine's forearm, afraid she might head for the telephone immediately. "That isn't why I came. At least, not entirely." She waited until her old friend sat again. "It's about Miranda."

A knowing look replaced Francine's excitement. "She doesn't approve?"

"No. She thinks I'm being reckless or thoughtless. Or both. And she's angry about it."

"I'm sorry."

Stephanie opened her purse to retrieve a tissue. "Frani, I don't want to lose my daughter's love. I don't want us to be separated by this. I thought ... I thought maybe you could give me some advice. You and Angie have worked out your differences. Tell me what I can do to make matters better between us."

"You want my advice?" Francine leaned back in her chair, steepling her hands and touching her fingertips to her lips. After a lengthy silence, she lowered her hands. "Steph, I lost count of how many mistakes I made with Angie. In the end, only God could fix things between us, and that's the only real advice I feel qualified to give you. Turn it over to him. Once I was willing to let go of Angie and get out of the Lord's way, the miracle happened. When things were at their darkest, I clung to the promise in Joel that says, 'I will give you back what you lost to the stripping locusts.' Angie and I were stripped bare in our relationship, but the Lord restored us."

With a nod, Stephanie turned her head to look out the window. She and Miranda weren't estranged. Not as Francine and Angie had once been. True, they often saw things from different perspectives, but they rarely argued. They had a good relationship—or at least, she thought they did.

*Am I making a mountain out of a molehill? Will she stop being angry if I give her some time?*

"Steph, why don't we pray about this together? I may not have an answer, but God does."

Stephanie agreed with a nod, thankful for the offer, and the two women joined hands and bowed their heads.

∼

JAMES COULD HAVE CUT THE TENSION AT SUPPER THAT NIGHT with the proverbial knife. Miranda Andrews was painfully polite, but there was no mistaking her true feelings about her mother's engagement.

Stephanie's grandchildren, Isabella and Foster, managed to keep the conversation going for the first hour, talking about what was happening at school and where Isabella hoped to go to college after graduation. But once the meal was done, James decided he was tired of tiptoeing around the real reason for the get-together.

Pushing his dessert plate back from the edge of the table, he said, "Miranda, I'm glad we finally managed to meet. I'm sorry it didn't happen sooner." His glance swept around the table, pausing briefly on her husband and children before returning to her. "You've got a terrific family."

"Thank you." Miranda's smile was brittle.

"I understand that you're concerned your mother and I are rushing into marriage. I want to assure you, we're not."

Miranda lifted her chin, and her eyes sparked with anger. "How can you say that? You're a stranger here."

"Not to your mother, I'm not." He reached for Stephanie's hand. "We know each other in here." With his free hand, he tapped his chest.

"You haven't seen each other more than a time or two in the past fifty years, Mr. Scott."

"Please call me James." He smiled, hoping to break through her defenses with a bit of humor. "I love your mother, and if I hadn't been so shy, I would've asked her to marry me even sooner."

The joke fell flat. If anything, Miranda looked appalled by his comment.

Vince, who'd said little throughout the meal, leaned toward his wife. "Honey, give the guy a chance. Hear what he has to say."

James didn't know who deserved his sympathies—Miranda, with her simmering hurt and anger; or her husband, for the glare his comment earned him; or their kids, who looked like two deer caught in the headlights, longing to escape.

Stephanie apparently felt the most sorry for her grandchildren. "Isabella, why don't you and Foster take these dishes into the kitchen?"

"Sure, Grandma."

The adults said nothing more until the grateful teenagers escaped from the dining room.

James glanced at Stephanie and gave her fingers a squeeze before turning his gaze on Miranda once again. "We're not like those crazy celebrities who decide to marry in Las Vegas on a whim and regret it the next day. We've lived a long time, your mother and I, and we know our own feelings." He paused to clear his throat. "I'll make your mother happy. I'll love and cherish her until the day I die. I'm not trying to take your father's place, in her heart or in yours. I hope you'll give me a chance to become your friend."

"You could never take my father's place, Mr. Scott," she answered. "And I don't need any more friends."

Stephanie gasped.

"If you know Mom in your heart the way you say, then tell me this. What's her favorite color? What's her favorite movie?" Miranda threw the questions at him like a knight's gauntlet.

James felt his composure slipping. What he wanted most was to give Miranda Andrews a piece of his mind, to tell her how childish she was being, to tell her to think of her mother instead of herself. But he didn't say those things. "The truth is, Miranda, I don't know yet. But it will be my pleasure to learn many of her favorite things the longer she and I are together."

"My father knew the answers." Miranda jutted out her chin. "He could've told you in an instant."

James drew a deep breath, then met Miranda's hostile gaze

with all the gentleness and compassion he could muster. "Your father had five decades with this wonderful woman beside me, and I'd wager he still didn't know everything about her. There are too many secret places in a woman's heart for a man to ever hope to find them all." He turned toward Stephanie, declaring his love once again with his eyes. "I want the chance to discover as many as possible in the years I hope to have with her. I promise I'll do everything humanly possible to make her happy."

"Vince," Miranda said, "please get the children. We're going home."

"Miranda—"

"Mom, you know I'm right. You know you shouldn't marry again this soon. You're just lonely. That's all. Dad was always there to help make the sensible decisions in the family. Well, I'm trying to help you in that way now. Don't do this." Miranda shoved the chair out of her way with the back of her legs, then fled the room in tears.

Vince rose slowly to his feet, setting his napkin on the table. "I'm sorry." He gave a slight shrug. "It's been rough for her since her dad died. She just needs a little more time."

James glanced from Vince to Stephanie and saw doubt flicker across her face. For the first time, he feared what would happen if Miranda didn't change her mind about him. If Stephanie was made to choose between his love or Miranda's, who would win?

## CHAPTER 10

**From:** "James Scott" <jtscott@fiberpipe.net>
**Sent:** Wednesday, October 12 3:47 AM
**To:** "Paula" <carpoolmom@fiberpipe.net>
**Subject:** October 29 or November 5?

Hi, honey. What did you find out about taking time off at work to come for the wedding? Any problems? We're looking at either the 29th of October or the 5th of November. Could you make those dates? Either? Both? Since neither Kurt nor Jenna said they would come for sure and you did, I thought you should have first choice of the date that's most convenient for you.

I had supper last night at Steph's home with her daughter, Miranda, and her family. I met Miranda's husband, Vince, and their children, Isabella and Foster, at a high school football game three weekends ago, but she wasn't able to be there, so this was our first meeting.

Miranda's reaction to our engagement isn't good. Worse than Jenna's. She's angry and thinks we're off our rockers. She didn't use that old expression, but she may as well have. Her demeanor said it all. I did my level best to help her think better of me and our plans to wed, but I wasn't successful. If anything, she was more hostile to the idea of our marriage by the time she left than when she arrived.

I think she's afraid I'm trying to replace her father. I'm not. Not in her mind or in the mind and heart of her mother. I tried to tell her that, but she was too worked up to listen to anything I had to say. I'm going to keep trying to win her over, but it's not going to be easy. Naturally, all of this is upsetting to Steph.

As you can see from the time of this email, I'm up in the middle of the night. Couldn't sleep. So if you get this before you go to work and can let me know about the dates ASAP, it will sure help us make our plans. As soon as I hear from you, we'll see the pastor and firm up the wedding plans.

I love you, Paula. Thanks for letting me spout off. No matter what I say, don't hold anything against Miranda. We'll work this out between us, just like things will work out with your brother and sister.

Give your girls a hug from their grandpa, and tell them I look forward to seeing them soon.

Dad

~

THE TINKLE OF BELLS ANNOUNCED STEPHANIE'S ENTRY INTO THE beauty salon.

From the back room, Terri called, "Is that you, Steph?"

"Yes, it's me."

"Have a seat. I'll be right out. Just throwing a load of towels into the washer."

Stephanie sat on the swivel chair in front of the mirror and glanced at her reflection. Did she look okay? She hadn't slept more than three hours last night, and she hoped her careful application of cosmetics would conceal that fact from others.

Terri entered the main room of the salon just as Stephanie turned the chair away from the mirror. "Hey, I hear from Frani that congratulations are in order for you and Mr. Scott."

Oh, dear. She'd meant to ask Francine not to tell anyone yet. Not until... Until what?

"So when's the big day?"

"A few weeks, we think."

"Wow! It's so romantic. You and your childhood sweetheart, together again." Terri shook out the cape and spread it over Stephanie, fastening it around her neck. "I'm happy for you. Everyone is—or will be as soon as they hear the news."

In her mind, Stephanie pictured her daughter's disapproving glare. *Not everyone.*

She'd hoped Miranda would accept this union once she met James. That hadn't happened. What if it never happened? Would she gain a husband but lose her only child? If there was a risk of losing Miranda's love, should she marry James anyway? What was the right thing to do?

She'd felt better after talking to James yesterday morning, and she'd found courage after praying with Francine. But the supper with Miranda had sent her spirits spiraling into confusion again. She'd been so sure she was doing the right thing when she agreed to marry James. She'd said yes without a moment's hesitation. But now? Now she doubted the wisdom of the choice she'd made.

A doubtful mind, the Bible said, was as unsettled as a wave of the sea that is driven and tossed by the wind. People like that can't make up their minds and they waver back and forth in everything they do.

*If ever a verse of Scripture described me, that's it.*

"I envy you," Terri said as she led the way to the shampoo bowl, oblivious to Stephanie's tormented thoughts. "I married my childhood sweetheart. Then he treated me like dirt before leaving me and Lyssa for another woman." There wasn't any bitterness in Terri's voice. Just acceptance of fact. "Unlike you, Steph, I won't be having a romantic reunion with the boy who stole my heart when I was a girl. That's for sure." She held the back of the shampoo chair as Stephanie sat down. "I think it's great you two got a second chance. Count yourself blessed."

Stephanie recalled the tenderness of James's gaze, the deep timbre of his laughter, the sweetness of his kisses, the sturdiness of his grasp, and the confidence of his faith. When she was with him, she felt young again, her stomach all aflutter, her heart full of joy. She was blessed. Blessed that he loved her and wanted to marry her.

If not for Miranda...

She leaned back in the chair, closed her eyes, and enjoyed the scalp massage Terri gave as she worked the shampoo into a lather.

After a period of silence, Terri asked, "What kind of wedding are you going to have?"

"I haven't really thought about it yet. There hasn't been much time."

"Hope you don't want a small one." Terri ran warm water over her scalp, rinsing away the suds. "All your friends will want to be there. There'll be enough of us to fill the church and then some."

In high school, Stephanie had dreamed about the day she would marry Jimmy Scott. As a teenager, she'd imagined herself walking down the aisle on her daddy's arm, wearing a satin dress covered in pearls and lace, her face hidden behind a beautiful veil.

But Jimmy hadn't proposed. Instead, he'd gone off to the army and college and then asked a different girl to marry him. Stephanie had stayed in Hart's Crossing, finished high school, fallen in love with Chuck Watson, and married him without a moment's regret.

Perhaps that was supposed to be the end of it. Perhaps

Stephanie was in love with the memory of the boy Jimmy had been and not the man James was today.

Was Miranda right after all? Was he a stranger to her? Stephanie thought she loved him, but was she absolutely sure? Perhaps she should have prayed about it a little longer. Wasn't she supposed to have absolute peace when she was doing the right thing? And if so, absence of peace meant she wasn't doing the right thing. Right?

"Steph?"

She opened her eyes and gazed upward. Terri leaned over her, frowning with concern.

"Are you okay?"

"Yes."

"You acted like you couldn't hear me. Are you sure you're all right?"

Stephanie sat upright. "I'm fine. I was lost in thought. That's all."

"Well, okay then." Terri wrapped a towel around Stephanie's head. "If you're sure."

The truth was, she didn't feel sure of anything at the moment.

∾

**From:** "Paula Scott" <carpoolmom@fiberpipe.net>
**Sent:** Wednesday, October 12 3:15 PM
**To:** "Dad" <jtscott@fiberpipe.net>
**Subject:** Re: October 29 or November 5?

HI, DAD. SORRY I COULDN'T GET BACK TO YOU SOONER. I checked on things at work, and it looks like the 29th would be better for me and the girls. I have enough vacation time saved that we could come early for a nice visit, then leave on Sunday the 30th.

So where will you and Stephanie go on your honeymoon? Make it some place special, Dad. Some place you'll always remember, like Paris. <g>

Better get to work on our reservations.

Love you, Paula

~

**From:** "Jenna Scott-Kirkpatrick" <jscottengland@yahoo.com>
**Sent:** Wednesday, October 12 6:37 PM
**To:** "Dad" <jtscott@fiberpipe.net>
**Subject:** Coming to see you

DAD, I TRIED TO CALL YOU SEVERAL TIMES YESTERDAY, as promised, but you weren't home. So I guess I'd better let you know by email that I've decided to come for a visit after all. I haven't been back to the States in two years, and it will be good for you and me to have some time together. You can show me around Hart's Crossing. I was just a kid the last time we went there to see Grandma before she moved in with us. I don't remember much about it except there wasn't much to do. So this will give you a chance to show me what you love about it.

Looks like I can get a flight for next week. Don't worry about driving to Twin Falls to pick me up. I'll get a rental car for the duration of my stay. All I need from you is a guest room, and you said you have that.

I still have a few things to work out. As soon as I've got all the details, I'll send you my itinerary.

I love you, Dad, and I'm looking forward to seeing you.

Jenna

~

James closed his email program and swiveled the chair so his back was to the computer screen. He was thankful Paula and her girls could come a few days before the wedding. Jenna's email was another matter. He didn't need his eldest daughter to spell out the reason for her hasty trip. She was coming to Hart's Crossing to make certain he hadn't lost all of his faculties, not because she hadn't seen him in a couple of years and most definitely not to celebrate his wedding.

At least Jenna didn't seem angry like Stephanie's daughter. That was something else he could be thankful for.

He sighed as he rose from the chair and left the room, walking slowly down the stairs and out to the porch. A full moon bathed the town in a blanket of white light.

He wondered why it was hard for some adult children to believe their aging parents could fall in love again. Did they think such feelings were reserved for the young? They weren't. Love was love at any age, and James Scott loved Stephanie Watson.

He recalled the final lines of a favorite poem by John Clare.

> I never saw so sweet a face
> As that I stood before.
> My heart has left its dwelling-place
> And can return no more.

That's what it was like for James. When he looked at Stephanie's sweet face—or, in her absence, when he thought of her—he knew his heart was lost for good. It would never return to him.

Now if only their children could understand that.

## CHAPTER 11

It was a beautiful morning, the air crisp, the sky clear. Fallen leaves crunched beneath Stephanie's sturdy walking shoes as she made her way toward the creek that was lined with cottonwoods and aspens.

For many years, this had been her private getaway, a place she came to think, to read her Bible, and to pray for answers to life's questions. She'd come here when Miranda went through her rebellious teen years. She'd come here when her husband considered a job that would have meant transferring out of state. She'd come here after Chuck's death when she couldn't face another visitor bringing well-meant but painful condolences.

With a sigh, she sat on a large boulder that nature had decorated with soft green moss. Time had also etched a small ledge into the granite, a comfy bench for her feet to rest upon.

As she placed her Bible on her lap, she squinted up through the trees and whispered, "Lord, show me what to do. I know what I want, but I don't seem to know what's right. What is it you want for me?"

The place to begin, she supposed, was with love. God's will always included love. She turned to 1 Corinthians.

Stephanie and Chuck, like countless other couples before and since, had used these words from the thirteenth chapter in their wedding ceremony. She'd read them many times, sometimes with joy, more often with conviction at how far from the mark she continued to fall. How seldom—if ever—did she love the way God called her to love?

Love was patient and kind, the Word told her. Love wasn't jealous or boastful or proud or rude, and it didn't demand its own way. It wasn't irritable, and it kept no record of when it was wronged. Love was never glad about injustice but rejoiced whenever the truth won out. Love never gave up and never lost faith. Love was always hopeful, enduring through every circumstance.

"I loved Chuck with all my heart. I tried to be a good wife always. And I love my daughter unconditionally. She must know that. Doesn't she?" Stephanie drew a slow, deep breath. "Lord Jesus, I love James, too. I want to be with him. But if marrying him costs me Miranda's love ..."

She riffled the well-worn pages with her left thumb and stopped when her eyes fell on an orange highlighted portion.

*So the person who marries does well,* it read, *and the person who doesn't marry does even better. A wife is married to her husband as long as he lives. If her husband dies, she is free to marry whomever she wishes, but this must be a marriage acceptable to the Lord.*

Stephanie's heart fluttered. A person who marries does well. A widow is free to marry whomever she wishes, as long as God approves.

"Is this marriage to James acceptable to you, Lord? He belongs to you, so we wouldn't be unequally yoked. Is this your will for me?"

She read on: *But in my opinion it will be better for her if she doesn't marry again, and I think I am giving you counsel from God's Spirit when I say this.*

She felt great irritation with the apostle Paul for adding that line. She wanted a clear, absolute, positive instruction, and what the apostle wrote, he said, was his opinion. She didn't want his opinion. She wanted an unmistakable answer. She wanted guidance, a clear, distinct path, like the trail she had followed to reach this creek.

"Jesus, I need to hear your voice."

*Love never gives up,* came the whisper in her heart.

Yes. That was true. But was it love for James that should never give up or was it love for her daughter that was to be her first priority?

Or was it possible that the two could be one and the same?

∽

JAMES TOLD HIMSELF NOT TO WORRY WHEN HE TRIED FOR THE fifth time that morning to call Stephanie and got no answer. He told himself that he wasn't her keeper when he stopped by her house just after 1:00 and found her still not at home. As he drove into town for a late lunch, he watched for her car at Francine Hunter's home, in the Smith's Market parking lot, and along the curb outside Terri's Tangles; he didn't see it anywhere.

Where could she be?

The Over the Rainbow Diner was empty of the lunch crowd by the time James arrived. Nancy Raney greeted him with her usual warm smile and escorted him to a booth.

"Anything besides water to drink?" she asked.

"A Diet Coke, please, Nancy."

"Sure thing. Back in a flash."

James took a menu from the rack and glanced at it. Nothing looked appetizing.

*Where is she?*

James and Stephanie had spoken by telephone twice yesterday, once before she left to have her hair done and again in the evening when he phoned to tell her that Jenna would be arriving for a visit the following week. Both times he'd felt Stephanie pulling away. He knew why—a safety measure, of sorts, in case things didn't work out between them.

Yes, he knew why, but he didn't know what he could do about it. He didn't know how to make her believe all would be well.

And if he couldn't make her believe it, maybe everything *wouldn't* be well. Maybe her worries would become a self-fulfilling prophecy.

Nancy arrived at his table, Coke glass in one hand, water glass in the other. "Have you decided?" She set the beverages before him.

"I'll have a toasted BLT."

"Wheat or white bread?"

"Wheat, please."

"Soup or salad?"

When a man ate from habit rather than hunger, he didn't want to make choices. "Surprise me."

She laughed. "You got it."

After Nancy headed for the kitchen, James turned his gaze out the window, looking across Main Street at the Apollo. He had lots of memories of that old theater, and many of them included Stephanie. Saturday matinees with black-and-white westerns flickering on the screen. V-J Day with its wild celebrations. Friday night dates when they were in high school and they'd talked about what they wanted to be and where they wanted to live.

He'd loved Stephanie Carlson, but he hadn't been ready for marriage when he was eighteen. Now, at the ripe old age of seventy, he was ready for it. More than ready.

He couldn't explain how or why this love for her had blossomed so quickly since his return. He only knew it had. He knew that it was real, solid, and lasting. It was an old love, yet it was like first love, too. He wanted to spend the rest of his days with Stephanie. He wanted to read love poetry to her by the fire on cold winter nights. He wanted to stroll with her through town on soft summer evenings. He wanted to be her husband, her lover, her best friend. God willing, they would have many good and healthy years together.

But first he had to keep her from bolting like a scared colt.

"You look like you could use a friend, Jimmy Scott."

He turned from the window as Till Hart slid onto the seat across from him. With a shake of his head, he said, "Is my mood that obvious?"

"Mmm. I'd say so."

"I don't suppose you've talked to Steph today. I haven't been able to reach her."

"Sorry. I haven't seen or talked to her all week. Not since you whisked her away to a fancy lunch at the resort and proposed marriage—or so I hear tell from Frani." Till clucked her tongue. "You certainly didn't let any grass grow under your feet, James. I'll say that for you."

He tried to smile but failed.

"You don't look like a happy groom-to-be. Why is that?"

"Our kids," he answered solemnly. "Except for my youngest, they don't approve of our wedding plans." He glanced down at his hands clenched into fists atop the table. "I don't mind getting old, Till. I can deal with the aches and pains that come with age. I figure I've earned them, living this long. But I resent being treated like a child by my own offspring."

"I believe I would, too."

"But that's not the worst part." He looked up again. "I'm afraid Steph's having second thoughts. I'm afraid Miranda and Jenna's attitudes are going to drive a wedge between us, and I don't know how to stop it from happening."

"Oh dear. We mustn't let that happen. Not if you and Steph love each other."

"We do, Till. I guarantee it."

∼

THAT EVENING, TILL HART CALLED AN EMERGENCY MEETING OF the Thimbleberry Quilting Club. If there was one thing the members of this group knew how to do even better than creating beautiful quilts, it was how to pray.

Through the years, they—and many former members of the club—had prayed for one another, for family and friends, and for complete strangers. They'd prayed when couples married, when babies were born, and when folks died. They'd prayed for elections, wars, and natural disasters in America and far corners of the world. They'd prayed for circumstances that seemed overwhelming, and they'd prayed for secret wishes of the heart. From the eldest member to the youngest, they were women who believed in the power of prayer and in a God who delighted in giving good gifts to his children.

On that evening in mid-October, five of the six Thimbleberry members—only Stephanie was absent and that was by design—gathered in the living room of Till's home to pray for their dear friend and for the man who loved her.

## CHAPTER 12

Stephanie had prayed that she would hear God's voice and know what she was to do, and early the next morning, in that halfway state between waking and sleeping, she received an answer.

*And the Lord God said, "It is not good for the man to be alone. I will make a companion who will help him."*

As the verse from Genesis floated through her mind, Stephanie opened her eyes, half expecting to see someone else in the room because the voice seemed so clear.

*I made you, beloved, for a purpose.*

Her pulse quickened.

*I made you to be his companion.*

Despite the rapid beating of her heart, Stephanie felt at peace. The special peace that came from knowing and doing God's will. Rare moments like this, when God spoke directly to her spirit, left her breathless with wonder. She heard and she understood. There was no room left for doubt.

She slid upright against the headboard and reached for the telephone on her nightstand. After punching in the number, she waited impatiently for an answer on the other end of the line.

Her heart skipped when she heard his sleepy, "Hello?"

"James, it's me."

"Steph?" He sounded more alert. "Thank God. Are you all right? Where were you yesterday? I kept calling, but you never answered the phone."

"I'm fine. Really. I needed to go off by myself for the day. I had some praying and soul searching to do."

Silence, then, "And?"

She smiled, hoping he could hear it in her voice. "And the children will simply have to accept that we're getting married." She brought her lips closer to the mouthpiece. "I love you, James. I want to be your wife more than anything."

"Don't go anywhere. Do you hear me? I'm getting dressed and coming right over. Don't go anywhere."

Stephanie looked at the clock. "It's only 6:30."

"I don't care. I'm up and you're up. What the clock reads doesn't matter to us."

She laughed softly. "All right. I'll put the coffee on. Come to the back door. It'll be unlocked."

The moment she hung up the phone, Stephanie tossed aside the bedcovers and hurried to the bathroom to wash her face, brush her teeth, and run a comb through her hair. She changed into a pair of slacks and a blouse, then went to the kitchen to make the coffee. It was just starting to brew when a soft rap sounded. An instant later, the back door opened.

If there had been any shred of doubt remaining about her decision to marry James, it would have disappeared at the sight of him. Her heart skipped, and she felt as giddy as she had at the age of sixteen when he'd arrived, clad in tux and cummerbund, to escort her to the junior-senior prom.

Strange, the pathways of life. She had loved James twice—first as a girl, then as an old woman. Yes, the pathways that had brought her back to him were strange ... wonderful ... unexplainable. No wonder her daughter couldn't understand what had happened in the past few weeks. Stephanie barely understood it herself.

"You're beautiful in the morning," James said.

Beautiful? Perhaps in her youth, but no more. Now her face was wrinkled, her hair was Ivory soap white, and her body was soft in too many of the wrong places. But as James drew near, she realized he meant what he said. She *was* beautiful in his eyes.

He gathered her in his arms. Arms still strong despite his age. Strong enough to hold her close. "You had me worried for a while. I was afraid I'd lose you."

"I know. I'm sorry."

One day she would share with him the words God had whispered to her. Perhaps on their anniversary as they reminisced about their whirlwind second courtship.

James kissed her softly on the mouth, and when their lips parted, Stephanie sighed with pleasure. Romantic love was not the property of the young, no matter what people believed.

"Tell me something," he said.

"Of course."

"What's your favorite color?"

She smiled as she touched his jaw, running her fingers over his close-trimmed beard. "It's a tie. Aquamarine and lemon yellow."

"And your favorite movie?"

*"Sound of Music."*

It pleased her that he'd remembered Miranda's questions. It pleased her that it mattered to him because it mattered to her daughter. It made her believe things would be well between Miranda and James. If not this week or next week, then perhaps next month or the one after that.

James brushed his lips against her forehead. "We'd better call John Gunn this morning and arrange for the church."

"Yes. I think we'd better. I'm ready to become Mrs. James Scott." She looked up at him. "The sooner, the better."

## CHAPTER 13

Twelve days later, the Thimbleberry Quilting Club hosted a bridal shower for Stephanie in the fellowship hall of Hart's Crossing Community Church. It was a joyous affair.

Francine and Angie Hunter led the guests in a few silly games that had everyone in stitches. Then they all clapped and teased as Stephanie opened her gifts, including a beautiful aquamarine negligee and robe. Afterward, the guests drank punch and ate cake while Till Hart regaled them with long-ago stories about Stephanie. One thing could be said about Till—there was nothing wrong with her memory!

"Mom!" Miranda exclaimed, looking at her with wide eyes after hearing about the night a bunch of kids from the junior class drove fifty miles to steal their arch rival's school mascot. "Did you really do that?"

"Well, it wasn't only me." Stephanie cast a mock glare in Till's direction. "There were a dozen of us involved."

"I can't believe you'd do such a thing." Miranda shook her head. "It's just not like you."

Interesting, how parents were viewed by their children.

Stephanie had no trouble seeing her involvement in that high school episode as being "just like her." She hadn't been what anyone would call wild, but she'd pulled her share of teenage pranks that got her in hot water.

Paula, seated on Stephanie's left side, leaned close and whispered, "No wonder Daddy fell in love with you. You rascal, you."

Although Paula had been Stephanie and James's greatest ally from the moment she and her daughters stepped onto the tarmac at the Twin Falls airport, the past week had seen a softening of attitudes with the other three children as well, giving Stephanie hope that one day the two families would become truly united.

Miranda had begun to warm up to James, despite herself. The more time they spent together, the less angry Miranda was and the less she seemed to fear that he wanted to replace her father. It was a good beginning.

Jenna had arrived in Hart's Crossing, expecting to find a treasure-hunting black widow who had trapped her unsuspecting father in a web. It hadn't taken long for the young woman to learn that Stephanie was anything but. While still not thrilled that her father had chosen to marry so quickly, neither had she raised more opposition.

As for the pragmatic Kurt, he'd accepted the inevitable with a "If you're sure, Dad," and a "Welcome to the family, Stephanie."

Most importantly, over the past few days, each of their children had let their parents know, in ways both large and small, that they were loved. And love, Stephanie knew, would see all of them through. Love never failed.

How blessed she was, she thought as she looked around the fellowship hall, to be surrounded by family and friends, some who had prayed for her countless times through the years, loved ones who'd lifted her when she had no strength to stand on her own. God had been good to her. He'd given her fifty years with her beloved Chuck. He'd entrusted her with their wonderful daughter. And now he'd brought James back into her life.

Autumn had always been Stephanie's favorite season of the year—and now she thought it might become the favorite season of her life as well.

Who, besides God, knew what the future held in store?

Storms? Probably.

Love? Most assuredly.

Stephanie couldn't wait for this new adventure to begin.

# DIAMOND PLACE

HART'S CROSSING #3

## CHAPTER 1

*February 2006*

Lyssa Sampson stared at her reflection in the bedroom mirror as she gave the brim of her baseball cap a slight tug. She did her best not to show any emotion. *Baseball Digest* said that's how Cardinal pitcher Chris Carpenter did it. The article, found in one of her older issues of the magazine, said concrete budged more easily than Carpenter's face. It called him "the Lord of Bored." That's how Lyssa wanted to look when she stood on the pitcher's mound.

"Lyssa," her mom called from downstairs. "Are you getting dressed?"

"Yeah."

"Well, hurry up. Your breakfast is about ready."

"Okay. Just a minute."

Lyssa removed the baseball cap and slipped it into her backpack along with her schoolwork and books. After a moment's hesitation, she shoved a couple issues of *Baseball Digest* into the backpack, too. She needed to memorize a few more stats before the next practice. She wanted Coach Jenkins to know she was serious about baseball.

Real serious.

∼

"Lyssa!" Terri walked to the foot of the stairs and looked up toward her daughter's bedroom. "Your breakfast is ready now. Hurry up or you'll be late for school."

"Comin', Mom."

Terri returned to the kitchen, where she scooped fluffy scrambled eggs onto a plate. She heard the telltale sound of her ten-year-old daughter's imminent arrival—athletic shoes stomping hard on the stairs as Lyssa took them two at a time. Moments later, she entered the kitchen, backpack slung over one shoulder.

"Do you have your homework with you?"

"Yeah."

She lifted an eyebrow and gave her daughter a hard look. "Are you sure? I don't want to have to leave the salon like I did yesterday to bring your papers to the school."

"I've *got* it, Mom." Lyssa dropped her backpack onto the floor before slipping onto a bar stool at the kitchen counter.

Terri turned to the stove, added two strips of bacon and a slice of buttered toast to the plate, and slid it across the counter. Lyssa took her fork and began shoveling eggs into her mouth as if it had been a week since her last meal.

"Slow down, honey."

Lyssa swallowed and grinned. "You told me I was gonna be late. I'm just doin' what you said."

Terri leaned her backside against the edge of the sink. She took enormous pleasure in her daughter. Watching her eat, watching her sleep, watching her play baseball—it all brought pleasure. Of all the blessings in Terri's life, Lyssa was the greatest.

Without looking up, her daughter said, "Don't forget you're gonna bake your special cake for the Cavaliers' carnival tomorrow night."

Terri winced. She had forgotten. Not the fundraiser itself, but that she'd volunteered to bring a cake. Why hadn't she written it in her day planner when she volunteered? She knew better than to trust things like that to memory. Her schedule and Lyssa's schedule were jam-packed during the school year. Without her list of "to do's," Terri was lost.

She would be the first to admit that it wasn't easy being a single parent with no other family to lend support. Some days she felt stretched to her absolute limit. Thankfully, she had many friends in Hart's Crossing and a wonderful church family who pitched in when needed.

She turned toward the recipe box, flipping open the lid with her left hand while reaching for a shopping list and pen with her right.

"Coach Jenkins says I'm pitching really good. Maybe he'll let me be a starting pitcher at least once this summer. Wouldn't that be something? First girl to start a game in the major division of the Cavaliers."

"Yes, it would be something." Terri had enough flour, but she would need more sugar and eggs. She scribbled on the notepad. "But remember, all the pitchers on your team are a year or two older than you are. You can't count on starting a game."

Lyssa laughed. "I'm a whole lot better than Bobby Danvers, and he's twelve."

"Pride goes before a fall, young lady."

"Huh?"

"I mean, you still have a lot to learn. Don't think you know it all."

"I don't think that."

Terri frowned as she stared at the notepad. Oh, yes. She needed two packages of frozen cherries, some unsweetened cocoa, and a carton of whipping cream. She would shop for groceries on the way home from work today and bake the black forest cake first thing in the morning before heading to the salon for her Saturday appointments.

"Mom? Did you hear me?"

Terri turned around. "I'm sorry, honey. What did you say?"

"I'm going now." Lyssa stood beside the kitchen stool, once again holding her backpack. "See you after school."

"Not without a kiss, you don't." She stepped forward and brushed her lips across her daughter's forehead. "And put your coat on. It's cold, and that sweatshirt isn't enough to keep you warm."

Lyssa rolled her eyes but obediently headed for the rack beside the back door.

Moments later, alone in the kitchen, Terri completed writing her shopping list, set it on top of her planner, then went upstairs to dress for work. She chose jeans, a rust-colored sweater with three-quarter sleeves, and—the most important item for a person who was on her feet all day—comfortable shoes. With a quick glance in the mirror, she determined a ponytail would have to do. No time for fussing with her hair.

She smiled ruefully at her reflection. *Good thing my clients don't judge my expertise based on how I look.*

It was a short drive from her home on the west side of Hart's Crossing to Terri's Tangles Beauty Salon, located at the corner of Main and Municipal. The car's heater didn't have time to take the chill out of the February air before she pulled her 1991 Toyota Camry into the reserved spot near the back of the shop.

"Brrr."

She rushed to the entrance, shoved her key in the lock, and pushed open the door. Before she had time to do more than shrug out of her coat, the telephone rang.

She lifted the receiver from the back room's wall phone. "Good morning. Terri's Tangles."

"Hey, Terri. It's Angie. Got a minute?"

Terri moved toward the coffeemaker, pressing the handset between shoulder and ear. "Sure. My first client isn't due for about forty-five minutes. What's up?"

"I wanted to see what you're doing on May 20th about 2:00 in the afternoon. It's a Saturday."

"I don't have any clients booked out that far." She filled the carafe with cold water and poured it into the reservoir. "You can pick whatever time you want. Hang on. Let me get my appointment book, and I'll—"

"I don't need an appointment for my hair, Terri. I need a maid of honor and a flower girl."

For an instant, Terri froze in place. Then she squealed. "Are you teasing me, Angie Hunter? Because if you are, so help me, I'll—"

"I'm not teasing. Last night, Bill asked me to marry him."

"It's about time." Terri couldn't think of better news. Bill Palmer and Angie Hunter were two of her favorite people, and she thought them perfect for each other. She'd been hoping and praying for this to happen for months and months. "I was wondering when Bill would get off his keister and propose. Sometimes that man is as slow as molasses."

Angie laughed.

"Did he give you a ring?"

"Yes. He did the whole routine. Candlelight dinner. Soft music playing in the background. He even got down on one knee to propose. When I said yes, he slipped the engagement ring on my finger. It was very romantic."

Terri sighed. "I'm sure it was. Bill's a romantic kind of guy."

"Mmm."

"Can you swing by the salon today? I'd love to see the ring and give you a hug. I'll be here until 3:00."

"Sure, I'll drop by. And you and Lyssa will be my maid of honor and flower girl, won't you?"

"Of course. As long as you don't make us wear something too atrocious or froufrou."

The two of them laughed in unison before exchanging a few words of farewell. Moments later, Terri hung up the phone and returned to the coffeemaker.

Angie, Bill, and a May wedding, how delightful. She wondered if they planned to be married in the church or outdoors. May weather could be iffy, but the gazebo in the park was a wonderful location for a wedding.

Terri and her ex-husband Vic had been married by a justice of the peace in Twin Falls. Neither of them had any family in Hart's Crossing, Terri's parents were deceased and Vic's family all lived back East. He hadn't wanted to wait to plan a more formal wedding. At the time, Terri had thought it romantic that he was in such a hurry to become her husband, but she should have wondered instead about his impatient nature. His spur-of-the-moment decisions had caused her much grief.

More than seven years had passed since Vic Sampson left town with that blonde he met at the ski resort—not the first woman he'd flirted with during his marriage to Terri, but the only one who'd convinced him to leave his wife and get a divorce.

Terri's love for her ex-husband had long since died, but time couldn't completely heal the wounds of a failed marriage. She'd never planned to be a divorced mom. She'd never wanted her daughter to grow up without a father. But that's what had happened anyway.

Terri gave her head a quick shake. Let sleeping dogs lie. That's water under the bridge. No crying over spilt milk. Pick a cliché. They were all true. Dwelling on the past couldn't change it.

Once, Angie had asked if Terri was interested in marrying

again. She'd answered, "I hope I can find the right guy, the one God means for me to marry. One day I hope Prince Charming will ride into town and sweep me off my feet."

So far Terri had seen neither hide nor hair of a tall, dark, and handsome prince and his white horse galloping down Main Street.

∼

"Hey, Coach Jenkins." Lyssa smiled at her Little League coach, who was standing in the hall outside the school office. "Whatcha doin' here?"

"Morning, Lyssa." He nudged his glasses with the knuckle of his right index finger, and then winked at her. "I've been called to the principal's office."

Lyssa liked the coach, but sometimes he was kinda weird. Even she knew the principal couldn't call just anybody to her office, not somebody who didn't have kids in the school, anyway. The coach didn't have kids or a wife.

"Are you ready for the carnival tomorrow night?" he asked. "We've got lots of money to raise for the Cavaliers."

"Uh-huh. I'm ready." She tried to stand a little taller, appear a little older, maybe not look so much like a girl and more like a pitcher. "My mom's gonna make her special chocolate cake for the cakewalk. It's really good."

"Terrific. I love chocolate cake. Maybe I'll win it."

The bell rang, announcing time for students to get to their classrooms.

"I better go, Coach. See you tomorrow night."

"See you there. And tell your mom I'm looking forward to trying out that cake of hers."

"Okay."

Lyssa suppressed a sigh as she walked away. What was she doing, talking about cake when what she wanted was to make the coach realize she was as good a pitcher as any of the boys on the team? Maybe she was only ten, and maybe they'd never had a girl pitcher before, but she oughta get a chance.

She should have quoted some of those stats she'd memorized or talked about the Little League teams that played in last year's World Series or even told him how often she practiced.

*"And tell your mom I'm looking forward to trying out that cake of hers."*

Her brow puckered. Sure would be nice if he'd said something about her pitching arm or her fastball instead of her mom's cake, even if Lyssa was the one who'd brought it up first. Of course, if the coach really liked chocolate cake all that much, and he got her mom's and thought it was good, maybe he would notice Lyssa a little more. And if he noticed her a little more, then maybe ...

Hmm. That gave her an idea.

CHAPTER 2

Mel Jenkins arrived later than he'd anticipated at Hart's Crossing Community Church, site of the Cavaliers' final fundraiser before opening day. By the time he entered the church's basement, where the carnival would be held, volunteers had finished stringing crepe paper across the ceiling and tying helium-filled balloons to whatever would hold them. Brightly colored booths—darts, fishing for prizes, ping-pong balls to win goldfish, even a pie-throwing booth—were set up on two sides of the room. In the opposite corner from where he stood, volunteers prepared for the cakewalk.

He shucked off his coat, tossed it onto a nearby folding chair, and rolled up his shirtsleeves. Then he looked for someone to tell him where his help was most needed.

Mel was a relative newcomer to Hart's Crossing—five years, which wasn't long in a small town like this—and he still felt like an outsider. But that was his own fault. He'd kept to himself after moving here from Montana. His relocation had come after he accepted a position as manager of a local bank. At the time, all he'd wanted was to be left alone with his memories and his grief—and his anger at God for taking Rhonda, his fiancée, from him.

Time had helped ease his sorrow, and finally he'd opened the door to let God into his heart to complete the healing. Becoming the coach of the Hart's Crossing Cavaliers was one step he'd taken to become a part of the community, another way to remind himself that he was among the living.

"Hey, Coach."

He turned his head. "Hey, Lyssa."

Mel liked the Sampson girl. Charming and funny, talented and determined, she had as much potential as any other player on the team. More potential than most, actually. One of only three ten-year-olds on the team, she needed a bit more experience as well as some time to grow. He figured the Cavaliers were in for a winning season and that Lyssa would play an important part in it, even if this was her first year in the major division.

"Wanna come help blow up balloons for the dart booth? It's takin' forever to get enough of 'em ready. That's where I'm headed."

"Sure, I'll help."

Strawberry-blond braids bouncing against her back, Lyssa led the way across the room to a purple booth. When she reached it, she stopped and looked over her shoulder. "You remember my mom, don't you?"

It wasn't until then that Mel saw the woman seated on the floor inside the booth, a half-blown balloon stuck between pursed lips. "Nice to see you, Mrs. Sampson."

Cheeks red, eyes narrowed, Terri exhaled forcefully, then took the balloon from her mouth and tied a quick knot in the end. "Thanks," she said once she caught her breath. "Nice to see you, too." She held out a package of new balloons. "Be my guest."

"Here's a chair, Coach Jenkins." Lyssa shoved the metal folding chair up against the back of his legs.

He sat on it at the same moment Terri rose from the floor. He'd have to say that this was the first time he'd noticed how pretty Lyssa's mom was. Of course, the other times he'd seen her had been at Little League organizational meetings; she'd sat in the back of the audience while he stood in front of the group. They'd never had the opportunity to talk one-on-one.

She had unusual eyes, he thought now that he was close enough to see them. Not quite green. Not really blue. Striking with her red hair, too. Unusual. Almost like—

Suddenly aware that he was staring at her—and also aware that she *knew* it—he lowered his gaze to the bag of balloons in his right hand. "Guess I'd better get to work."

It had been a long time since he'd noticed the color of a woman's eyes or hair. Doing so now surprised him.

In the first couple of years after Rhonda's death, he'd been numb to everything. After that, he'd put up an invisible shield whenever he was around women, not willing to risk an involvement that might later cause him heartache.

So when had he lowered that protective shield?

"Coach, don't forget you're gonna try to win my mom's chocolate cake in the cakewalk tonight."

"What?" He looked at Lyssa. "Oh. Sure. You bet."

~

A MAN HADN'T BEEN TONGUE-TIED IN TERRI'S PRESENCE IN AGES. If Mel Jenkins was always this flustered around women, it would explain why he was a bachelor at his age.

She subdued a smile and put another balloon between her lips before casting a surreptitious glance in Mel's direction. He was a man of good looks, medium height, and muscular build. The creases between his eyebrows and the slight squint of his blue eyes made her wonder if the prescription for his eyeglasses needed adjustment. He had pale blond hair and fair skin that probably required 45 SPF sunblock. As a redhead who burned easily, she sympathized.

Terri didn't know much about the coach other than that he managed one of the two banks in town, had moved to Hart's Crossing from somewhere in Montana, and was enthusiastic about Little League baseball. Most gossip eventually spilled into Terri's salon, but nothing of significance had reached her ears about Mel Jenkins. Folks said he was friendly but reserved. Now she suspected extremely shy would be a better description.

Bill Palmer had recommended Mel for the coaching position when it became vacant. League rules called for a thorough background check of coaches and other volunteers, and Terri wouldn't have wanted it otherwise. Not the way things were these days. Still, it was Bill's endorsement that made her feel truly comfortable with Mel's involvement with Lyssa and the other kids on the team.

"How's it going here?"

Terri turned toward John Gunn, the pastor of Hart's Crossing Community Church. "Fine. We've got enough balloons ready to start tacking them to the board."

"Need more help?"

"I don't think so." She glanced at Mel. "Do we?"

He shook his head. "I think we can manage."

"We're doin' okay," Lyssa added before putting another balloon to her lips and breathing into it.

"I guess not," Terri said, looking at the pastor again.

"Good. Then I'll see who does need my help." With a wave, John moved toward the next booth.

Terri picked up a thumbtack before reaching into the large box of inflated balloons.

"Do you go to church here, Mrs. Sampson?" Mel asked after a brief period of silence.

"Please. Call me Terri." She poked a tack through the lip of a pink balloon and into the corkboard behind it. "Yes, this is my church. It has been since before Lyssa was born." She attached another balloon to the board. "What about you?"

"I attend services at the Methodist church over on Idaho Street. It's a small congregation, but I like it."

"I have a number of good friends who go there. Has Reverend Ball decided to retire yet?"

"No, not yet."

"He's talked about it for years."

"I've heard him say it, too, but I don't think he means it. Not yet."

Terri glanced over her shoulder. Although she was naturally attracted to tall, lean, dark-haired cowboy types, she conceded that Mel had a certain appeal, for a banker. Oh, and that dreadful haircut. Davis Wiggin, the local barber, must have cut it.

Now, if she could get her hands in Mel's pale hair, she would—

"Hey, Mom," Lyssa interrupted Terri's thoughts. "Mrs. Bedford's calling for you."

Terri felt heat rush to her cheeks, knowing she'd been caught staring, just as Mel had been caught earlier.

"I guess I'd better see what Patti wants," she said before hurrying away.

Patti Bedford, four months pregnant with her first child, stood near a table that held an array of beautiful cakes and pies, each covered with plastic wrap. She frowned down at a small, portable CD player.

"What's wrong, Patti?"

"Oh, this miserable thing won't work. I told Al it was broken, but he insisted he'd fixed it." She looked at Terri. "I'd better run over to Radio Shack and buy a new one, or we may not have music for the cakewalk. Will you finish getting the numbers on the floor with the masking tape?"

"Sure. I'll get it done. And make certain you get a receipt so the league can reimburse you for the cost of the CD player."

"I don't know why Al thinks he can repair everything electrical." Patti reached for her coat and purse. "Sometimes he even puts the batteries into a flashlight backwards." She rolled her eyes. "Men."

Terri nodded as if in agreement, but she thought Patti was one of the fortunate ones. Al Bedford, young as he was, was a peach of a guy. He and Patti had been married almost two years, and he still hung on her every word, as if each one was made of pure gold. If Vic had treated Terri half as good …

Well, it was pointless for her thoughts to go there. Besides, it looked too much like envy for Terri's comfort. First Angie, now Patti.

"Shame on me," she muttered. "I've been blessed too much to envy others. Shame on me."

***

THE COACH KEPT BLOWING UP AND TYING OFF BALLOONS, ONE right after another, but Lyssa was pretty sure he'd watched her mom most of the time since she went over to the cakewalk area.

"Mom's cake's even better than it looks."

The coach turned his head. For a second, she thought he didn't understand what she'd said, but then he grinned. "Is that right? There looks like a lot of choices over there."

"Nope. Hers beats them all." Man, there she was, doing it again. Talking about her mom's cake when she should impress the coach with baseball stuff. She reached for another balloon while mentally scrambling for something better to say. Finally, it came to her. "Coach Jenkins, can you name the four pitchers who had twenty or more strikeouts in a single game?"

His eyes narrowed behind his glasses. "No, I don't think I can."

Lyssa grinned. "Tom Cheney of the Washington Senators had twenty-one back in 1962. Roger Clemens of the Boston Red Sox had twenty in two different games, one in 1986 and one in 1996. Kerry Wood of the Chicago Cubs had twenty in—" *Oh, oh. What year was it?* "Oh, yeah. That was in 1998. And the last one was Steve Carlton of the St. Louis Cardinals. He had twenty in 1969."

"Mighty impressive, Miss Sampson."

She beamed. If those stats impressed him, just wait until she—

"Hey, Jenkins. I could use your help."

Lyssa and the coach turned in unison to see Angie Hunt and Bill Palmer standing beyond the booth's front counter.

*Not now! I was so close.*

Bill motioned toward the stairs. "I've got cases of soda pop to bring down. Can you give me a hand?"

"Sure thing." The coach stood. "See you later, Lyssa."

The two men strode away, leaving Lyssa with baseball statistics racing through her head.

"Don't look so disappointed, squirt," Angie said. "I'm staying."

"Sorry."

Angie settled onto the chair the coach had vacated moments before. "Maybe you can help me decide on the colors I want to use at the wedding."

Like she cared about that when she could have been talking baseball with the coach.

∽

TWO HOURS LATER, THE BASEMENT OF THE CHURCH WAS JAM-packed with people. Voices buzzed and laughter rang as carnival-goers moved from booth to booth, happy to win silly prizes.

Terri greeted each person and took tickets for the cakewalk.

"Thanks so much for coming tonight. Hope you win a cake. The Cavaliers appreciate your support. Do enjoy yourself."

Till Hart, granddaughter of the town's founding father, approached Terri, a smile wreathing her face. The woman never missed a community event if she could help it.

"Good evening, Miss Hart. Quite the crowd tonight."

"Always good to see folks turn out to support our youth." She offered Terri a ticket. "I hear you baked your famous black forest cake."

"I don't know how famous it is, but yes, I did."

"Well, that's the one I want to win. I've been thinking about it ever since Lyssa told me that's what you brought."

Terri looked over at the long table that held the desserts. At the end of it, Lyssa stood beside the brand-new CD player and a glass bowl full of numbers. "We're about to start a new walk, Miss Hart. You're the last one in for this round. Go stand on that empty number there." She pointed at the floor. "And good luck."

Till moved with surprising swiftness for someone her age. Sometimes Terri found it hard to believe the woman was approaching seventy. She acted decades younger.

*I should be so spry.* Which reminded her she needed to be more faithful about riding the stationary bike she had in a corner of her bedroom.

Till Hart came to a standstill on the lone remaining number. She turned, looked at Terri, and winked.

Terri might have returned the wink, except her gaze was drawn to the man on the number in front of Till. It was Mel Jenkins. Terri didn't remember taking his ticket. How had he—

Music blared forth from the player, and Lyssa shouted, "Everybody walk. Follow the numbers. Everybody walk until the music stops."

"Step lively, Mr. Jenkins," Till said loudly as she passed by

Terri. "I'm about to step on your heels. Men should never dawdle."

He responded, but Terri missed his words. However, she saw the teasing look in his eyes as he glanced back at the older woman following close behind him.

The music stopped abruptly. Participants shuffled forward or back to make certain each stood on a number. Lyssa reached into the glass bowl and pulled out a slip of paper.

"Number fourteen. Who's on number fourteen?"

There was a moment of silence before Mel answered, "I am."

Lyssa dropped the paper back into the bowl. "All right, Coach! You get your pick." She pointed toward the black forest cake Terri had baked that morning. "That's the one you want."

Terri didn't miss the quick look he stole in her direction. "You promise it's the best one, Lyssa?"

"I promise. My mom made it."

The number on the slip of paper *could* have been fourteen. Of course, Lyssa would never know if it was or wasn't because she hadn't looked before dropping it back in the bowl. She'd sorta faked reading it.

Was it really lying if she didn't know for sure?

It wasn't like anybody spent a whole lot on those tickets anyway. Everybody came to the carnival to help raise money for the Little League, so win or not, they would've spent the same amount of money. Right?

CHAPTER 3

Mel had been home from church a couple of hours when the telephone rang. Bill Palmer was on the other end of the line, calling in his official capacity as owner and editor of the *Mountain View Press*, the local weekly newspaper.

"Mind answering a few questions for the paper on a Sunday?" Bill asked after they'd exchanged a few pleasantries.

"No. Go ahead."

"Did the Cavaliers meet their financial objective last night? Would you call this year's carnival a success?"

Shifting the telephone receiver from his right ear to his left, Mel looked to the black forest cake in the center of his kitchen table. Eighteen hours after he'd brought it home, more than a third of it was missing. "Yes, on both counts."

"Coach Jenkins, it's not long now until the season opener. How do you think this year's team will fare?"

"We've got a strong bunch of experienced players. Most of them already have two years in the majors, and the rest have come up through the minors, many of them starting with Tee Ball. I think we'll see a winning season from this team."

Bill cleared his throat. "This is your first year as head coach of the Cavaliers. How are you feeling about the experience thus far?"

"It's been terrific. I like working with the kids, and the parents have really pitched in to help whenever and wherever they're needed. I've got no complaints. I hope they all feel the same way about me."

"Great." Bill chuckled. "Official interview over. Now tell me the truth. How's it going?"

"I *am* telling the truth."

Over the past year, he'd come to think of Bill as a trusted friend. They'd met at the local Chamber of Commerce meetings when Mel first came to town, but it wasn't until last year that he'd been willing to be more than business acquaintances. He was thankful Bill wasn't the sort to be easily put off. The two men had plenty in common—never married, fortyish, interested in sports and current events, avid readers, Christians.

"The kids are great," Mel continued, "and so are the parents. We never lack for enough volunteers, no matter what needs done. I'm glad you talked me into coaching."

"Well, that's good to know. I'd hate to be responsible if you were miserable."

Mel reached for the cake in the center of the table and drew it toward him, recalling the pretty redhead who'd baked it. As quickly as the image popped into his head, he tried to shake it off by changing the subject. "Hey, I hear you've got a bit of news of your own. Something about you and Angie Hunter and a wedding."

"Man, that didn't take long to get around town. Who told you?"

"Betty Frazier was in the bank on Friday afternoon, checking about a loan for one of her real estate clients. I overheard her talking to a teller about the proposal."

Bill laughed again. "I don't know why I bother to publish a

newspaper. Everybody knows everything before I can get the thing to press."

"True enough, but I promise to keep subscribing anyway."

"Thanks. I'll soon have a wife to support, so I've gotta sell lots of subscriptions."

A familiar heaviness weighed on Mel's heart as memories of Rhonda and what might have been pricked his thoughts. "You know I wish you and Angie the very best."

"Thanks."

"How about we meet for lunch or dinner later this week? That way I can get the straight facts instead of the gossip."

"Sure. What day?"

"Let me check my appointment schedule at the office, and I'll get back to you in the morning."

"Okay. Thanks for the comments for the paper."

"Not a problem. Be sure to remind folks to turn out for the season opener." Rising from the chair, Mel said good-bye, then hung up the phone.

He turned, and his gaze swept over the kitchen. It was a room devoid of personality. Sterile, even. He'd bought the newly constructed house when he came to Hart's Crossing and lived in it for five years, but there was little evidence of that.

He looked at the black forest cake on the table. *I'll bet Terri Sampson's kitchen has plenty of personality.*

Maybe it was no accident that he'd noticed her green-blue eyes and the fiery color of her hair. He'd signed up to coach baseball as a reminder that he was among the living, but it might be time that the land of the living included more than his co-workers and a baseball team of ten-, eleven-, and twelve-year-olds.

Maybe it should include a woman, too.

Terri added another log to the fire, then returned to the couch, a soft blanket, a comfy pillow, and the latest novel from her favorite Christian author.

She loved lazy Sunday afternoons, especially in winter. Sunday was the one day of the week when she allowed herself to be selfish, doing only things she wanted to do, activities that brought her pleasure. Today she didn't even mind the constant drumbeat coming from the compact audio system in Lyssa's bedroom.

"Mmm." She scrunched down into a comfortable position and opened the novel.

Although cool weather would be around for several more weeks—according to Punxsutawney Phil and his shadow—there wouldn't be many more days that begged Terri to build a fire. Spring was almost upon them. Spring and baseball followed by summer and baseball.

The telephone rang, but she made no move to answer it. Nine times out of ten these days, calls were for Lyssa, shades of the teen years to come.

Terri shuddered. She was nowhere near ready to contemplate *that*.

"Mom! It's for you."

Glancing toward the stairs, she laid the book against her thigh. "Thanks, honey." She moved aside both book and blanket and rose from the sofa. "I need a cordless phone," she muttered as she walked into the kitchen and lifted the receiver. "Hello?"

"Mrs. Sampson? Terri. It's Mel ... Mel Jenkins."

"Oh. Hello." She couldn't imagine why he might be calling. Other than last night's fundraiser, Terri's volunteer duties for the Cavaliers didn't start until the season opener.

"Sorry to disturb you on a Sunday afternoon."

She cast a longing glance toward the living room couch. "No problem."

"I … uh … I wanted to tell you how delicious your cake is. The best I've ever eaten."

"Oh." She blinked. "Thank you."

"To tell you the truth, it's providing a bit too much temptation for one person. I'm afraid I'll eat the whole thing before the weekend's over."

Her brow puckered in a frown. Why on earth had he called to tell her that?

"Lyssa said this is her favorite cake, and I thought … Well, maybe I could bring some of it back to her. Unless, of course, you made two of them while you were at it."

"No, I didn't make two."

"Well, would you mind then? If I brought some of the cake over for Lyssa to enjoy?"

"I'm sure she would like that a lot—"

"Great. Why don't I bring it now? Unless that's an inconvenience."

Having discovered the previous evening how shy Mel was, Terri decided it wouldn't hurt to be kind to him. "No, it isn't an inconvenience. I'll let Lyssa know you're coming." She gave him directions to her house and then hung up the phone.

So much for an afternoon by the fire reading a good book.

A few moments later, she rapped on Lyssa's bedroom door, a knock that was drowned out by the pounding music. She opened the door, saying loudly, "Hey, honey. Turn that down, please."

Lyssa gave her a pained look but obeyed.

"That was your coach on the phone."

"Did we raise enough money?"

"I don't know. I didn't ask." Terri stepped into the bedroom. "But you can ask him yourself when he gets here. He's bringing over the cake he won last night."

Lyssa's eyes widened. "Didn't he like it?" Crestfallen, she sank onto the edge of her bed. "I thought he'd like it."

Terri chuckled. "Just the opposite. I think he liked it more than he should." She motioned with her head toward the door. "Come downstairs and give me a hand. He's on his way now."

"How could he like it more than he should?" Lyssa asked as she followed Terri.

"He said a whole cake is too much for just one person."

"Not *your* cake, Mom. I could eat it all by myself."

She laughed again. "True enough. But you don't have to think about your waistline the way adults do."

∽

Mel parked his Ford F150 in the driveway of the Sampson home. It was a two-story house but not large, just big enough for a divorced mother and one daughter. He wondered how long Lyssa's dad had been out of the picture. Did he see his daughter and ex-wife? Did he live in Hart's Crossing? Were they on good speaking terms? What if there was a chance of reconciliation? Mel didn't want to get in the middle of something like that.

Maybe coming here wasn't such a good idea. Terri Sampson was a friendly, attractive woman, but dating was difficult enough without outside complications. Maybe—

The front door flew open, and Lyssa appeared on the stoop. "Hey, Coach!" She waved an arm.

Good idea or not, it was too late to change his mind. He reached for the cake platter and got out of the truck.

"Mom said you couldn't eat that all by yourself."

He followed the sidewalk toward the front door. "Not quite what I said. I *could* have eaten it all, but I knew I shouldn't."

She gave him a look that said he was nuts. "C'mon. Mom's waiting."

As Mel stepped through the doorway into the living room, he noticed the blanket and book on the sofa and the dancing flames in the fireplace. Looked like he'd interrupted her plans. He shouldn't have come.

"Want me to take the cake?" Lyssa asked. "You can hang your coat in the closet there."

"Thanks." He handed her the platter, then shrugged out of his jacket.

Before he could open the closet door, he saw Terri step into the archway between living room and kitchen. She smiled in welcome, and the room seemed to grow brighter because of it.

Maybe this was a good idea after all.

∽

Over cake and beverages—coffee for the adults and hot chocolate for Lyssa—the conversation turned quickly to Little League baseball. It was the one thing the three of them had in common, as far as Terri knew. Mel mentioned his hope for warmer weather by the season opener. Terri asked about the fundraising results from the previous night. Lyssa announced she'd been working hard on her curveball.

"I'm proud of you, Lyssa," Mel said. "You've come a long way since team practice began."

Terri smiled, thankful that he took seriously her daughter's desire to improve. A few of the Cavalier team members gave Lyssa a hard time. She was the only girl in the major division and among the youngest of the Cavaliers. Some of the boys— and undoubtedly some of their parents—didn't think Lyssa belonged in the majors.

"Good enough to start a game next month?" Lyssa asked her coach, her voice filled with hope.

He gave a slight shake of his head. "This is your first year in the majors. This is the third year for both of our other pitchers, and they want to start as badly as you do. We'll have to see how the season goes. I'm not saying it won't happen. I'm saying we'll have to wait and see."

Terri noticed the way he looked directly at Lyssa as he spoke. His tone of voice was kind but firm. He didn't talk down to her daughter, as if her question was frivolous or unimportant.

Determination narrowed Lyssa's eyes. "Coach Jenkins, I'm gonna get good enough to start at least one game this year. You'll see."

"I hope you do, Lyssa."

Something warm blossomed in Terri's heart as she observed the two of them. A feeling so long unfelt she couldn't quite put a name to it.

CHAPTER 4

Lyssa pushed open the door to the *Mountain View Press.* "Hey, Mr. Palmer. Mom said you wanted to see me."

"Yeah, I did." The newspaper editor rose from behind his cluttered desk. "Didn't expect you so soon though. I just talked to your mom half an hour ago."

"She had to run some errands after I got outta school, so she dropped me off on her way to the store."

Bill motioned her forward. "Come on back here. I ran across an old article from the Associated Press that I think you'll want to read." He picked up several sheets of paper. "After I read the first one, I searched out a few more on the Internet. Pretty interesting stuff. Did you hear about this girl when it happened?" He handed Lyssa the papers before sitting down again.

She recognized the name in the headline immediately. "Are you *kidding*, Mr. Palmer? *Everybody's* heard of Katie Brownell. She pitched a perfect game. She even got honored by the Baseball Hall of Fame."

The editor laughed softly. "So where was I when all that happened?"

211

"D'know." She shrugged as she sat in a chair opposite him, then started reading the top article.

*Katie Brownell is a shy 11-year-old girl of few words. But when she gets on the baseball field, she lets her pitching do the talking.*

*Brownell is the only girl in the Oakfield-Alabama Little League baseball program in this community about halfway between Buffalo and Rochester. On Saturday, that didn't stop her from accomplishing something league officials can't remember anybody—boy or girl—ever doing.*

*She threw a perfect game ...*

Wow, Lyssa thought. Wouldn't that be something? And if Katie Brownell could do it, why couldn't she? She could if her coach believed in her enough.

*Katie said she knew she had a chance for something special in the fourth inning. Fortunately, Katie's coach, Joe Sullivan, realized that, too.*

*He had intended to pull Katie at some point during the game and was ready to do it when the scorekeeper told him she had a no-hitter going ...*

"She's lucky she's got a coach who let her start a game and keep playing."

"What's that?" Bill asked.

Lyssa looked up, only then realizing she'd spoken aloud. "Oh, nothin'."

He watched, waiting for her to say more, his eyes saying he knew she hadn't told him the whole truth. The look made her squirm inside. She hated it when adults did that, especially since it usually worked. She couldn't seem to keep her thoughts to herself.

She laid the papers in her lap. "I guess I'm jealous. I want what happened to her to happen to me."

"Who's to say it won't?" He smiled. "Your coach tells me you've got a great arm."

Strange. She'd felt pretty good about things yesterday when the coach came to her house and he sat at the table, talking with her and her mom. Lyssa had convinced herself she could prove to him she was good enough to start a game, even if she was only ten and a girl. Now it felt impossible. "Mr. Palmer, you can't pitch a perfect game if you don't get to *start* a game, and Coach Jenkins says I'm not ready to start one yet."

"I see." His expression grew serious. "Do you think maybe he's right?"

She looked down at the girl in the photograph in the article. "No," she muttered. "I'm ready."

"You know, Lyssa. The season hasn't even opened yet. Lots can happen in a couple months. That girl's perfect game was in May. Maybe by this May your coach will think you're ready."

"Yeah. Maybe." Lyssa slunk down in the chair. "It's just I want it so bad. Know what I mean? Have you ever wanted somethin' so bad it makes your insides hurt?"

He was silent awhile before answering, "Yes. Believe it or not, Lyssa, I have."

∽

The last errand on Terri's list was a visit to A to Z Arts and Crafts. She needed a new curtain for the back window at the salon. She hoped she could find fabric she liked and make it herself. She wasn't much of a seamstress, but she could manage a curtain: bit of cutting, a bit of hemming, relatively simple.

She was browsing through the bolts of fabric when Francine Hunter, Angie's mother, appeared on the opposite side of the table.

"Oh, good. I'm glad I ran into you, Terri. I planned to call you as soon as I got home. The Thimbleberry Quilting Club is making a wedding quilt for Angie, and we hoped you'd want to participate. But it's a surprise. Don't say anything to her about it." As she spoke, she came around the end of the table.

"A quilt?" And Terri was hoping she could manage to sew a simple curtain.

"Well, we're not asking you to make an entire quilt, dear. Just one of the squares. Something that would be meaningful for Angie from you."

"I haven't done much needlework, Francine, but I'll do my best."

The older woman laughed softly. "Don't you worry. What I'm asking isn't nearly as difficult as you might think." She patted Terri's shoulder. "Trust me. The Thimbleberry gals will make sure you know what you're doing."

Terri wondered if she could bribe someone else to make her square in exchange for a perm or a haircut and color or even a French manicure.

"I don't know why we waited so long to get started," Francine said, oblivious to Terri's thoughts. "Everyone knew Bill would propose. Only the when was in question."

Terri smiled as she nodded in agreement. "He was smitten from the first moment he saw her after she returned to Idaho. He never stood a chance."

"So true." Francine paused and gave Terri a thoughtful look. "What we need now is to find a nice young man for you."

As if bidden by the woman's words, the image of Mel Jenkins sprang into Terri's mind. "Nice" would certainly describe him, she thought as she recalled the way he'd interacted with Lyssa yesterday. But Francine meant a love interest, and Terri wasn't attracted to Lyssa's Little League coach in that way.

∽

Mel rounded the corner from Park onto Main in time to see Terri and Lyssa Sampson exit the offices of the *Mountain View Press*. Hand in hand, they crossed the street and disappeared into Terri's Tangles Beauty Salon. If he'd left the bank five minutes earlier, Mel would have met up with the mother and daughter. Too bad. He'd wanted to say how much he enjoyed his time with them.

He strode across the street, then followed the sidewalk to the brick building that housed the newspaper. When he opened the door, he caught a whiff of dust and newsprint. He wondered when the last time was that the office had been thoroughly cleaned. He knew he couldn't work amidst all this clutter.

Not finding his friend in the front office, Mel called, "Hey, Bill. Are you back there?"

"I'm here." A few moments later, he appeared in the doorway to the print room.

"Would you mind going to eat a little earlier than we planned?"

"Not a bit. Let me grab my jacket."

A short while later, the two men sat in a booth at the Over the Rainbow Diner, the only restaurant in town, if one didn't count the Big Burger Drive In, the Suds Bar and Grill, or the quaint tea shop Pearl Ingram opened last fall over near the senior center. They didn't talk as they perused the menu. In the end, they both ordered the baby back ribs special.

After the waitress left, Bill said, "Lyssa Sampson was in to see me not long before you came."

"I saw them leaving. Lyssa and her mom."

"I found an article about that girl who pitched a perfect game, and I showed it to her."

Mel suppressed a groan, knowing what reading about Brownell would do to Lyssa.

"I guess you don't think she's ready yet," Bill said as he loosened the paper napkin wrapped around his table service.

"Not yet. She will be, but not yet."

"She wants it bad."

Mel released a soft laugh. "Don't I know it." He shrugged. "The good thing is, she plays hard even when she doesn't get what she wants. She never acts spoiled, the way some kids do."

"Lyssa isn't spoiled. Terri's done a good job raising her."

Mel tried to sound casual as he asked, "What about Lyssa's dad?"

"Vic Sampson?" Bill shook his head. "Who knows? He deserted the two of them years ago. Must be at least seven years by now. Never showed his face in Hart's Crossing again. He hasn't made any effort to stay in touch with his daughter."

"That's tough."

"I don't know how a man could do that to his family."

Mel glanced out the window. Clouds had drifted in from the west, turning the sky pewter in this last hour before sunset. "We live in a throw away society. You don't want something, you chuck it."

"If there's anything I'm determined to do, it's to be a good husband to Angie, and if God blesses us with children, then a good father to them."

His friend's comment drew Mel's gaze from the window. "You will be." The truth was, he envied Bill Palmer. Mel hadn't meant to be unmarried and childless at his age. He'd wanted a wife and kids, same as Bill.

Terri Sampson's pretty green-blue eyes flashed in his memory, the sound of her laughter lingering in his ears. He pictured Lyssa in her baseball uniform, her cap pulled low on her forehead, determination setting her mouth as she wound up to release the ball.

Maybe, God willing, it wasn't too late for him.

## CHAPTER 5

"I'm driving down to Twin Falls on Saturday morning to look at wedding gowns." Angie settled onto the chair in front of the shampoo bowl. "Could you and Lyssa go with me? I'd love to see if we can find dresses for the two of you, ones you'll like."

Terri shook her head as she eased Angie back against the neck rest. "I couldn't do it this Saturday. I've got several appointments scheduled, and Lyssa has baseball practice." She turned on the water and ran it until the temperature was right. "How about Monday afternoon, after Lyssa gets home from school? We could go then."

"Mmm. Let me think." Angie closed her eyes. "Yes, Monday will work for me."

Terri pressed down on the pump of the shampoo dispenser, then worked the golden liquid into Angie's dark brown hair.

"Oh, that feels heavenly."

"That's what I hear." Terri tried to remember the last time she'd had her scalp massaged by another hair stylist. Maybe back when she was in beauty school? Could it have been that long?

"Bill and I ordered the wedding invitations yesterday." Angie opened her eyes. "You know, it was kind of scary. Does that make sense? I love him and want to be his wife. Most of the time, I'm really excited. But it was still scary placing the order for those invitations. I guess it made it seem more real somehow. Am I crazy?"

Terri rinsed the shampoo from Angie's hair, sat her up, and wrapped her head in a towel before answering. "You're not crazy, Ang. It makes perfect sense. This is a big change in your life."

"Did you feel that way when you married Vic?"

"Not really." She shrugged and released a tiny laugh. "I guess I didn't know enough to be nervous. We didn't have a long engagement or a fancy wedding. It all happened too fast for nerves or common sense to get in the way."

Angie rose from the chair. "I'm sorry," she said softly. "I didn't mean to bring up bad memories."

"Don't be silly. It's too long ago to hurt me now." Terri motioned for Angie to follow her to the styling chair. "Besides, whatever else Vic did wrong during our marriage, he did give me Lyssa, and I wouldn't trade her for anything."

No, she thought as she began trimming Angie's hair, she wouldn't trade Lyssa for anything, not even a happy marriage, but she wouldn't mind having both. She wished Vic had been a better man. She wished he'd been a Christian. She wished he'd wanted to be a husband to her and a father to Lyssa. And although memories of Vic didn't hurt any longer, she did sometimes wonder what was wrong with her that he'd felt the need to cheat.

"Bill and I want children," Angie said, interrupting Terri's thoughts. "I hope it's not too late for us."

Terri smiled at her friend in the mirror. "Women lots older than you are having babies, Ang. You're what? Thirty-six? I wouldn't worry if I were you."

The chime above the salon door rang. Before turning to see who'd come in, Terri cast a quick glance at the clock to make certain she wasn't running behind schedule. Thankfully, she wasn't.

"Hey, gorgeous."

Terri looked at Bill standing just inside the door. "Are you talking to me or my client?"

"Ah, I'm too smart to fall for that." He laughed. "You're both gorgeous. Ask any guy in town."

That was sweet of him to say, but it was obvious, as Bill gazed at Angie, who was truly beautiful in his eyes.

Okay. Terri might as well admit it. She would love to have a man look at her like that. Could it possibly be in God's plan to send someone her way who would?

∽

Mel leaned back in the chair and swiveled it toward the window of his office. The vertical blinds were halfway open, enough to let in the daylight. If he opened them completely, it was like being in a fishbowl. Every passerby on the sidewalk could look right in at him.

Across the street, Dave Coble, the police chief, entered the post office moments before Harry Raney, owner of the Over the Rainbow Diner, came out the same door. Familiar sights. Familiar faces.

But the face that persisted in his thoughts belonged to one particular and very attractive redhead.

It was already Wednesday, and he still hadn't come up with another excuse to call Terri Sampson. There wasn't any more chocolate cake to share with her daughter, and he couldn't use Terri's involvement as a Little League volunteer too often. Of course, he *could* try the truth. He could tell her he liked her and wanted to invite her out to dinner or a movie or both.

He hated this feeling in his gut, all nerves and uncertainty. Normally, he was a confident guy, a fellow able to make decisions and then act on them, but the thought of asking Terri out made Mel nervous.

Through his twenties and into his early thirties, he'd had a number of girlfriends. He hadn't been what one would call a ladies' man, but he'd enjoyed the company of women. Then he'd met Rhonda and he knew he was ready for that home in the suburbs with a jungle gym in the backyard and everything else that went with marriage and a family. After proposing, he'd thought his dating days were over for good.

But here he was again.

Mel shook his head slowly. He'd thought dating was like riding a bike. That one never forgot how. But it didn't seem to work that way. He felt more like a fifteen-year-old trying to stir up courage to ask a girl to the prom than a man hoping to enjoy an adult relationship with a woman.

His gaze moved to the telephone on his desk. Did he have the courage to take that next step?

Mel rose, walked to the window, and pulled the cord to open the vertical blinds wide. It was a gray and windy day, appropriate for the first of March, roaring in like a lion.

From the vantage point of his office, he could see up Park Street to the north. Main Street Drug was on the opposite corner from the bank and beyond the drugstore was Sawtooth Dentistry. To the south lay the offices of Randy Dickson, Attorney at Law, and the red brick First Baptist Church with its white steeple.

He'd come to like Hart's Crossing—and the people in it— over the years he'd lived here. At first it had been a place of escape, but it had grown on him. Somehow, despite himself, it had become home when he wasn't looking.

*I don't have to feel empty and alone any longer.* He raked the fingers of his right hand through his hair. *I can do something about it.*

He turned, strode to his desk, and yanked open the drawer where he kept the slim Hart's Crossing phone directory. He opened it, flipped through the pages to the *T*s, and then followed his finger down the list until he arrived at Terri's Tangles Beauty Salon.

Drawing a deep breath, he picked up the handset and punched in the numbers.

~

Using the blow dryer with her right hand and a brush with the left, Terri had almost finished styling Angie's shorter hairdo when the salon's telephone rang.

*What I wouldn't give for a receptionist.*

She glanced toward Bill, who sat in the dryer chair, flipping through a magazine while he waited for his fiancée.

*He'll have to do.*

"Bill, would you mind getting that for me?" she asked above the whirr of the blow dryer.

"Sure thing." He got up and headed for the counter.

Catching Angie's gaze in the mirror, Terri asked, "Do you two have plans this afternoon? Or does he just need something to do?"

Angie laughed. "We've got plans. We're going to look at new living room furniture. The things I had in my place in California aren't right for Bill's house, and his furniture isn't fit for—"

Bill walked back into view. "That was Mel Jenkins. He asked you to call him at the bank. I wrote his number on the slip of paper by the phone."

Terri hoped Lyssa's coach didn't need her to volunteer for

something else. One more thing on her calendar, and she would collapse.

She flipped the switch on the blow dryer, plunging the salon into sudden silence. "All done." She set the dryer in its slot. "What do you think?" As she swiveled the chair around, she gave Angie the hand mirror, then waited for the verdict.

"I like it."

Bill grinned. "Me, too."

Terri retrieved the hand mirror from Angie. "You should consider how you want to style your hair for the wedding. It could make a difference in the type of veil you choose. Or vice versa."

"Okay. I'll think about it. When we go to Twin, you can help me pick out a veil that'll work."

With the cape removed from around her neck, Angie rose and walked to the counter, where she wrote a check to pay for the cut and style. Then she and Bill said good-bye and left the salon, holding hands, their heads close together as they spoke softly to each other.

Terri sighed as she opened the register and slipped the check into the appropriate slot. As she closed the drawer, her gaze fell on the note Bill had scribbled.

She sighed again.

Might as well find out what Mel wanted. She just hoped she remembered how to say no if she needed to. She already felt as if she were running in three directions at once, not that she didn't enjoy her volunteer work with the Cavaliers. She did. She had many friends among the other moms and dads, and she loved watching Lyssa play. Still, she wasn't Super Mom, despite how often she pretended otherwise.

Settling onto the stool behind the counter, she tapped the numbers and waited as the phone rang.

"Farmers Independent Bank. How may I direct your call?"

"Mel Jenkins, please."

"Certainly. May I tell him who's calling?"

"Terri Sampson."

"Oh. Hi, Terri. Didn't recognize your voice. It's Isabella."

Isabella? Isabella … Miranda Andrews' daughter? "Hi. I didn't know you worked at the bank."

"Only part time. But I'm hoping I'll get to stay on this summer after graduation. I'll need all the money I can save. I'm going to attend Boise State in the fall." The girl paused a moment before saying, "I'll put you through to Mr. Jenkins."

"Thanks."

Terri felt a twinge of envy. Wouldn't it be great to be in Isabella's shoes, eighteen years old with all of life still before her? Dorm rooms. Football games. Studying in the library. Pizza parties. Boyfriends. A girl with a clean slate, free of major mistakes.

Terri hadn't gone to college, and she'd often regretted it. Not that she'd had much choice. She hadn't had the money, and although her grades had been good in school, they hadn't been good enough to earn a scholarship.

"Mel Jenkins. May I help you?"

"Mel, it's Terri. You left a message for me to call." She pressed her lips together rather than asking what he needed. After all, he might have found some other volunteer already.

"Yes, I did." He cleared his throat.

*Please don't let it be that he needs a driver for the van for away games. Anything but that.*

"I was hoping to see you on Friday. Any chance you're free on such short notice?"

Relief flooded through her when she realized his call wasn't about the Little League. *Thank goodness.* She reached for her planner. "My last appointment is at 4:00. I could fit you in right after that."

"No. That wasn't what I meant." He half-chuckled, half-coughed. "I ... uh ... I wondered if you'd like to go to the movies with me. There's a *War of the Worlds* double feature playing at the Apollo, first the 1953 version, then the newer one. I've seen them both before, lots of action and special effects. The Tom Cruise one's kind of gory but not too bad." He cleared his throat. "They aren't great movies, but they're what's playing."

It took Terri a moment to process his words. Was he asking her out on a date?

"I thought we could have dinner at the diner first."

Yes, he was definitely asking her out. Dinner and a movie was a date. She wasn't sure what to do. Mel was a nice, likable guy, but he was a banker, not a cowboy.

"Terri? Are you there?"

"Yes, I'm here."

"If you're busy right now, you could call me back later with your answer." Obviously, he was giving her an out, if she chose to take it.

She opened her mouth, planning to do just that, but surprised herself. "No, I'm not busy, Mel. I'd like to see the movies with you."

"Great." He sounded pleased. "How about I pick you up at your house at 5:30?"

"That would be fine."

"See you Friday."

Terri returned the handset to its cradle. Talk about out of practice. It was almost a year since a man had asked her out, and that time she'd seen it coming long before it happened. Why had this invitation caught her off-guard?

She let the memory of her few encounters with Mel play through her mind, and for the life of her, she couldn't think of one instance—not even last Sunday when he'd brought the cake over to share with Lyssa—where he'd indicated a personal interest that might have prepared her.

What if she'd made a horrible mistake in agreeing? He was Lyssa's baseball coach. If Terri and Mel didn't get along, if their date was a complete bust, what would that mean for her daughter? Mel could make Lyssa's experience on the team miserable.

Terri pictured him in her mind again, sitting at her kitchen table, talking to Lyssa, and her worries eased.

## CHAPTER 6

"Mom! Mom, wake up!"

Terri heard Lyssa's voice through the mist of a dream. A dream she wasn't ready to leave.

"Mom!"

A hand shook her shoulder, and Terri came awake with a jolt. "Lyssa?" Her gaze shot to the digital clock at her bedside: 2:47 a.m. "What's wrong?"

"I'm scared." Lyssa lifted the covers and crawled into bed beside her mother.

"What is it, honey? Did you have a bad—" As she began to ask the question, she felt a blast of wind shake the house, giving her the answer. "It's storming, isn't it?" She put an arm around Lyssa's back and drew her close. "Well, don't worry. March likes to come in with a lot of wind. We'll snuggle down under these blankets and get some sleep. By the time we wake up, it'll be over."

Her words were true for Lyssa, but sleep evaded Terri as the storm continued to batter the house, whistling around the eaves. A leafless tree danced eerily outside her bedroom window, the shadows cast upon the blinds by a nearby streetlight. Then the lightning began, a bright flash, followed by a crack of thunder, another gust of wind, another flash of lightning, more thunder, again and again and again.

Terri hated storms like this one. They made the old place creak and moan. They made this small house feel fragile, and then Terri felt small and fragile, too. In the middle of a stormy night, she felt too alone, too frightened, and too insignificant to handle what life tossed her way.

She glanced toward the clock. It was past 3:30. It seemed much more than an hour since Lyssa had awakened her.

Drawing a deep breath, Terri searched her mind for memorized words from Psalm 107, comforting words that she'd turned into a personal prayer for times such as this.

*God, you can still the storm to a whisper. You can hush the waves of the sea. I will be glad when it grows calm because I know you will guide me to my desired haven.*

The fear in her heart receded as she silently repeated more words from the Psalms.

*In peace I will lie down and sleep, for you alone, Lord, make me dwell in safety.*

At last, the thunder moved into the distance, rolling across the heavens but no longer close and threatening. The gusting winds slowed. Raindrops began to rat-a-tat-tat against the windowpane, a moment of warning before the skies opened in earnest.

Unlike wind, lightning, and thunder, Terri loved the sound of falling rain. She rolled onto her side, kissed Lyssa's forehead, and closed her eyes.

*In peace I will lie down and sleep.*

Perhaps she could find her way back to that lovely dream. She didn't recall what it had been about, only that she'd felt happy in that misty playground of her mind at rest. She felt her thoughts growing fuzzy, the dreaming coming closer.

The doorbell rang once, jolting her back to awareness. Then

it rang a second time. At this hour, it couldn't be for a good reason.

Terri's heart felt as if it missed several beats as she sat up, alarmed, and tossed aside the blankets. Grabbing her robe first, she rushed from the bedroom. A fist pounded on the door as she descended the stairs, unnerving her even more.

She reached the door and jerked it open. Dave Coble stood on her stoop, his police hat and uniform covered with protective rain gear. "Dave?" She reminded herself that Lyssa was safe and asleep in the bed upstairs. "What is it? What's happened?"

"Sorry to get you up at this hour, Terri, but I thought you should know. That tree between your shop and the real estate office. The storm snapped it in two, and the top half came down on the roof of your building. Tore clean through." He jerked his head toward the rainy street. "I imagine things are getting mighty wet inside about now."

Her heart sank. "The salon's damaged?"

"Yes, ma'am." He put a hand on her shoulder. "Nothing you can do until the rain stops, far as I can tell. Too slick to let anybody get up on the roof while it's still dark. Powers out over on that side of town, something must've hit a transformer. Come first light you should be able to assess the damage."

Dawn was about three hours away. How much of the roof was gone? Would water destroy the inside of the salon? Shouldn't she go down there now and see for herself? No, she couldn't leave Lyssa all alone, and she couldn't wake her up and take her along; it was a school night. Besides, what could she do by herself anyway?

"I'd best be on my way, Terri. Sorry for waking you in the middle of the night with news like this, but I figured you'd want to know so you can get an early start."

"I'm glad you told me." She wasn't sure she meant that. A part of her would have preferred ignorance for a few more hours. Maybe she would have fallen back to sleep. She wouldn't sleep now, that was certain.

Dave Coble pinched the brim of his hat between index finger and thumb, gave a brief nod of his head, and turned to walk away. "'Night, Terri."

"Good night, Dave." With a sigh, she closed the front door.

*How bad is it?* She had insurance on the building. Where had she put the policy? How much would it cover on the repairs? *Oh, Lord. If I can't work, how can I take care of Lyssa? Where will the money come from?*

∼

As soon as Mel heard that a tree had fallen on Terri's building in the previous night's storm, he left the bank and walked down Main Street to see if he could be of help. He found Terri, Angie, and Bill standing on the sidewalk at the southwest corner of the salon. Angie's right arm was around Terri's shoulders in a comforting embrace, and from the look on Terri's face, she needed plenty of comfort.

"Morning, Mel," Bill said.

"Morning." He stopped beside the threesome. "I heard the storm did some damage." He turned and looked in the direction the others had been staring a short while before. *Oh, man.* The old gnarled tree that stood between the two buildings had snapped in two, the top crashing down on the roof of Terri's Tangles Beauty Salon.

Terri turned toward Angie and pressed her face into the curve of her friend's shoulder as she wept.

"Have you been inside yet?" Mel asked Bill softly.

"Not me, but Terri has."

"Come on. Let's have a look."

Bill glanced at his fiancée. "Wait here for us."

Angie nodded.

The two men walked away.

As soon as they were out of hearing, Mel said, "Is she okay?"

"Terri? She's pretty shaken up. She's worried about the insurance coverage and how soon she'll be able to return to work."

Mel opened the door and stepped inside. Rainwater covered the floor in the main room. The water wasn't deep but it was enough to do serious damage to the floor and drywall. Bottles of hair care products were scattered across the salon, mingling with twigs, broken tree limbs, dried leaves, and small pink curlers. A thick branch of the fallen tree hung through the ceiling above one of the chairs. Looking up, Mel saw the cloudy sky above the large hole in the roof.

"We'd better get a tarp over that before it dumps more rain on us," he said.

"I was thinking the same thing. I'll head over to the hardware store to get a tarp and some rope. We'll need guys with chainsaws, too. I'll put out the word for help."

Mel thought of the expression on Terri's face. "Maybe you should ask Angie to take her home."

"She won't go." Bill shook his head. "Trust me on that. She's tiny, but she's tough. She's had to be."

"What do you mean?"

"She's never had it easy. She lost both parents when she was a teenager. Then she married Vic, who's a classic deadbeat dad. He doesn't pay child support so she's got to financially care for Lyssa on her own. There aren't any living family members for them to lean on in hard times." He made a sweeping motion with his hand. "She took a risk, buying this building, but she made it succeed. Now look at it." He shook his head again. "She's taking it hard, but she'll rally. She always does."

∽

By early afternoon, the rain had passed. Men with chainsaws—under the direction of Larry Tatlock, owner of a local tree service—had cut the broken trunk into sections and stacked the wood in the parking space behind the shop.

*At least I'll have plenty of firewood next winter,* Terri thought as she carried a plastic garbage bag to the Dumpster in the alley.

Tears threatened, but she swallowed them. She hadn't any time to give in to self-pity. Besides, look at all the people who'd turned out to help as soon as they heard what happened. She was blessed with many good friends.

BJ Olson, her insurance agent, had said he would have information for her this afternoon regarding estimates, and Bill Palmer had a friend who was a contractor. Someone else—she didn't remember who—had said he thought she could be working inside her salon again in two or three weeks. It might be inconvenient with some construction continuing, but it would be doable. She hoped he was right.

She tossed the trash bag into the blue Dumpster and turned to face the rear of her building. Hers and the Farmers Independent Bank's building, that is. The mortgage payment for the brick and frame structure wasn't much, all things considered, but neither was her income most months. If she had to close the salon for two weeks or more …

*Lord, please let the insurance cover the cost of repairs.*

The Idaho Bureau of Occupational Licenses was strict about how and where a licensed cosmetologist practiced her trade. Otherwise, Terri could cut hair in her kitchen until the repairs to the salon were finished. But the law wouldn't allow her to do that, and she didn't believe in breaking the law.

Mel Jenkins exited the back door of the building, packing an armload of branches that he'd cleared from the interior of her salon. At some point during the day, he'd changed from business attire into faded Levi's and a blue sweatshirt. It was a good look on him.

He dropped the debris on top of a growing pile of the same, then brushed dried leaves from the front and sleeves of his sweatshirt. When he turned, he saw her. After a moment's hesitation, he strode forward. "How're you holding up?"

Oh, those blasted tears! There they were, threatening again. "I'm okay. Thanks." She glanced at her wristwatch. "School will be out soon. I'm not sure Lyssa should be here during the clean-up."

"Why don't you go on home? There isn't anything we're doing that requires you to be here. We'll make sure nothing important gets tossed out."

"I don't know."

"Let Angie drive you home," he said gently. "You're exhausted. You should get some rest."

His image swam before her.

"Hey." His hand alighted on her shoulder. "It's going to be okay."

She choked on a sob.

A heartbeat later, he drew her into his embrace. "It'll be okay." He patted her back. "It'll be okay."

Despite her tears, she smiled a little, sensing his uncertainty. It had been a long while since a man held her in his arms. Had it been as long since Mel held a woman the way he was holding her now?

∼

IT TOOK EVERY OUNCE OF MEL'S WILL NOT TO BRUSH THE TEARS from Terri's cheeks with his thumbs and then kiss her quivering lips. He wanted to comfort her. He wished he could draw her closer, hold on tight, not let her go for a long, long while, not until he could make everything better for her.

Except he'd learned that he couldn't always make things better. He couldn't stop people from hurting—or from dying.

"Life is hard," Mel's mother had often said. "But God is good."

For a time, such comments had made him want to rage. How could a good God allow bad, senseless things to happen? Why did the innocent so often suffer? He'd found no human answers to those questions, but somehow, some way, the rage in his heart had ceased. He'd begun to trust again, trust that the God of heaven had a plan and a purpose in all things.

Terri drew a shuddering breath and stepped back. "Sorry," she whispered. "I didn't mean to lose it like that."

He wished he could pull her into his embrace a second time. He wished he could comfort her a little while longer. Instead, he said, "It's understandable. You have a tree sitting in your beautician's chair."

That drew a little smile. "You're kind."

"I'm glad I can help." He motioned with his arm toward Municipal Street. "Now, let's have Angie take you home."

## CHAPTER 7

"Don't you dare cancel," Angie scolded over the telephone the next afternoon.

Terri lay back on her bed, staring at the ceiling. "I don't *feel* like going out."

"Of course you don't, but you need to anyway."

"I won't be a fun date. I'm tired, and I'm worried."

"Mel will understand. And going out will take your mind off the salon for a few hours. You need that. Sometimes escape can be a good thing. Instead of thinking about your building's roof, you can watch Tom Cruise save civilization from the pod people or whatever they are."

Worry churned in Terri's stomach. There was a wide gap between the early estimate for repair costs and what she thought the insurance policy would cover. Since the adjuster hadn't finished assessing the damage, she couldn't be sure of much. BJ had told her to relax, but Terri wasn't doing a good job of following that particular piece of advice.

Fear was the opposite of faith. She knew that. Yet fear persisted. She couldn't keep appointments at her shattered salon, and the law wouldn't allow her to work out of her home without major renovations.

The facts were, no appointments, no income. She had some money in savings, but nowhere near enough. She and Lyssa had never done without any necessity. God had been faithful to provide. But if she couldn't work, what would—

"Terri, are you listening to me?"

"What?" She blinked. "Oh … No … Sorry."

Angie laughed softly. "I'm taking Lyssa for the night, and *you* are going out to dinner and a movie with Mel. Get used to it. I'll see you about 5:00."

"Okay. Okay."

"That's a little over an hour from now."

"I know. Lyssa will be ready for you."

"And you need to get ready, too. You know what I mean. Do something with your hair. Put on some makeup."

"Yeah, yeah, yeah. All right. Quit nagging."

They said good-bye, and Terri hung up the phone.

She could have told Angie it wasn't *that* kind of date. She liked Mel, but it wasn't as if she expected fireworks. They barely knew each other. Besides, now wasn't a good time for her to contemplate romance. Not with her salon wrecked and her money worries. No, she and Mel would probably end up as friends and that would be fine with her. A person could never have too many friends.

She rose from the bed and crossed the room to the closet, feeling better now that her expectations for the evening had been set in order.

"Wear that sweater you got in the mail, Mom."

Terri glanced over her shoulder to look at Lyssa striding into the bedroom, holding a small bag of chips in her left hand.

"That one there." Her daughter pointed to the soft teal sweater Terri had received from a catalog order a couple of weeks before. "It's almost the same color as your eyes."

Terri pulled the sweater, tags still attached, from the shelf in her closet, shook it out, then held it in front of her as she turned to look at her reflection in the mirror. She shouldn't wear it. She should return it for a refund. Money would be tight for a long while to come. She needed to save and cut corners every way she could. She had plenty of sweaters already, and summer would be here soon. She wouldn't need her sweaters then.

"Mr. Jenkins thinks you're pretty, Mom."

"Does he?" She felt a flutter of unanticipated pleasure.

"Sure." Lyssa hopped onto her mother's bed and pretzeled her legs. "'Cause you are. Everybody thinks so."

"I doubt everybody does. You do because you're prejudiced."

"What's that?"

"Prejudiced?" She sank onto the bed beside her daughter. "It means you're predisposed to be biased for or against something."

The frown on Lyssa's forehead told Terri the definition hadn't clarified the meaning.

She ruffled her daughter's hair with one hand, then stroked her cheek. "You see me as pretty because you love me, because I'm your mom, not because of how I really look."

Lyssa's mouth pursed and her eyes narrowed. "Nope," she said after a lengthy pause, her smile returning. "I think you're pretty 'cause you are."

As she rose from the bed, Terri smiled briefly, knowing she wouldn't change her daughter's mind and glad of it. She walked to the mirror and held the blue-green sweater against her torso. Lyssa was right. It was a close match to the color of her eyes. She supposed it wouldn't hurt to keep it. It hadn't been all that expensive.

A wave of panic hit her like an unexpected punch in the stomach. *God, how will we manage until the salon can reopen?* The room seemed to sway, and her stomach hurt.

"Mom, I like Mr. Jenkins. He's really nice."

*I've got enough money in the bank to make the next mortgage payment. But how long will it be before I can work again? What if my clients go elsewhere? What if I can't get them back once I reopen? They might find someone they like better. How much will I need to borrow to make the repairs? I don't know if my credit is good enough for what I'll need. If it isn't ...*

She lowered her gaze from the mirror, unable to look at her reflection any longer.

"You like the coach, too. Right, Mom?"

She shook her head from side to side, not listening to her daughter as a litany of her problems—existing and potential—played in her mind.

∾

AFTER LEAVING HER MOM TO GET DRESSED, LYSSA WENT INTO HER bedroom and closed the door. She sank onto the floor near the built-in shelves that held her most prized possessions—her various sports trophies, an autographed baseball, a collection of stuffed teddy bears and Breyer horses, her favorite books.

She felt awful. She'd heard her mom talking on the phone, saying she didn't want to go out with Coach Jenkins tonight. Her mom didn't like the coach after all. She was unhappy, and it was Lyssa's fault. If Lyssa hadn't tricked the coach into winning the cake at the carnival, then he wouldn't have asked her mom to go to the movies with him; and if her mom hadn't agreed to go, then she wouldn't be sad now.

Lyssa should've told her mom she didn't have to go anywhere with the coach. She didn't want to be a starting pitcher badly enough to make her mom do something she didn't want to do, something that made her miserable. Besides, Coach had said Lyssa wasn't ready yet. She shouldn't be so impatient. Worse, she shouldn't be so selfish. And she never should've lied about the number she pulled out of the bowl at the cakewalk.

"Dear Jesus, please don't let my mom be unhappy. I'm sorry for what I did, really sorry. I'll make it up to her somehow. I promise."

∾

Two thoughts crossed Mel's mind when Terri opened the door for him: she looked tired—understandable, considering what had happened to her salon yesterday—and she looked beautiful. How she managed to do both at the same time amazed him.

"How's it going?"

She gave a slight shrug. "Okay."

He might not know her as well as he hoped to, but he knew her well enough to recognize the worry in her eyes. Maybe he should tell her they didn't have to—

"Let me grab my purse and coat, and we can go."

Minutes later, they were in his car, headed for the Over the Rainbow Diner. Mel had considered taking Terri to a nicer restaurant up at the resort or down in Twin Falls, but something had told him it was best to keep this first date simple and casual.

Simple and casual, yes, but maybe it shouldn't be dead silent. He cleared his throat. "Is Lyssa ready for our practice tomorrow? We've got lots to work on before the season opener."

"She's always ready to play baseball. Practice or an actual game, she loves it. She has since she was about four years old. Instead of *Sesame Street*, she wanted to watch baseball games on ESPN."

"She's a good kid. I've enjoyed coaching her." He glanced to his right. In the glow of the streetlights, he saw Terri smile as she stared out the front windshield.

"She *is* a good kid." The simple words were laced with a mother's love.

"Does Lyssa remember her dad?"

Terri didn't reply.

"Sorry." His grip tightened on the steering wheel. "That's none of my business."

"No. It's okay. I guess I assume everybody in Hart's Crossing already knows the whole pitiful story."

"We don't have to—"

"I don't mind talking about it, Mel." She laughed softly. "And isn't that why we're going out? So we can get to know each other better and become friends?"

Mel hoped they would become more than friends, but he kept that to himself.

"First dates are awkward, aren't they?" Terri added.

He chuckled. "Can't say I remember. I haven't been on a first date in years." He felt her looking at him but kept his gaze on the road.

"I suppose that's something you should tell me about."

He supposed so, too.

"In answer to your question," Terri said, "Lyssa's dad doesn't see her. After he moved away, he broke off all contact, with me and with his daughter. Lyssa was a toddler when Vic left, so she doesn't remember him. That makes things a little easier, I suppose." She paused before adding, "But not having a dad leaves a void in her life, all the same. Every little girl wants a dad to love and to love her back."

Mel wondered if Terri felt a void in her life, too. "Must have been rough for you both."

"Hard enough."

A number of follow-up questions filled Mel's head, but he had no time to ask them before he pulled into a parking space not far from the diner.

∼

SEATED IN THE REAR BOOTH AT THE OVER THE RAINBOW DINER, red baskets of Tin Man Fish and Chips and tall glasses of ice water on the table between them, Terri found herself relaxing in Mel's company. He made her feel comfortable, as if she'd known him all of her life. Perhaps it was the gentle tone of his voice or the way he leaned forward whenever she spoke, as if he didn't want to miss a single word she said. Being with him made her forget her worries about the salon and the insurance and her too-low bank account balance.

Responding to his questions, she told him more about the end of her marriage after Vic left town with another woman. She shared the challenges of being a single mom, but she also talked about the joys of motherhood and Lyssa's dreams of playing in the Little League World Series.

She felt her cheeks grow warm when she realized how long she'd talked about herself. She couldn't remember the last time someone had plied so much information out of her at one sitting.

She took a quick sip of her water. "Now it's your turn. Tell me about yourself. What brought you to Hart's Crossing?"

"Besides my job?"

She nodded.

"I lost someone, too. I was engaged. We'd been planning the wedding for months when my fiancée passed away suddenly. She was sick only a short time. No one realized she was that ill. Not me. Not her parents."

"I'm sorry."

Mel nodded, acknowledging her sympathy. "I shut down for a long time. I was angry at God and felt cheated by life. I took the job in Hart's Crossing so I could get away from all the memories that lurked around every corner in our hometown. You know how that is."

"Yes."

"It's a wonder God didn't give up on me."

He smiled gently, and Terri saw peace in his eyes, a deep kind of peace that came with trusting God. She returned the smile, feeling a kinship with him, a kinship of loss, a kinship of faith.

"I'm glad I came to Hart's Crossing," he said, his gaze locked with hers.

*Me, too.*

After a lengthy silence, Terri lowered her eyes, not wanting Mel to see her jumbled emotions. She wasn't as relaxed as she'd been minutes before, but she was not relaxed in a good way. In a way she hadn't experienced in years, in a heart-fluttering, this-can't-be-happening-to-me sort of way.

It was then she looked at her wristwatch and realized how long they'd been in the diner. "We missed the start of the first movie, didn't we?"

A crooked smile lifted one corner of his mouth higher than the other. "Yeah."

"I'm sorry. I—"

"I'm not." The smile slowly faded. His blue gaze was intense.

Terri remembered the feel of his arms around her yesterday. She'd thought the embrace a bit awkward at the time, but now she recalled the breadth of his shoulders and the strength of his biceps as he wrapped her close.

*"Mr. Jenkins thinks you're pretty, Mom."*

Mel's crooked smile returned, as if he'd read Terri's thoughts. Heat rose up her neck and flowed into her cheeks once again, and she longed for the darkness of the theater where she could hide her embarrassment.

"Come on." Mel slid to his feet beside the booth. "I'll bet we haven't missed anything but commercials and previews." He offered his hand.

She reached for it, amazed by how right it felt, her smaller hand enfolded within his larger one—and she completely forgot that Mel Jenkins was expected to become a good friend and nothing more.

## CHAPTER 8

The telephone rang shortly after 8:00 the next morning. Terri knew the time only because she had to open her eyes to find the noisy instrument.

"Hello," she said, her voice gravelly with sleep.

"You're not up?" Angie laughed. "Must've been a late night."

Terri closed her eyes again. "Late for me. We got to my place around 11:30."

"And?"

She smiled. "We had a good time, Miss Nosey."

"Oh, I knew you would. I just knew it." In a soft, wheedling tone, Angie asked, "Did he kiss you good night?"

"No, but it was only our first date." What Terri didn't tell her friend was that she'd been disappointed when he didn't *try* to kiss her. She'd thought he might. She'd hoped he would.

"So, what's on your plate today?"

Terri groaned. "More cleaning up at the salon. I've got a contractor coming to look at it on Monday morning so I want to be ready for him. And Lyssa's got her baseball practice this afternoon. It's the last one before the opening game."

"Listen, you take care of business at the shop, and I'll take Lyssa to her practice and stay until you get there."

"I can't ask you to do that, Ang."

"You're not asking. I'm offering."

"Are you sure?"

"I'm sure. It's going to be a lovely day. I can sit in the bleachers and work on my laptop."

"What are you writing now?"

"Nothing creative, if that's what you mean. I'm making long lists of things I must accomplish before the wedding." She laughed. "It seems that's all I've been doing from the moment Bill proposed. I didn't know planning a wedding took so much time. There's always something new to add to the list, something I didn't anticipate."

Terri smiled as she slid up against the headboard. "Don't forget to enjoy yourself, too."

"Good advice. And don't *you* forget that we're driving down to Twin on Monday as soon as school's out to look at bridesmaid dresses for you and Lyssa."

Terri winced. Was that this Monday?

"I know you've got lots of other things on your mind, Terri, but you can still go, can't you? We don't want to put this off too long. Finding the right gowns can be hard."

"Yes. Of course Lyssa and I can go." She hoped the contractor would be done long before then.

∼

Lyssa had lain awake in the middle of the night, staring at the ceiling of Angie's guest room, trying to figure out how to fix the mess she'd caused. She didn't want to tell her mom how she'd lied about the number she drew out of the bowl at the carnival.

Well, she hadn't looked at the scrap of paper, so she didn't know for *sure* it was a lie.

Only something in her heart told her it was the same thing. She'd told Jesus she was sorry, but now she needed to fix it so her mom wasn't unhappy about the coach.

When she'd asked her mom if she liked him, Lyssa hadn't expected her to shake her head no. Why didn't her mom like him? He was nice. Lyssa liked him a lot.

But she loved her mom even more, and she'd do just about anything to make her mom happy. She would even give up playing in a Little League World Series if that's what it took.

Of course, if she didn't get to pitch much for the Cavaliers that would never happen anyway.

∽

Mel whistled as he reached into the back of his pickup for the oversized box that held bats, balls, and a few extra gloves. He hadn't felt this good in ages—and that was thanks to a pretty redhead with blue-green eyes and a sad-sweet smile that made his heart race.

"Good afternoon, Mr. Jenkins."

Leaving the box on the tailgate, he turned around. Till Hart walked toward him, clad in a bright pink warm-up suit, athletic shoes, and a sun visor. "Afternoon, Miss Hart. Nice day for a walk."

"Yes, indeedy." She glanced up at the cloudless sky, then back at him. "Getting ready for practice, I see."

"Yes, ma'am."

"If you don't mind, I'll sit and watch a spell."

"I don't mind, but the team won't start arriving for another half hour or so." Wrapping his arms around the box, he pulled it against his chest and lifted it off the tailgate.

"Well, then, you and I can have us a chat while we wait for them."

"Sounds good." He started walking toward the baseball diamond, shortening his stride to accommodate the older woman.

"I'm told you and Terri Sampson had dinner together last night."

Mel chuckled as he looked at Till. "I think that made the rounds quicker than the news of Bill and Angie's engagement."

"If you'd wanted it to be a secret, you wouldn't have taken Terri to the diner." She winked at him, but when she continued, her tone was somber. "I hope you managed to cheer her spirits some. Such a shame what happened to her salon."

Mel set the box on the lower bench of the metal bleachers. "She'll bounce back." *And if she'll let me, I'll help her do it.*

"I know she will. Terri's made of sterner stuff." Till settled onto the second row. "More importantly, she puts her trust in Christ. Knowing the Lord makes the burdens easier to carry."

"Yes," he agreed softly. "It does."

Till gave her head a nod, and Mel had the feeling he'd passed some sort of test.

"By the way, Mr. Jenkins, I have an idea for where Terri might do hair until her salon is repaired. There's a—"

The crunch of tires on gravel drew both of their gazes toward the parking lot. A cloud of dust settled as the driver and passenger doors opened, releasing Angie Hunter and Lyssa Sampson.

Mel swallowed his disappointment. He'd looked forward to seeing Terri this afternoon.

"Hello, Miss Hart," Lyssa called. "You gonna watch the practice?"

"I thought I might."

Mel said, "I could use your help, Lyssa."

"Okay." She seemed a little reluctant as she walked toward

him, her cap pulled low on her forehead. "What d'you want me to do?"

"Let's get these out." He handed her one of the white rubber bases. "You take third. I'll take first and second."

"Sure." She turned and ran down the baseline toward third.

Mel took the other two bases and strode toward first. By the time he reached second, Lyssa was there.

She met his gaze briefly, then look up and studied the sky. "So how was the movie last night?"

Mel knelt to fasten the base in place. "Pretty good."

"I heard it's kind of creepy. Were you scared?"

"No." He shook his head. "I wasn't scared." He smiled to himself. "But I think your mom was a few times."

Lyssa was silent awhile before saying, "Most of Mom's boyfriends take her dancing and to dress-up places like that. She likes doin' that kind of fancy stuff better than going to the Apollo."

*Most of her boyfriends? Dancing?* He'd gotten the impression Terri didn't go out much.

"She thinks scary movies like *War of the Worlds* are dumb."

Mel sat back on his heels and looked at Lyssa. "She seemed to enjoy herself last night."

"Yeah, well." Lyssa shrugged. "Mom was trying to be nice to you. You know. She didn't want to hurt your feelings. Do unto others and stuff like that." A touch of pink painted her cheeks as she lowered her gaze to the ground. "I'll go get the bats out." She took off at a run, straight across the pitcher's mound.

"She was being *nice* to me?"

Had he misread Terri? He'd thought she enjoyed herself last night. He'd believed something good was happening between them. Sure, the sci-fi movies were just okay, but the dinner had gone great. At least, he'd thought so. He'd liked listening to her talk about her life and about Lyssa. When she spoke of her ex-husband, there hadn't been any signs of bitterness. Even in her concern about her beauty salon, she'd carried a spirit of hope in her voice and in her eyes. He suspected her faith ran deep, as Till Hart said.

He looked toward the bleachers where Angie sat beside Till, the two of them engrossed in conversation.

Why had Angie brought Lyssa to baseball practice? Was Terri avoiding him? He hadn't dated in a long time, but he'd thought he could read women better than that.

A cloud seemed to fall across the sunny day as Mel stood and walked across the baseball field toward home plate.

~

TERRI PLACED A HAND IN THE SMALL OF HER SPINE AND ARCHED backward, a groan escaping her lips. It surprised her, how much damage rainwater and wind could do. But she was done with her salvaging. When the contractor showed up on Monday, she would be ready for him. God willing, he wouldn't be tied up with another job that would delay him starting on hers soon.

Her cell phone vibrated in her pocket. She grabbed it, saw Angie's number in the ID, and flipped it open. "Hey, Ang."

"What happened to you? Don't tell me you're still at the salon."

"I just finished up. I should be over to the field in five minutes. Ten tops."

"Don't bother. Practice is over. The kids are clearing out."

Terri looked at the wall, but the clock was no longer there. It had fallen victim to the storm. Her gaze dropped to her wristwatch. "I didn't know it was this late. I'm sorry, Angie. I never meant for you to stay with Lyssa the whole day."

"To tell the truth, I enjoyed it. Who'd have thought I'd become a fan of Little League baseball?"

Terri laughed, remembering the first Cavalier game Angie attended, shortly after her return to Hart's Crossing. She hadn't liked the cold weather or the noise made by the spectators, and she definitely hadn't understood how a Little League team's victory over their arch rivals could cause an entire town to celebrate.

Angie's voice lowered almost to a whisper. "There's something you should know, Terri. I think Lyssa's had a falling out with Mel."

"What do you mean?"

"I'm not sure. It's a feeling I've got." There was a moment of silence, then she added, "Here comes Lyssa. Looks like she's ready to go. Want me to bring her to the shop or take her home?"

"Home, thanks. I'll lock up now and meet you there."

"Okay. See you soon."

Terri frowned as she closed the cell phone. Why would Angie think Lyssa and Mel were at odds? Had he criticized her pitching? Had he left her off the play roster for opening day? Lyssa wasn't prone to pouting, but she could be stubborn, especially when it came to baseball.

Well, Terri wouldn't know if a problem existed until she talked to Lyssa. It was probably nothing. Angie didn't have children of her own, so she most likely misread something in Lyssa's behavior.

Terri slipped the phone into her pocket and headed for the rear door of the salon.

∽

MOST OF HER BOYFRIENDS ... SHE'D RATHER GO DANCING ... JUST being nice ...

Mel sat in his truck in the empty parking lot and dialed Terri's number. The phone rang numerous times before the answering machine finally picked up. As soon as the beep sounded, he said, "Terri, it's Mel. Sorry you didn't make it to

Lyssa's practice. Hope nothing's wrong. I'll ... uh ... I'll give you a call later."

After flipping the cell phone closed, he stared at it. Maybe he should have asked her to call him back when she had time. Then the ball would have been in her court, not his. If she wasn't interested, she should say so. Right?

He felt stupid. How could he have misread her that way? But maybe he hadn't. Maybe Lyssa was the one who was wrong. Still, Lyssa didn't seem like the kind of kid to misunderstand what her mom had said, and Terri must have said something or where else would Lyssa have gotten the notion she was only being nice to him. Whatever Terri had said couldn't have been good.

*"Do unto others and stuff like that."* Lyssa's words still stung. A ten year old didn't think up that phrase on her own. Either Terri had said it to her or Lyssa had overheard her mom saying it to someone else. No matter which, he felt like an idiot.

What had he been thinking, wanting to get involved in a relationship again? Especially with a divorced woman and her daughter. It was safer to keep to himself.

∽

It was suppertime before Terri broached the subject of the coach with Lyssa. One reason she waited was because Lyssa had homework to finish, but she also waited because she'd hoped Mel would call again as he'd said he would in the message left on her answering machine.

But he didn't call again.

"I'm sorry I didn't make your practice game," Terri said as she passed the bowl of mashed potatoes to Lyssa.

"It's okay." Her daughter shrugged. "It was only a practice."

"Did Mr. Jenkins have you pitch?"

Lyssa hooked a loose strand of strawberry-blond hair behind

her ear before putting two scoops of potatoes on her plate. "Yeah, I pitched a couple of innings."

"Was the coach pleased with your game?"

"I guess." She sounded listless, very unlike herself.

"Lyssa, is something wrong between you and Mr. Jenkins?"

"Me and the coach?" Lyssa shook her head, her gaze fastened to her supper plate. "No," she mumbled.

"Honey?" Terri was getting concerned now. "Tell me what's wrong."

"I don't know. It just feels weird. You know. To have you and the coach you know." Her daughter wrinkled her nose. "Dating."

"But I thought you liked him. I thought you wanted me to go out with him."

"I do like him, Mom. But—" Lyssa looked up at last. "I don't think he oughta be your boyfriend. Do *you?*" Her question rose on an anxious note, as if the idea caused her pain.

Terri lifted the bowl of corn and passed it to her daughter. "I suppose not." *Not if it makes you unhappy.* She swallowed a sigh. *Not if he doesn't call and ask me out again.*

"I didn't think so."

Neither one of them said much more as they ate their supper.

## CHAPTER 9

Terri didn't sleep well that night. She tossed and turned, tossed and turned, her thoughts racing.

It shouldn't bother her this much, that Lyssa didn't want her to see Mel Jenkins socially. After all, they'd only had one date, and he hadn't even kissed her.

Besides, Terri had seen the sort of problems that came with step-parenting. Blended families were no piece of cake. Mel was good with the kids on the team, but was he the right kind of man for a step dad?

Step dad? What was she thinking? Why worry about blended families after one date? Besides, maybe she was wrong to want to marry again. She hadn't exactly chosen well the first time around. How could she know she would choose better if given another chance?

Yet there was something about Mel that drew her to him. She wanted to know him more, better. He was gentle, yet strong. Nice looking, but not full of himself. Sometimes he was funny, other times serious. He was intelligent and had a responsible position with the bank. The kids he coached liked him.

Lyssa liked him. Terri had witnessed his caring patience with them. He was a man of faith, a faith that had been tested by the loss of his fiancée, and he'd come out stronger on the other side.

She pulled the pillow from behind her head and placed it over her face.

Hadn't she enough to worry about? She had a building in disrepair, a home to run, a living to earn, a daughter to raise. Why complicate her life with a man? She should remember that marriage wasn't always happy and romantic. Even when two people loved each other, there was stress and strain involved. And if Lyssa didn't want her to date Mel, that was enough reason to keep her distance.

Wasn't it?

∽

*So what am I going to do?*

Mel stared at his reflection in the bathroom mirror, his razor held close to his lathered jaw.

He should have called Terri again last night, like he'd said he would in his message. Why hadn't he?

Because he was a coward, and he was afraid he would find out Lyssa had told the truth. Because he cared for Terri Sampson more than he should after only one date. Because he didn't want to discover that she didn't feel the same about him.

Worry about nothing. Pray about everything. That's the advice he would give someone else in his shoes. Maybe it wouldn't hurt to practice some of it himself.

∽

"Terri," Till Hart called from a corner of the narthex as church members exited the sanctuary.

Terri waved to acknowledge she'd heard her, then made her way through the crowd of folks. "How are you, Miss Hart?"

"Fine and dandy, thanks. Do you have time to do something with me?"

When Terri got home, she would probably start mulling over the same thoughts she'd had during the night. Any distraction from that would be welcome. "Of course, Miss Hart. What do you need?"

"It's about your hair business."

"My salon?"

"Mr. Palmer tells me it will take some time before you're able to get back into your building."

"I'm afraid that's true."

"Well, I have found a place for you. My friend has a basement room that is perfect, and she's agreed to let you use it."

"Oh, Miss Hart. That's very kind. But the state of Idaho has very strict laws regarding square footage and separate entrances and—"

Till waved a hand in dismissal. "Yes, yes. I've been told all that, and that's just what I've found for you. Could you drive me over to Willow Lane so I can show you? I promise not to keep you from your Sunday dinner more than an hour."

Terri saw no polite way out of it. "Of course. I'll be glad to drive you anywhere you wish."

∽

HOME FROM CHURCH, MEL SAT AT HIS KITCHEN TABLE, STARING at the portable phone, debating whether or not to call Terri.

He hadn't heard much of Reverend Ball's sermon, although it probably was a fine one. The minister might be retirement age, but he still knew how to deliver a powerful message. However, Mel's thoughts had been focused on a woman and her daughter who lived in a small, two-story house.

*Should I call her or not? Are we meant to be together? Or have I made a major blunder?*

~

TERRI COULDN'T BELIEVE HER EYES. THE WELL-LIT BASEMENT HAD a stylist chair, a shampoo bowl, two large mirrors, shelves for supplies, even an outside entrance with a ramp for wheelchair access. The style of the furnishings was straight out of the 1960's, but everything looked in pristine condition except for a layer of dust.

"Why didn't I know you were a cosmetologist, Mrs. Osborn?"

Elizabeth Osborn, a woman in her late seventies with an impeccably coifed head of snow white hair, laughed softly. "It's been almost twenty years since I closed my salon, dear girl. There's no reason you should have known."

"You're sure you wouldn't mind me using it?"

"Of course, I wouldn't mind. I'd be delighted. Think of the people who'll come to see you for an appointment and then they might stop upstairs to say hello to me, too. I don't get around as well as I used to. My bad hip, you know. I miss the company." She patted her hair. "Besides, I'd hate to see your clients go to Mary Lou Hitchens out on the highway. That woman couldn't find her way around a perm rod to save her soul."

Terri subdued a laugh before asking the inevitable. "About the rent?"

"Oh, goodness gracious. I don't need a thing."

"I insist, Mrs. Osborn. I'd be using your power and heat and water. I must pay something. I could be here for a month or more."

"I'll tell you what. I know a woman who leases a station down in Twin Falls. I'll ask what she pays for rent in that salon she's in, then we'll come up with something reasonable for this location and the service provided. How does that sound?"

"It sounds more than fair." Terri grinned as some of her money worries slid off her shoulders.

And if God could take care of the detail of finding her a place to work while Terri's Tangles was restored, surely he would take care of other things in her future as well, such as her feelings about Mel Jenkins.

## CHAPTER 10

"That's it!" Angie exclaimed. "That's the one."

Terri stood in the oversized dressing room at Baskins Formal and Bridal in Twin Falls, looking into the floor-to-ceiling mirror. The tea length matte satin dress was a shade of mossy green that the sales clerk had called celadon. It had off-the-shoulder sleeves and a modest neckline. The cut was simple, the style classic.

"That's a dress you could wear out. It doesn't look like a bridesmaid dress that you wear once and hang in your closet. You know what I mean?"

"I know what you mean. But I don't know where I'd wear it. Too dressy for church."

Angie tilted her head slightly to one side, meeting Terri's gaze in the mirror. "I meant on a date, silly."

"Hmm."

"What's up?" Angie stood and stepped to Terri's side. "Something's bothering you."

Terri listened to Lyssa's muffled chattering with Angie's mom in another dressing room. Francine Hunter had graciously taken Lyssa and about a dozen different dresses into that room a short while before.

"Can't you tell me?" Angie asked.

"It's Mel ... and Lyssa." *And me.*

"So I was right about Saturday? Lyssa had a falling out with him."

"Not exactly. Well, not that I know of, anyway."

Once Terri got started, the words tumbled out in a rush. She told Angie how much she'd enjoyed her date with Mel, how she hadn't expected to like him so much, how disappointed she'd been when Lyssa said she didn't want Terri to have Mel as a boyfriend, how awful it made her feel that he hadn't called again. By the time she finished, she was holding a tissue to her nose and hoping she wouldn't stain the bridesmaid dress with her tears.

Angie was silent as she helped Terri out of the satin gown and returned it to its padded hanger. It wasn't until the two were seated side by side on the bench in the dressing room, Terri wrapped in a soft robe provided by the dress shop, that Angie said, "If you like him so much, is it a good thing to allow your ten year old daughter to determine your future? Shouldn't that be something you let God decide?"

The question brought her up short.

Angie took hold of one of Terri's hands. "Have you had a heart to heart with Lyssa to find out what happened?"

"No."

"Don't you think it's time you did?"

Terri sniffed and wiped her eyes again. "Yes. I think it is."

~

MEL WAS SEATED ON THE SOFA, WATCHING THE EVENING NEWS ON television, when a voice in his head said, *What are you waiting for? Get over there and talk to her.*

This time, he didn't second guess himself. He got up, put on his coat, and headed for the garage, truck keys in hand.

~

TERRI AND LYSSA HAD BEEN HOME FROM TWIN FALLS ABOUT AN hour when Terri tapped on Lyssa's bedroom door, waited a moment, then cracked it open. "Sweetheart?"

Her daughter sat cross-legged on her bed, headphones plugging her ears and CD player in hand. Even from the doorway, Terri could hear the music pounding away.

Raising her voice, she asked, "May I come in?"

Startled, Lyssa looked up. After a moment's hesitation, she pressed the stop button on the CD player and removed the headphones.

"Lyssa, we need to talk."

"About what?"

"About Mr. Jenkins."

Tears pooled in her daughter's eyes. "I'm sorry, Mom."

"Sorry for what?" Terri moved to the bed and sat down beside Lyssa.

"I didn't mean to lie to you or Mr. Jenkins. It just sorta happened. I thought if the coach liked your cake, then maybe he'd notice me more and not just think of me as a girl, and he'd give me a chance to start a game." Tears rolled down Lyssa's cheeks as the words tumbled from her lips with ever-increasing speed. "Then when he liked you, I kinda thought that was even better 'cause I like him, too, but then you were unhappy and didn't want to go out with him, and I knew it was all my fault 'cause I lied. I don't know what the number was on that piece of paper at the cakewalk. I just said it was his so he'd get the cake, and then I told another lie so he wouldn't ask you out again. I never meant to lie, but I did. I'm so sorry, Mom."

"I know. I know." Terri took hold of Lyssa's hand. "But

honey, what made you think I didn't want to go out with Mr. Jenkins?"

Tears glittered in her daughter's eyes. "I heard you tell Angie you didn't want to go out with him."

Terri tried to remember when she'd said any such thing.

"You looked so sad, Mom, and it was all my fault." Lyssa released a tiny sob.

Understanding began to dawn.

"Shh." She drew her daughter into her arms. "Sweetheart, whatever it was you did or said, I love you. Nothing will change that. We'll sort this out, the two of us. Okay?"

Lyssa sniffed and uttered a muffled, "Okay."

Smiling as she held Lyssa close, Terri felt a glimmer of hope in her heart.

∼

MEL FORCED HIMSELF TO OBSERVE THE SPEED LIMIT AS HE followed the tree-lined streets. When he arrived at the Sampson home, he stopped his truck next to the curb and killed the engine, then took a deep breath.

"Father, give me the right words to say when I see her," he whispered. "I can't do this without you."

He got out of the truck, rounded the cab, and came to a halt on the sidewalk. Staring at the front of the house, he folded his arms over his chest and took another deep breath. Maybe he should have rehearsed what he meant to say before he came over.

*Help me, Lord.*

After another steadying breath, he strode up the walk and rang the doorbell. It seemed forever before the door opened.

Surprise—and an emotion Mel couldn't define—flickered in Terri's eyes. "Mel," she said softly.

"Terri. Listen, I'm sorry for not calling again."

She acknowledged his apology with a nod.

"I tried to call, but you didn't answer." He pushed away the doubt as he cleared his throat. "I ... uh ... I'm not quite sure how to say this."

She seemed willing to wait for him to figure it out.

"Terri, I like you. A lot. I enjoyed being with you Friday night. I was hoping ... well, I hoped we might see more of each other. I felt something with you that I haven't felt in a long while. But Lyssa said you—"

"Mel, she was wrong."

His heart thrummed with sudden hope. "She was?"

"Yes." A slight smile curved the corners of her mouth. "I'd like to spend time with you, too." She glanced over her shoulder toward the stairs, then back at him. "Won't you come in and sit down? I have a story to tell you about a girl, a chocolate cake, and Little League baseball."

Faith, the Bible said, was being sure of what he hoped for and certain of what he didn't see. As Mel looked into Terri's eyes, his heart told him that he needed to have some of that faith now—and let God work.

# EPILOGUE

Lyssa wrinkled her nose as Bill Palmer fed his bride a piece of wedding cake, then kissed her with the frosting still on her lips.

But it wasn't the kiss that bothered Lyssa. It was this silly dress she wore. The lace around her neck was scratchy, and the satin fabric felt funny against her skin, all clingy and slick. Besides, it made her look like a dork.

While the photographer snapped more pictures of the bride and groom, Lyssa turned away, her gaze scanning the church's fellowship hall. The place was packed with people, standing and sitting everywhere. It seemed like the whole town had turned out to see Angie Hunter and Bill Palmer get married.

Lyssa thought weddings were okay, but baseball was a whole lot better. Good thing this wedding fell on one of the Cavaliers' free game days or she would have been really upset. Especially since her team was on a major winning streak.

Through the crowd of wedding guests, Lyssa saw her mom. Mom didn't look like a dork in her satin dress. She looked like a princess. Her whole face sparkled with happiness.

And the coach, who stood close to her mom, talking and smiling, looked pretty good in his fancy suit, too. Almost like the Prince Charming her mom said she used to hope and pray for.

Sometimes, grownups were weird.

# SWEET DREAMS DRIVE

HART'S CROSSING #4

# PROLOGUE

August 2002

The sanctuary of the Hart's Crossing Community Church was draped with blue satin and white netting. Candles flickered in candelabras. Soft music from the organ drifted to the rafters as guests were ushered down the aisle.

As a friend of the bride, Patti Sinclair sat on the left side of the church, although in a town this size, it didn't matter. Everybody pretty much knew everybody. Patti hadn't lived in Hart's Crossing in seven years, but she had no trouble picking out familiar faces among the guests.

Close to the front sat Till Hart, the unofficial grandmother of the town. Hart's Crossing was named for one of her ancestors. Miss Hart had the sweetest smile and kindest eyes of anyone Patti knew.

Next to Till sat Francine Hunter, Chuck and Steph Watson, and Ethel Jacobsen. The four women were all part of a group of quilters. What did they call themselves? The Huckleberries? No, that wasn't it. She smiled as the name came to her. The Thimbleberries. The Thimbleberry Quilting Club.

Amazing that she could remember it all these years later.

One row behind the quilters were Nancy and Harry Raney. Who could forget the owners of the Over the Rainbow Diner? That was *the* place to hang out when she was a teenager. The only place.

She saw Police Chief Coble a couple rows further back. Who was that blonde beside him? Could that be his daughter? The last time Patti saw her, Cassandra had been a gawky kid in middle school. No more.

The music changed. Patti looked over her shoulder to see the mother of the bride being escorted down the aisle. Patti's gaze shifted to the usher. The church went silent, and the world shifted on its axis.

The ceremony was half over before Patti fully recovered.

∼

THE WEDDING RECEPTION WAS HELD OUTDOORS AT HART'S Crossing's golf course. Patti congratulated the bride—Olivia, her best friend in elementary school—and the groom before moving to the refreshment table, where she was handed a cup of punch.

"Patti Sinclair. Is that you?"

She turned to see another familiar face.

"I'm Eric Bedford. Remember me?"

"Of course. You played the drums in the middle school band one year. That was the year Toby Kasner broke your nose with a drumstick."

"Ouch." He touched the bridge of his nose. "I'd almost forgotten."

"I'll never forget. Blood gushed everywhere. It was like a war zone."

He laughed, then asked, "So where are you living now?"

"Nampa. How about you?"

"Right here. The old Bedford roots go pretty deep. Dad's still farming. My brother got his degree and is teaching school here." His eyebrows raised. "Speak of the devil. Hey, Al. Come over here."

Patti turned her head, ready to greet Eric's brother, and the earth tilted for the second time that day. That golden hair. Those green eyes. That crooked smile. Those broad shoulders.

"Al, this is Patti Sinclair. She used to live in Hart's Crossing. Did you two ever meet?"

"Not sure. Maybe." Al held out his hand. "Nice to see you again, Patti."

If they'd met before, Patti would remember. Either that or Al Bedford had changed a lot in the past seven years.

Eric said, "She's living in Nampa."

"Do you like it there?"

She nodded, tongue-tied and breathless.

"Care to sit down?"

"That would be nice." Hopefully she could walk on her rubbery legs.

She didn't know what happened to Eric. By the time she and Al reached one of the white plastic tables placed under a large canopy, Al's younger brother was no longer around. Just as well, since the table Al chose had only two chairs. He held one for her.

So he was a gentleman as well as handsome. When was the last time she'd stumbled upon that combination?

"What do you do in Nampa?" Al sat in the other chair.

"I'm an editor at a small publishing house. I was hired part time while in college, and they offered me a full-time position after I graduated."

"Do you enjoy the work?"

"Yes." The way he watched her made her insides go all aflutter. She lowered her gaze to her hands. "Eric says you're a teacher. What subject?"

"Everything. I teach sixth graders at the elementary school."

His answer surprised her. For some reason, she'd expected him to say history or algebra or some other class taught at the high school level.

She asked another question. He answered and asked his own.

Patti shared about her mom's divorce when she was in middle school. Al shared about the recent death of his grandfather, a farmer like his dad. She shared about her move to Boise at the age of sixteen and how difficult it had been to feel comfortable with city life, though she loved it now. He shared how eager he'd been to finish college and get his teaching certificate so he could return to Hart's Crossing. She shared her love of books and the theater. He shared his passion for golf and basketball. She mentioned her cat. He told funny stories about his dog.

And in the midst of it all, there came a moment when Patti knew that Al Bedford was destined to be part of her future. At least she hoped so with all her heart.

CHAPTER 1

August 2006

Soft mewling sounds awakened Patti at 3:00 a.m. She lay still, hoping Al would get up and be able to walk the baby back to sleep. Trouble was, if she waited too long, the cries of one twin would wake the other.

She heard Al's breathing, a sound not quite a snore but close enough. As she slipped from beneath the sheet and lightweight blanket, she felt a spark of irritation. Not at their precious twins, but at her husband. Why did he get to sleep when she didn't?

The two bassinets—one pink, one blue—were set in the far corner of the master bedroom. Moonlight, falling through the window, illuminated her way across the room. Placing one hand on each bassinet, she leaned over to see which baby was fussing. Like his father, Weston didn't budge. Sunni, however, punched the air with tiny fists, warming up for a good cry.

"Shh," Patti whispered as she lifted her infant daughter. "Mommy's here. Shh."

A short while later, as the baby nursed at her breast, Patti set the rocking chair in motion and stared out the window of the family room. The silvery-white moonlight bathed the rooftop of the house across the back fence. Somewhere in the neighborhood, a dog barked. Soon another dog replied. It was a strangely comforting sound.

She and Al had purchased this home in a new subdivision on the east side of Hart's Crossing last spring. She'd fallen in love with it upon entering through the front door. If they were going to stay in this small town, then this was the home she wanted to live in. Yes, the mortgage was higher than what they wanted, but whose wasn't? At least they were investing their money instead of throwing it away on rent. She just wished there was a little more of Al's paycheck left over each month after they paid their bills.

She leaned her head against the back of the rocker and closed her eyes as the memory of their latest argument played through her head.

"We could move to Boise. You'd make more money in a larger school district, and you'd have more opportunities for advancement."

"There's more to life than money, Patti. I want our kids to grow up in Hart's Crossing. We've talked about that. I like my job. I like the people I work with. I know and love the kids I teach. There's no reason to leave."

"Raising children is expensive. Have you seen the doctor and hospital bills?"

"We'll manage."

Tears spilled from beneath her eyelids, trailing down her cheeks. She and Al never used to fight. Now they seemed to disagree about everything. Her mother said it was whacked-out hormones and too little sleep. Maybe that was true. Maybe not.

Her gaze lowered to the infant in her arms. Sunni slept again, her mouth gone slack.

*Why can't I be content with things as they are?*

Guilt surged. She had much to be thankful for. And she *was* thankful. Truly, she was. The babies were healthy and strong despite their early arrival. Al loved teaching at Hart's Crossing Elementary. Her wonderful mother-in-law dropped by as often as she could to help with the twins. The ladies of the Thimbleberry Quilting Club and her friends from church had showered the Bedford family with gifts.

And yet ...

*I'm sorry, God. I don't mean to complain.*

There was something else to feel guilty over. Her spiritual walk was almost nonexistent, except for church on Sundays. For several years it had been her habit to rise early to read her Bible and pray before she got ready for work. She'd loved those quiet times, sitting in the Lord's presence, waiting for him to speak to her heart. When was the last time she'd read her Bible? When was the last time she'd heard God's voice? Weeks? No. More like months.

With a sigh, she rose from the rocker and carried the baby to the pink bassinet in the bedroom.

*If I just weren't so tired all the time, maybe ...*

As if on cue, Weston whimpered.

Patti cast an envious glance toward her sleeping husband before stepping toward the blue bassinet.

~

THE BEEP-BEEP OF THE ALARM CLOCK AWAKENED AL AT 6:30. With a flailing arm, he managed to hit the snooze button without opening his eyes. He wanted five more minutes of sleep, and he didn't need the alarm waking the twins.

This first week of the new school year had been rough. In the past, he'd looked forward to meeting his students and discovering more about each one of them, but he hadn't had much rest since the babies were born. A sleep-deprived teacher had few defenses against the wiles of a bunch of sixth graders still getting into the groove after summer vacation.

"Al?"

So much for those last five minutes. "Hmm."

"I didn't make your sandwich last night. I forgot."

He opened his eyes. Morning light filtered through the bedroom curtains. "That's okay. I'll get hot lunch with the kids. I think it's burger day." He turned his head on the pillow to look at his wife. Her eyes were closed.

"I was up and down with the babies three times in the night." Patti pulled the sheet over her head as she rolled onto her side. "Try not to wake them."

"I'll do my best."

He slid out of bed and made his way to the master bathroom, closing the door without a sound. He didn't bother to flip the light switch. Enough daylight came through the block-glass window over the jetted tub.

Minutes later, freshly shaved, he stood beneath the shower spray, suds from the shampoo sliding in globs down his cheeks and neck as he used the bar of soap to lather the rest of his body. He wasn't normally a guy who took long showers, but this morning he had to resist the desire to stand there, eyes closed, and catch those five extra minutes of sleep.

But he didn't. Duty called and so did eighteen eleven-year-olds.

After dressing in clothes he'd laid out the night before, he left the bathroom and walked to the edge of the bed, where he leaned down and kissed his wife on the forehead. Next he moved to the bassinets, where he smiled at his son and daughter, so sweet in slumber.

*See you tonight*, he mouthed before leaving the bedroom.

Al was thankful the twins had arrived during the summer months. It had given him time to bond with them in a way many dads couldn't because of their work schedules. He didn't mind changing diapers or burping or bathing them. The only thing he couldn't do was feed them. And even though there were times he might prefer his children had arrived one at a time, with a couple years in between, he wouldn't trade Sunni and Weston for a million bucks.

He yawned as he grabbed his briefcase and car keys from the table near the back door, already planning to get a few minutes of shut-eye during the lunch break.

## CHAPTER 2

"*H*oney," her mother said, "it's time you found someone to watch the babies and give yourself a few hours out of the house."

"How can I do that?" Patti shifted the cordless handset to her left ear and pressed it close with her shoulder, then continued folding towels. "Do you know how much sitters want per hour these days? Even in a small town like this one."

"Are you telling me you have no friends who would watch those adorable babies for a couple of hours?"

"Of course I have friends who would do it if I asked. But I think they're intimidated with two babies." *I know I am sometimes.* "I'd hate to impose on them." She released a sigh. "I wish you could have stayed in Hart's Crossing longer."

"Me too. But I've used the last of my vacation time for this year."

"I know." She swallowed another sigh.

"You heed my words. Get out of the house for a while. Even if it's just long enough to get yourself a cup of coffee at the diner. You'll have a better perspective on things if you do."

Her mother made it sound so easy.

"I've got to run, dear. I'm about to burn your stepfather's dinner."

"Bye, Mom. Give Doug my love."

"I will. You do the same with Al."

After setting aside the phone, Patti sank onto a chair at the kitchen table. Wouldn't she love to take her mom's advice? How much fun it would be to go down to Twin Falls to spend a few hours at the mall. Or maybe drive up to the resort for a nice dinner with her husband. It felt as if she and Al hadn't talked to each other in ages, other than to say, "Would you change her diaper?" or "Can you fold the laundry?" or "Where's dinner?"

Or to argue. Again.

And though she was loathe to admit it, she started too many of those arguments. What was wrong with her? Why did she pick fights with him? It wasn't for sport. She preferred peace. She preferred laughter.

Patti swept loose strands of hair back from her face as her gaze moved around the kitchen. Breakfast dishes were in the sink, and the dishwasher needed to be emptied. Clean baby clothes, sheets, and towels—about four loads of laundry—had yet to be folded. Al would be home in less than an hour, and she hadn't given a thought to dinner. Was anything defrosted?

After she and Al had moved into their new home last March, Patti had kept everything in perfect order. Little Miss Susie Homemaker. That was Patti. She loved cleaning and shining and decorating, and her pregnancy hadn't slowed her down one bit. She couldn't have imagined the day would come when her home looked like a cyclone hit it.

She heard a knock on the back door and turned to see who it was. Amy Livingston, the thirteen-year-old girl from next door, grinned and waved at her through the glass.

"Come in, Amy. It's unlocked."

The girl opened the door. "Hey, Mrs. Bedford. How're the twins today?"

"They're sleeping." She glanced at the baby monitor on the counter. Not a sound came through the speaker, to her great relief.

"Mom said it was okay if I came over as long as I'm not in the way. Will I be in the way? Can I help with something?"

"Amy, you're a lifesaver. I could definitely use some help. Would you mind folding the laundry while I clean the kitchen and see what I can fix Al for dinner?"

"No, I don't mind. Is there any special way you fold things?"

Patti laughed. "Any way that gets it done is okay with me."

She rose from the chair and moved toward the dishwasher. In short order, she had the clean dishes in the cupboards and the dirty ones closed inside the machine. Then, with a bottle of spray cleaner in one hand and a damp cloth in the other, she wiped the countertops, the front of the microwave, and the handles on the refrigerator.

She was staring into the pantry, contemplating dinner, when she heard the first whimper through the monitor. The fullness in her breasts told her it was feeding time. It looked like Al would have to wait for his supper again.

∽

"Hey, Bedford!"

Standing beside his 1991 Alfa Romeo Spider convertible—a college graduation gift from his parents—Al looked over his shoulder and watched as Jeff Cavanaugh, the town doctor, strode toward him.

"What's up, Doc?"

Jeff rolled his eyes at Al's Bugs Bunny impersonation—an old and overused joke—and ignored the question. "You look tired, buddy."

"Yeah, it's hard to remember what a good night's sleep feels like."

"But your babies are thriving. I was pleased when they were in for their six-week checkup."

"That's what Patti said."

Jeff jerked his head toward the building. "I'd better get inside. I promised Penny I'd help her with a school project her first graders are doing." He flexed his right arm. "I'm the muscle."

"Things getting serious between you two?"

"Could be." Jeff shrugged.

Love was definitely in the air in Hart's Crossing. Al and Patti had been to two weddings in the past nine months. First there was James Scott and Steph Watson, childhood sweethearts who'd fallen in love again after fifty years apart. They'd wed in late autumn, before the first snows flew. In May, Angie Hunter and Bill Palmer, owner of the local weekly newspaper, tied the knot in a ceremony with the whole town turned out to witness the union. Now, word was Mel Jenkins had proposed to Terri Sampson, the mother of one of Al's current students, and the wedding was set to take place in December.

Yes, love was in the air. Why not for Jeff and Penny?

Al opened the car door and tossed his briefcase onto the passenger seat. "Cavanaugh, you're the most eligible bachelor this town's got left. Good looking and a doctor to boot. What mother wouldn't want you for her daughter? I'd say your days are numbered."

Jeff gave him a good-natured punch in the shoulder, then walked toward the main entrance to the school.

On the drive home, Al's thoughts drifted to the day he and Patti first met. He'd been taken with her from the start. Lucky he hadn't tripped as he walked Olivia's mother to her seat at the front of the church. In the months that followed, he'd made countless trips to Nampa, about a three-and-a-half hour drive from Hart's Crossing. The more he'd seen her, the more he'd known he wanted to spend his life with her. One of the best days of his life had been when he proposed and she'd said yes.

Maybe Patti was right. Maybe he should look for work outside of Hart's Crossing. His teaching salary was stretched to the limit with a wife, two babies, payments on a used Honda Odyssey, and a hefty mortgage. Only he didn't want to leave his hometown. Patti had known that was how he felt before they got married. She'd been in agreement with him. At least, that's what she'd told him in the beginning.

Approaching their house on White Cloud Drive, Al pushed the button on the remote clipped to the visor, slowed as the garage door opened, then drove in beside the Odyssey. He glanced at the front yard as he exited the car. The lawn needed to be mowed, but he wasn't keen on doing it with the temperature still hovering around the ninety-degree mark. Cooler weather couldn't get here fast enough to suit him.

As he opened the door into the house, he called, "I'm home."

A moment later, Amy Livingston poked her head into the kitchen. "Hi, Mr. Bedford. Mrs. Bedford's upstairs feeding the twins. I was on my way home." She waved before making a beeline for the back patio door. "Bye!"

"See ya."

Two years ago, Amy had been one of his students. She was bright, friendly, and as kids her age go, dependable. From the moment the Bedfords moved to this house, she'd been a presence in their lives. Maybe because she was an only child with a working mom and a father who traveled a lot for his business. Plus she was crazy about the twins.

She wasn't the only one who could say that.

Al dropped his briefcase near the entrance of the den before taking the stairs two at a time. He paused in the doorway of the master bedroom.

Patti sat in an overstuffed chair, her legs tucked to one side, one of the babies nursing at her breast. Her long, black, wavy hair was pulled into a ponytail, keeping it out of her face and out of reach of an infant's grasping fingers.

"Hey, beautiful."

She looked up with a smile. "I didn't know you were home."

"I came in as Amy was leaving." He strode across the room to look at the baby in her arms. "Wes's turn?"

"Mmm. Sunni ate first."

He stepped to the side of the pink bassinet. His daughter stared up at him with wide, dark eyes. "Aren't you supposed to be sleepy after you eat?" He lifted her into his arms and kissed the top of her downy-haired head.

Did every dad feel like his heart might explode with joy when he held his child? There wasn't anything else like this. Nothing to compare.

"Al, I've been thinking I might want to start supplementing with formula."

"Really?" He turned to look at Patti.

"I'm not sure I'm making enough milk."

"Jeff said their weight's good."

Tears flooded her eyes and slipped down her cheeks. She lowered her gaze to Weston, but not before Al felt like a complete heel for making her cry, even though he didn't know what he'd said wrong.

"Patti, I thought breast-feeding was the better way to go. That's all."

"Better for you, maybe," she said softly.

"What?"

"Nothing." She shook her head. "I'm sorry. I'm just tired."

Al sank onto the ottoman near the chair. "Hey, if you think that's what you should do—"

"I don't know what I think I should do." She met his gaze again, giving him a tremulous smile. "I love the ease of nursing, and I know it's better for them. I've tried using that pump I got at my baby shower, but ... Oh, I don't know. I just feel like if the twins were on bottles, things would be easier. We could even ask someone to watch them for a little while. Maybe you and I could go to dinner or to a movie instead of staying home all the time." Patti moved Weston to her shoulder and started patting his back. "Would you order a pizza to be delivered?"

Pizza? That would make the fourth time in two weeks.

Al swallowed his objection. His wife was in one of those moods, and he didn't want to make her cry again.

"Sure. I'll call it in now." He glanced at the baby in the crook of his arm. "Come on, Sunni. You can help me decide what to get."

# CHAPTER 3

Patti paused a moment in her housecleaning to watch Al as he mowed the back lawn. A blue baseball cap covered his blond hair and shaded his eyes from the sun as he strode toward the east. Clad in a loose tank top and khaki shorts, he walked with a long, easy gait, his bare legs and arms tanned to a dark bronze after a summer of yard work.

Most Saturdays the hum of his mower was one of several. But on this first weekend in September, many of their neighbors were gone for the final three-day holiday of summer, leaving the neighborhood oddly silent.

Last Labor Day weekend, she and Al had borrowed a tent trailer from a friend and gone camping in Grand Teton National Park. During the days, they'd hiked trails, ridden horses, and eaten copious amounts of food. At night, they'd huddled together near the campfire and talked about their future and what God might have in store for them.

That had been the same weekend Patti first suggested they should start a family. Her job with the publishing company, which she'd been able to continue after their wedding via telecommuting, had ended due to in-house changes. Maybe now, she'd said, was the time to think about having children of their own. She hadn't shared with Al that her heart longed to be part of a family, a family that was whole, where the husband loved his wife and the dad loved his kids. She hadn't told him because it was a truth she barely acknowledged to herself.

The doorbell rang, drawing her thoughts to the present. She hurried to answer it.

Sven Johnson, the mailman, stood on the front porch. Grizzled, gray-haired, and bent at the shoulders, he smiled at her through thick spectacles. "Morning, Patricia."

"Good morning, Mr. Johnson."

"Have a package for you." He held a box toward her, the rest of the mail stacked on top of it.

"Thanks." She took hold of the items with both hands.

"Give my best to Alfred."

She swallowed a chuckle. No one but Sven called Al by his given name. "I'll do it."

As soon as the door closed, she carried the mail into the kitchen and set it on the table. The return label on the box told her these must be the books she had ordered a week ago. She grabbed a knife from the drawer and sliced open the packing tape.

"Wow," she whispered as she pulled the first of two coffee-table books free of its wrapping. "It's even more beautiful than I expected." She flipped through the pages, admiring the nature photos and reading the captions.

"What's that?" Al asked from the back doorway.

She set the book on the table and closed its cover before looking in his direction. "The mail. Mr. Johnson brought it to the door."

Al removed his grass-stained athletic shoes before entering the house. "I meant the book."

"Oh, it's the most beautiful collection of photographs from

around the world. The captions are all Bible verses. I bought the pair for the coffee table in the living room."

He looked at her for a few moments before picking up the receipt. "Forty dollars?"

"That includes the shipping. They were marked way down. I saved 50 percent."

"We didn't *need* them, Patti."

She sent him a glare that told him what she thought of his tone.

Al let the receipt float to the table before stepping toward the sink to wash his hands. Patti stared at his back, all the while hoping one of the twins would cry so she would have an excuse to leave. She didn't want to continue this conversation. It would lead to another argument, the same old argument they'd had for months.

But no sounds came through the baby monitor. She was stuck where she was.

Drying his hands on a dishtowel, Al turned to face her. "Honey, I know you want our home to look nice. So do I. But we've got to stick to our budget." He spoke slowly, as if afraid she wouldn't understand. "We're already carrying too high of a balance on our credit cards. The interest is killing us. We're barely touching the principal each month."

She wasn't a complete fool. She knew their finances were stretched to the limit. But sometimes she wanted to buy things because she *liked* them, not because they were a necessity. Was that so terrible? Did her whole world have to consist of diapers and laundry soap? Couldn't he cut her some slack? Didn't he know she did it for him?

∽

There had been a time when Al thought that stubborn tilt of Patti's chin was adorable. Not so much lately.

"You know what?" He tossed the towel onto the counter. "Maybe *you* ought to pay the bills for the next month and see what it's like. Maybe then you wouldn't be so quick to order things we don't need or to order pizza delivered two nights a week."

"I could do as good a job as you're doing, *Alfred* Bedford. And without so much bellyaching."

Al clenched his jaw. He didn't want to say something he would have to apologize for later.

"But if I'm paying the bills, buster, you can take care of the babies while I do it."

"You mean, take care of them without so much bellyaching?"

Her eyes went wide, and her mouth formed an *O* as she sucked in air.

Well, now he'd gone and done it. Said something he'd have to apologize for. But he wasn't apologizing right now. "I need gas for the mower. Be back in a while."

He was still mad when he pulled up to the pump at the Main Street Service Station ten minutes later.

"Women," he muttered as he opened the driver's side door.

He retrieved the gas can from the back of the minivan—no way did he haul gas in his sports car—and set it next to the pump. Straightening, he pulled his wallet from his back pocket and checked to see how much cash he had. After the words he'd exchanged with his wife, he preferred not to use the credit card.

Three bucks. That should get him through the last mowing of the year. He lifted the nozzle for regular gasoline and stuck it into the can.

He shouldn't have said what he did to Patti. He should have kept his temper in check. He knew she was tired. She didn't get enough sleep. But neither did he, and he had to face a classroom of eleven- and twelve-year-olds five days a week. She didn't have to go to an office every day where someone judged her performance.

Besides, Patti was the one who'd wanted to buy the new house. He would have been just as happy with something smaller and less expensive in an older part of town. He'd told her they would have to cut corners if they bought the new house, and she'd agreed to it.

Lost in thought, he was past the three dollar mark before he realized it. "Idiot." Now he would have to use his credit card.

He saw himself in his mind, scowling at the gas can while talking under his breath. He acted like charging three dollars and twenty-seven cents was the end of the world.

Recalling what he'd said to Patti before storming out of the house, his amusement faded. He'd hurt her, and that wasn't funny. It didn't matter if he had a good reason to be angry. He shouldn't have said what he did.

He needed to get home and apologize. Fast.

∽

PATTI HID HER FACE IN HER FOLDED ARMS ON TOP OF THE KITCHEN table, the sound of the slamming door echoing in her mind. Her chest ached.

*Oh, God. What's wrong with me?*

She recalled another slamming door, the one that closed behind her father the day he'd walked out for good. Her parents had fought a lot too. Her childhood home had been filled with tension whenever her parents were together. Even at thirteen, Patti had promised herself that when she got married her home would be different. She would make it a haven for her family.

What if she drove Al away, spending money she shouldn't, getting angry at the drop of a hat? What if he walked out that door and never came back?

She heard the garage door open. Seconds passed, counted by the ticking of the mantel clock.

"Patti?" Al stepped into the kitchen, stopping when he saw her at the table. "Patti, I'm sorry."

She rose from the chair. "Me too."

"I lost my temper and said things I shouldn't."

"I shouldn't have bought those books."

He moved toward her. She stepped into his arms, pressing her cheek against his chest.

"I'll curb my spending, Al. I promise."

"I love you. We'll be okay."

*Please, God. Let it be true.*

## CHAPTER 4

"Remember to bring your permission slips to school tomorrow," Al called to his departing students the following Thursday.

Not that any of them listened. Once that dismissal bell sounded, they tuned him out. He'd been the same at their age.

After everyone was gone and he'd performed a quick sweep of the room to see if anything important had been left behind, Al sank onto his desk chair and reached for the top paper in the stack of essays that awaited him. He liked to begin the year by asking his students to write about the favorite thing they'd done during the summer and three reasons why they'd liked it so much. Sure, it was a knock-off on "How I spent my summer vacation," but it worked. It helped him get to know the kids.

The first essay was by Lyssa Sampson. If he was a betting man, he'd bet hers was about Little League Baseball. He would have lost that bet. She'd written about a camping trip with Mel Jenkins, her soon-to-be stepdad.

He smiled as he read the essay. Lyssa had a way with words that brought the vacation experience to life on the page. Her writing also made him see Mel, manager of the Farmers Independent Bank, in a whole new light. He hoped his own kids would write as affectionately about him when they were Lyssa's age.

His gaze drifted to the framed photo on his desk. In it, Patti sat on the living room sofa, holding a baby in each arm. The twins were about two weeks old at the time, their eyes closed and frowns creasing their brows, as if to say, "We don't want our picture taken." Hard to believe those two small bundles would be writing essays for their sixth grade teacher eleven years from now.

He shook his head. Eleven years ago, he'd been a cocky college student, staying up too late, living on pizza and breakfast cereal. Despite his youthful antics, he'd managed to graduate with honors, but in the meantime, he'd been responsible for more than a few of his parents' gray hairs.

"Knock, knock."

He looked toward the classroom doorway. "Hey, Cassandra."

"Am I disturbing you?"

"Not really. What's up?"

Cassandra Coble—a tall, model-thin brunette—leaned her shoulder against the doorjamb and crossed one ankle over the other. "Nothing, really. I just needed to hear an adult's voice for a few minutes before I tackle my lesson plan."

"The natives restless today?"

"You said it. None of them seem able to concentrate. Their bodies are here, but their minds are elsewhere." She twirled a strand of hair with an index finger as she spoke.

Like Al, Cassandra had grown up in Hart's Crossing, but she was seven years younger, so he hadn't come to know her until she returned to town last year with her degree and had been hired to teach fifth graders in the room next to his.

"Another week, and they'll settle into the routine," he said, leaning back in his chair.

"I hope you're right." She laughed softly. "Were they like this last year?"

"They're like this at the start of every school year."

"I guess I was too excited about my new job to notice."

"Probably."

She pointed toward his desk. "Is that a new photo of the twins?"

"No. Same one."

"You ought to have Walt Foster come over to take some family photos. He's a great photographer."

The cell phone on Al's desk vibrated, drawing his gaze. Seeing his home number in the ID, he picked up the phone and flipped it open. "Hey, hon."

"Did I call too soon?"

"No. The kids are long gone. I was just talking with one of the other teachers."

Cassandra straightened away from the doorjamb, gave him a smile and a little wave, then disappeared from view.

"We're invited to a party at Jeff's house on Saturday. He and Penny are having a group of friends over for a game night. I hope it's all right that I said we could go."

"What about the babies?"

"Jeff said to bring them along. If they're fussy, we'll have plenty of people there to help."

"You sure you want to go?" He thought of how much stuff they would have to take with them. Was it worth it for a few hours playing Scene It or Cranium?

She laughed. "I'm sure. I'm ready for some fun. Getting more rest has made a world of difference."

Over the past week, the twins had slept for longer stretches at night, a change that had improved the moods of both parents.

"So what do you say, Al?"

"Sure. Why not?"

∼

After hanging up the phone, Patti hurried into the walk-in closet to look for something to wear on Saturday. She'd lost a good portion of her baby weight but not enough to squeeze into her favorite jeans.

"I need to diet," she whispered as she slid hanger after hanger along the rod. Things either didn't fit or were out of season or out of style.

Maybe she could run down to Yvonne's Boutique on Saturday morning and find a nice pair of jeans that wouldn't make her look too fat. As quickly as the thought came, she discarded it. The boutique didn't have much in the way of fashionable jeans, and even if they did, Al would have a fit about the cost.

She sighed. She would have to make do with what she had.

If only Al wasn't such a penny-pincher. She hadn't expected that of him when they were courting. Why would she when he'd driven to Nampa often, taking her to movies and to dinner, buying her gifts? Of course, back then he'd lived in a basement apartment, driven a car that was over two decades old, and carried a zero balance on his one and only credit card. Now he had a family of four to support.

*He does the best he can.*

She shook her head. Al wasn't a penny-pincher. It was unfair to think such things about him. He was a good provider, a good husband, a good father.

Patti left the walk-in and headed out of the bedroom, hoping the twins would sleep another thirty minutes. That would give her time to start dinner. She'd almost reached the kitchen when the doorbell rang.

*Please don't wake the babies.*

She opened the front door as the UPS truck pulled away

from the curb. On the stoop was a box. She leaned forward to see who it was from: Sweet Baby Things.

"Oh no."

She'd forgotten. Completely and totally forgotten. Last weekend, around four o'clock on Saturday morning, upset with Al, unable to sleep, continuing to debate adding formula to the twins' diet, she'd found this breast pump system while browsing online. "Amazing!" the consumer reviews said. "The most advanced system available to mothers," the manufacturer promised.

*"Patti, I thought breast-feeding was the better way to go."* That's what Al had said the day before she ordered the pump. He hadn't wanted her to stop nursing the babies.

And so she'd ordered the fancy pump.

For $320, plus tax and shipping.

Her stomach churned as she lifted the box and carried it inside.

She'd meant to tell him about it the day she ordered it. Really she had. But how could she, after he made such a big deal over the forty dollars she spent for those books? And when they'd made up after the fight, she hadn't wanted to spoil things again. So she'd waited.

Now they had plans for an evening of fun. She didn't want to spoil that either. No, she would have to wait a little longer. Another couple of days wouldn't matter that much. Monday. She could tell him on Monday.

She carried the box upstairs and stuck it in the corner of the closet.

## CHAPTER 5

Patti chose a frilly pink dress with matching tights and a bonnet with white lace trim for her daughter to wear on Saturday evening. For her son, she chose a tiny pair of jeans with a blue shirt and suspenders.

"Look at you, little cowboy." She held Weston up to the mirror. "You're too adorable for words." She kissed the soft crook of his neck. "Mommy loves you."

"And Daddy loves Mommy."

She met Al's gaze in the mirror. He stood in the bedroom doorway, smiling at them.

"Are you ready?"

"I think so." She turned. "The diaper bag is packed, and their blankets are already in the car, in case it turns cold while we're out."

Al walked toward her. "Here. Let me have Wes, and you can get Sunni." As he took the baby from her arms, he leaned forward and kissed her on the cheek. "You look pretty tonight."

Her cheeks grew warm. Silly to blush at a compliment from her husband, but the words were so nice to hear. "Thanks."

"I'm glad we're doing this."

"Me too."

"Let's go."

With a nod, she turned toward the pink bassinet and lifted Sunni into her arms. Her daughter was all smiles. Patti hoped she would stay that way for a few hours.

Twenty minutes later, they pulled into Jeff Cavanaugh's driveway. Before they had the babies out of their infant car seats, their friend was waiting for them on the sidewalk.

"Good to see you two." Jeff came around the minivan to stand near Patti. "Can I help with anything?"

"If you wouldn't mind, there's a large diaper bag and a couple of blankets in the back. Could you get them for me?"

"Glad to." He moved to comply.

Al asked, "Who else did you invite over tonight?"

"Your brother and his girlfriend. A couple more of Penny's teacher friends. And you two. That makes eight adults. Pretty much packs my living room." He slapped Al on the back. "Come on. You're the last to arrive. Everybody's in the kitchen, eating snacks. We'd better join them before the food's gone."

"If my brother's in there, it's probably gone already."

Patti laughed as she headed up the sidewalk. Her husband spoke only half in jest. Eric Bedford, five years younger than Al, was tall, thin, and always hungry.

They were barely in the door before Penny and the three other women gathered around the babies. In moments, both Sunni and Weston were out of their carriers, *oohed* and *ahhed* over, and passed from one set of arms to another.

Penny touched Patti's shoulder. "Patti, you know Susan."

She smiled at Eric's girlfriend. "Good to see you."

"You too."

"And you know Cassandra and Rene."

"How are you, Cassandra? Hi, Rene."

Rene Brewster had been in the same grade in school with Patti, although they'd never been close friends. Married at eighteen and divorced before she was twenty-five, Rene was plain and plump, her smiles never quite touching the perpetual melancholy in her dark eyes.

In contrast, the never-married Cassandra Coble sparkled with laughter. Whenever Patti saw her, she was struck by the younger woman's stunning beauty. She'd wondered more than once why Cassandra chose teaching in Hart's Crossing instead of modeling or acting or some other glamorous profession. She was certain Cassandra could have written her own ticket in Los Angeles or New York.

"Hey, Sis!"

Patti barely had time to turn before she found herself embraced by her brother-in-law.

"Man, you've gotten skinny." He gave her a peck on the cheek.

"Hardly." She kissed him back. "And you won't stay skinny if you keep eating everything in sight."

He feigned offense. "Where's that nephew of mine? He won't insult me."

"Good luck getting him away from Susan."

∽

IT'S GOOD TO SEE PATTI ENJOYING HERSELF, AL THOUGHT AS HE watched from the opposite side of the kitchen island. His wife hadn't looked this carefree since before the twins were born.

How much of that was his fault?

Things had been better between them this past week. They hadn't fought once, and he was grateful. He didn't like to argue with his wife. He wanted to make her happy, and he seemed to fail at that too often. Half the time he didn't know what he did to start their disagreements, but he did seem to be responsible the majority of the time.

"Troubles, Al?" Cassandra stepped to his side.

"No." He shook his head. "I was thinking it's been awhile since Patti and I got together with friends like this."

"Well, I imagine being the parents of twins keeps you more than a little busy."

"Yeah." He looked across the kitchen again, watching as Patti placed Weston in Eric's arms. "It can be crazy."

"But you love being a dad." Cassandra laid her hand lightly on his wrist. "I can see it in your eyes."

"Yeah, I love it."

"It's a big responsibility. A wife and kids, mortgage and a job." Her voice lowered. "I admire you, Al. You're a special guy."

His skin felt hot beneath her fingertips. The musky scent of her cologne filled his nostrils as she leaned closer.

"Your wife's a lucky girl."

Something dangerous coiled inside Al, an awareness of a woman who found him ... interesting.

A slight smile curved the corners of Cassandra's mouth. Her eyebrows arched, as if she'd asked a question. Was she flirting with him? No. They were talking about his wife, for Pete's sake. He was imagining things—and not the sort of things he should imagine.

"Hey, everyone," Jeff said in a loud voice. "Let's get started. The Balderdash game board's set up in the living room."

Cassandra's smile broadened. "This should be fun. I love word games."

Al watched her walk away, then turned to look at Patti. But his wife's back was toward him as she, too, followed Jeff into the living room.

∽

SOME THINGS A WIFE KNEW. NO ONE HAD TO TELL HER. SHE JUST knew. Like that instant her husband noticed Cassandra in a new way.

The joy went out of Patti's evening, right then and there.

Within a half hour of the start of the first game, she had to step out of the room so she could nurse Sunni. Seated in the eating nook, she listened to the sudden bouts of laughter coming from the living room. She swore she could pick out the exact lilt of Cassandra's laugh mixing with Al's deeper one.

The room turned cold. Her breath felt labored.

Was she jealous? She needn't be. Al might notice a beautiful woman like Cassandra, but he wouldn't stray. He loved her.

So why did she feel alone and rejected? And afraid.

She thought of the extra weight clinging to her hips and thighs, of the loose skin on her belly that hadn't yet snapped back to its previous firmness. Would it ever? Did it bother Al that she wasn't as lithe as when they'd married? He never said so. He told her she was beautiful. But was that true? Or was it something he thought he needed to say?

Tears pooled in her eyes, and a lump formed in her throat.

*"And Daddy loves Mommy."*

The memory of Al's words soothed her a little. Cassandra was her husband's colleague. Nothing more. She had nothing to fear.

Did she?

No, of course not. She was letting her hormones run away with her emotions again.

After Sunni was fed and burped, Patti placed the baby in her infant seat and returned to the living room just as Al was declared the winner.

Jeff said, "I never knew you were such a good liar, Bedford."

"Liar? Please. It was pure skill, my friend. I'm adept at language arts."

"Yeah. Sure."

Cassandra leaned forward and plucked her game piece off the board, then moved it back to the starting point. "I was only three spots behind. Next time I'll win."

"Not if I can keep you from it." Penny looked at Jeff. "Is there a kid's version of this game?"

He shrugged. "Don't know."

"It might be a fun way to teach word definitions. Especially for older kids." Penny turned toward Al. "Maybe the winner could get special privileges on that combined field trip for the fifth and sixth graders."

Cassandra clapped her hands together. "Oh, I have something even better. We could pit my fifth graders against Al's six graders. My students would love it. And we'd win, too."

"Hey!" Al wore an insulted expression. "You're forgetting that the sixth grade teacher ... that would be me ... already beat the fifth grade teacher." He grinned. "That would be you."

"He's got you there, Cassandra," Jeff said.

Patti listened to the good-natured banter and felt herself shriveling on the inside. Left out. Excluded.

Did Al even remember she was there?

∽

It was nearly midnight by the time Al drove the minivan into the garage and cut the engine. "I'm glad you accepted Jeff's invitation. It was fun."

"Yes," Patti replied softly as she opened the passenger side door.

He got out, too, and went around the car to help her with the babies, both of them sound asleep. "Didn't you have fun?"

"It was alright." She headed into the house, diaper bag on one shoulder, Sunni's infant carrier gripped with two hands.

He followed with Weston. "Did something happen to upset you?"

"No."

"Something's wrong."

"Nothing's wrong." Her tone held an edge of warning.

"You're sure?"

"I'm sure."

He frowned. She wasn't telling the truth. Something was wrong. She'd enjoyed herself when they first got to Jeff's, but then she'd suddenly stopped participating. The twins hadn't been a lot of trouble. Not enough to keep her from playing the game with the others.

As they put the babies to bed, Al's thoughts replayed the events of the evening. For the life of him, he couldn't figure out what had spoiled things for Patti. She'd been all smiles for a while. Had someone said something to hurt her feelings? If so, he didn't know what.

He went downstairs to turn off the lights and check the locks, stopping long enough in the kitchen to put a couple of glasses into the dishwasher. When he looked up, Patti was watching him from the doorway.

"Al?" Her voice was soft and sad. "Why don't you tell me about what's happening at school? I didn't know any of the things you and the others talked about tonight. Jeff knows more from Penny than I do from you, and he's only her boyfriend."

He straightened. "What should I have told you?"

"Well, what about the field trip you're planning for the fifth and sixth graders."

He had the feeling he should understand more than she said. "We haven't firmed anything up yet. What's to tell?"

"Jeff knew." Tears slipped down her cheeks.

Why was she crying? Over a field trip?

"Penny isn't even involved, but she told Jeff about it."

Weariness washed over Al. He was tired of doing or saying the wrong thing all the time. Why couldn't something go right between them? Why couldn't Patti sustain a good mood for longer than five minutes?

Swallowing a sigh, he said, "Honey, I'm sorry. I didn't know you wanted me to tell you everything about my workday. But if that's what you want, I'll tell you." He stepped around the kitchen island and pulled her into his arms. "I promise."

## CHAPTER 6

I went to church alone the next morning. Patti said she was too tired to go. She and the twins would stay home.

To be honest, it was a relief. No minivan. No diaper bags. No infant carriers. No temperamental wife who was either angry or in tears.

*Great attitude for a Sunday.*

But who could blame him? He felt as if he were trapped in a pinball machine, never knowing what was going to bang into him next. *Boing! Boing! Boing!* One minute Patti was in a good mood, and the next she was mad or crying. Or both.

Arriving late, he slipped into the empty back row and joined with the singing in progress, but his worship wasn't heartfelt. He didn't get lost in the lyrics and music, not like he did most Sundays. His thoughts kept drifting to Patti. He kept wondering what he was doing wrong, why they weren't as happy as they used to be.

She was unhappy too often.

He was unhappy too often.

*God, what's wrong with us?*

The music ended, and the people in the row in front of him turned to say good morning and shake his hand. He pasted on a smile, pretending all was well.

*Hypocrite.*

~

Patti carried the box from Sweet Baby Things into the nursery. Two matching cribs were placed against opposite walls, two matching dressers beside them, the drawers packed with baby clothes. The way the twins were growing, they would soon be sleeping here rather than in their bassinets in the master bedroom.

Kneeling on the floor beneath the large window, she cut the packing tape on the box and opened the lid to look at her latest purchase. Al wouldn't be happy when he saw the price tag.

But how could he complain? She needed this. Wasn't he always telling her they had to cut the *wants* and buy the *needs*? Well, this was a need. Even he would have to see that.

Except she should have discussed it with him before placing the order. Over three hundred dollars. How could she spend that kind of money without checking with him first? But hadn't he said he didn't want her to use formula? So wasn't this the next logical step?

Her stomach churned as she imagined their raised voices. She sat on the floor, leaned her back against the wall, and closed her eyes.

*I don't want to fight anymore. I don't want to be a nag.*

A nagging wife was as annoying as the constant dripping on a rainy day. That's what Proverbs said. That's what she'd become to Al. A constant dripping. A spendthrift who spent three hundred dollars in the middle of the night.

The image of the carefree Cassandra popped into her head, and she felt sick to her stomach. Sick with dread. Cassandra liked Al, maybe a little too much. Cassandra was gorgeous, thin, and employed in the same profession that Al loved with his whole heart.

There wasn't anything interesting about Patti. Not anymore. When she and Al were dating, she'd often talked to him about various manuscripts as she shepherded them through the publishing process. She'd sung the praises of some wonderful new author. Sometimes she'd asked him, as a man, if he would read a story about this or that.

Nowadays, her conversations were about babies and diapers and housework and how tired she was. Some days she felt lucky to make it into the shower. She spent money she shouldn't, lost her temper too easily, and cried over nothing.

Speaking of tears...

She grabbed a cloth diaper from the stack on the nearby changing table and dried her eyes. Then she allowed her gaze to sweep the nursery, remembering when she and Al had painted the room a few months before the twins were born.

It had been a warm Saturday in early May, warm enough to open the windows while they worked. Al had stood on the stepladder, carefully applying the sky blue paint on the wall near the ceiling, while Patti had worked with equal care around the white window casing. They'd been at it about an hour when she paused to stretch. Her back had ached, and she'd felt starved for air. Sometimes she would have sworn one of the babies slept on top of her lungs. A tiny moan escaped her lips as she'd released a deep breath of air.

Al had been down the ladder in an instant. "You okay?" he'd asked, his face wreathed in concern. "Maybe you should go sit down."

"Don't be silly. I just needed to stretch. I'm all right."

"I should have asked Eric to help. You shouldn't be around these paint fumes."

She'd set the brush on the edge of the paint can, then with

hands on his shoulders, had pulled him forward for a kiss, her distended belly trying its best to keep them apart. "Stop worrying. The window's open. There's plenty of fresh air."

She'd started to draw away. He'd pulled her close again.

"I like those flecks of blue in your hair. Did I tell you that?" Laughter had filled his eyes.

"I've got paint in my hair?"

He'd nodded. "I like it. Goes with the paint on your nose."

"I don't have paint on my nose."

He'd taken his right thumb and drawn it across the tip of her nose, then held it up for her to see. Sure enough, there had been a smudge of blue paint on it. His smile had broadened as he watched her.

In a flash of insight, she'd guessed the truth. "The paint was on your thumb. You just put it on my nose. Why you …" She'd clasped his head between her hands and pulled him downward, as if for a kiss. But at the last moment, she'd turned and rubbed the end of her nose against his, Eskimo-style. "Ha! Got you back."

"Mrs. Bedford, you're in serious trouble now." He'd swept her off her feet and into his arms, carrying her out of the nursery and into their bedroom while he'd peppered her with kisses and spread the blue paint around.

Oh, that had been a happy day. Just one of many happy days as they'd painted and decorated this room and dreamed of what it would be like when the babies arrived.

It hadn't been so very long ago. Only a matter of months. Could they be happy like that again?

*Please, God. Let us be happy like that again.*

∽

THE SERMON THAT MORNING WAS ON STEWARDSHIP, AND AL FELT God trying to tell him something through the pastor's words.

He had an awful feeling that he wasn't doing much of a job of managing God's blessings.

He shouldn't have let Patti talk him into buying their house. It was too much for them with only one salary. And it wasn't only the mortgage. It was the heat and electricity and water and sewer, too. And the insurance.

But what could he do about all of that now? Sell the house? Patti would be heartbroken. Wasn't she sad enough already?

With those glum thoughts roiling in his head, Al arrived at the side exit of the church at the same time as Till Hart.

"Good morning, Al." The older woman smiled at him. "Where's that pretty wife of yours? Not to mention those precious babies."

"They stayed home this morning, Miss Hart. Patti was feeling a bit run-down and wanted to rest."

"Oh? I hope she isn't catching that bug that's been going around. Francine was sick last week and has been coughing up a storm ever since. Tell Patti I'll pray for her."

*Pray for us both. We need it.* "I will."

Her brows drew together. "You look a little peaked yourself. Are you all right?"

"Yes," he lied. "I'm fine." He pushed open the glass door and motioned her through.

"Well, all right then." She didn't sound convinced. "Be sure to tell Patti that she can call on me if she needs a hand with the little ones. I'm a good babysitter."

"Thanks, Miss Hart. I'll tell her."

They said their farewells on the sidewalk before turning in different directions, Al headed for the parking lot, Till Hart walking home as she always did in nice weather.

He made it to his car without running into others who might want to pass the time of day. Thankful for that—not wanting to feel more of a hypocrite than he already did—he slipped into the red Spider, then sat there, hands on the steering wheel, not wanting to go home yet, not sure what he would say to Patti when he got there.

Maybe a drive would help clear his head.

He started the engine, left the parking lot, and followed the road out of Hart's Crossing, picking up speed as he reached the main highway. The wind felt good in his hair, and for a time, he thought of nothing except the way the sports car hugged the road. But eventually, he remembered why he took the drive in the first place. To figure things out. To figure Patti out.

He'd driven several miles into the mountains by the time he slowed the car and turned off the road at a lookout point. He parked near the Idaho highway historical marker and got out, walking to the metal railing that overlooked the valley.

*Figure out Patti.*

Was that even possible? Could a man really understand a woman? He used to think he could, but lately ...

He thought back to their honeymoon. They'd planned their wedding to coincide with the beginning of spring break and had left the next day for a week in Hawaii. Each night, they'd taken long walks on the beach, holding hands, sharing their hopes and dreams for the future. Even when they'd said nothing, it seemed they'd been in communion with each other.

When had that stopped? When had he stopped knowing what she wanted before she asked? It seemed to him it was about the same time that he started waking up in the middle of the night, wondering how he could make his paycheck stretch another week, wondering if their credit was going to end up in ruins. Or worse. He tried to make Patti understand without letting her know how worried he was. He tried, but he wasn't doing a good job of it. They never talked about money these days. They fought over it.

How could he make things better? They never should have bought that house. Not after Patti lost her editing job. Not when they were about to start a family with two babies at once. Oh, their finances looked tight but okay on paper. But most of the time, he felt like he couldn't breathe when his thoughts turned to money.

He shook his head, a rueful smile touching his lips. He'd come up here to think about Patti, and where were his thoughts? Back on their finances instead. Only maybe the two were tied together.

He loved his wife. He wanted her to be happy all the time, not just now and then. He wanted her to laugh the way she used to. He wanted her to look at him with trust, with eyes that said, "I know you'll never hurt or disappoint me."

*How do I make that happen, God? How?*

∽

A TWIN IN EACH ARM, PATTI GLANCED AT THE MANTEL CLOCK IN the living room, turned, and walked back to the kitchen. The clock on the stove said the same thing: 1:37.

Where was Al? He should have been home more than an hour ago.

She paced to the living room window and stared out at the street.

This wasn't like him, not to come home, not to call if delayed. Even when he was angry with her, he wasn't the thoughtless sort. He was dependable, the type of man who did what he said he would do, who checked his day planner so he never missed an appointment, and who kept the budget in a spreadsheet so the bills were paid on time. She liked those qualities about him. He made her feel safe.

Her own father had none of those qualities. Soon after he left her mother, her dad had moved away from Hart's Crossing. Phone calls had dwindled from once a month to once a year to an occasional birthday or Christmas. He hadn't made it to Patti and Al's wedding.

Weston started to fuss, an outward expression of his mother's inward feelings. With a soft moan, she turned from the window and carried the babies toward the stairs. Her right foot was on the bottom step when she heard the garage door open. She turned toward the kitchen. A few moments later, Al came into view.

*Where were you? Why didn't you call me?*

"Sorry I didn't come straight home. I ... I went for a drive. I needed time to think."

She pictured Cassandra, placing her fingers against Al's wrist. "What about?" Her heart raced. Maybe she didn't want to hear his answer.

"About why we fight so much when neither one of us wants to."

Her heart stopped racing. It hardly seemed to beat at all. "Did you figure it out?"

"Not yet, but I will."

She swallowed the lump that had formed in her throat. "I was taking the twins upstairs. Their diapers need to be changed, and Wes is getting hungry."

"Here." Al moved toward her. "I'll help you." He took Weston into his arms.

What should she say to him? Was it better to talk or be silent? She wasn't sure. She used to be sure about everything. Now nothing seemed certain.

She turned and ascended the stairs, Al following right behind. They entered the master bedroom, took identical changing mats, baby wipes, and disposable diapers from the small bureau near the bassinets, then placed the mats and babies on the floor and knelt beside them.

"Miss Hart asked about you after the service," Al said. "She said to call her if you need a babysitter."

Here it was. The golden opportunity to tell him about her extravagant purchase.

"Al, I ..." She swallowed, searching for the words.

"Yeah?"

"Maybe we *can* use Miss Hart sometime. I ... I've decided to give the babies a bottle every now and then. So I don't have to be with them for every feeding. Not formula, though."

*Tell him. Tell him the whole truth.*

She glanced up, and the words stuck in her throat. He looked as uncertain as she felt. He didn't want to fight, and neither did she.

Tomorrow would be soon enough. She would tell him tomorrow.

## CHAPTER 7

Somehow, one day became two, which became three, which became more, and still Patti didn't tell Al about the charge on the credit card. Why make waves when they were getting along?

But her reprieve couldn't last forever. The credit card bill would arrive one of these days. Delaying would only make things worse. Unless she could get a little help. And there was only one person she could ask.

Early on Friday morning, she picked up the phone and dialed, punching in the extension when asked for it.

"Janet Alexander."

"Hi, Mom."

"Patti?"

"Sorry to call you at work."

"That's all right, dear. Let me close my office door." There was the sound of movement from the other end of the line. "There. Now tell me. What's up?"

"Nothing much. You know how it is in Hart's Crossing. One day's pretty much like another. The twins are growing like weeds, and Al and I are both well even though there's a virus or the flu or something going around since school started."

"Are you getting more rest?"

"Yes. The twins are sleeping longer stretches at night. Not all the way through but almost."

"Good. That's always a relief."

Patti chewed her lower lip for a moment. "Mom you know how you told me that I needed to get out more? You know, have a breather from the babies, see a movie, go to the diner."

"Of course I remember."

"I haven't been able to yet, but I decided to start feeding the babies sometimes from a bottle so they'll get used to it. Then we can hire a sitter, and Al and I can go out together. Only we're both against the idea of using formula." Her words came faster. "Anyway, I was looking around online, and I found this breast pump that all the mothers rave about, so I ordered it. It's absolutely the perfect thing. It's making a huge difference." She drew a quick breath. "Only, I need a little help with the cost of it."

"How much?"

Her voice lowered. "Three hundred dollars."

"Three hundred dollars? My gracious, Patricia Ann. It must be made of pure gold."

"No." She choked on a sob. "It isn't."

"Patti? What's wrong?"

"Nothing." Her voice dropped to a whisper. "Everything."

"Take a deep breath, honey."

Patti wiped at the tears rolling down her cheeks. "I'm so tired of crying, Mom. I feel like such a baby. I'm trying to make a nice home for Al and the twins. I love them so much. But it seems like I can't do anything right. Al and I have been fighting a lot. Mostly about money."

Her mother was silent for a while before saying, "Did you argue about the three hundred dollars?"

"Not yet."

"You haven't told him you bought it?"

"No."

"Oh, honey. Keeping secrets isn't good for a marriage."

Patti stared out the window at the backyard. "I know. And it won't be a secret for long because the credit card statement is about due." She sucked in a breath and let it out. "Will you help me, Mom? If you lend me the money, I'll pay you back a little each month."

She hated the silence that followed. She could imagine the wheels turning in her mom's head as she debated the pros and cons of bailing Patti out of trouble. The amount of money wouldn't bother her mother. Janet and Doug Alexander lived comfortable lives, and both made good incomes in their respective careers. Her mom's concern would be whether or not giving Patti the money was the right thing to do, the best thing to do.

At last, the silence ended.

"I'll give you the money, dear, on one condition. Actually, several conditions. First, you tell Al what you did. No more secrets. The two of you need to have a serious conversation about your finances and then live within the boundaries. Second, if you two are fighting as much as you say you are, you need to consider counseling. Two people can love each other and still need help learning to communicate. There is no shame in that. And third, tell your doctor how you're feeling. Maybe the problem is more than lack of sleep or a need to get out of the house a bit more."

Patti didn't protest the conditions her mom set. She had no right to protest. Besides, it was good advice. Even in her emotional state she recognized that. "Okay."

"I'll put the check in the mail today."

"Thanks, Mom. I really appreciate it. Really."

"I know, dear. I love you very much. You take care of yourself, and give my love to Al and the babies."

"I will. I love you too. Bye."

"Good-bye."

With a sigh, Patti returned the handset to the charger, her thoughts racing ahead to that evening and the promised conversation with her husband.

∽

AL STOOD ON THE SPOT WHERE BLACKTOP MET SCHOOLYARD AND watched the kids at play during their lunch break. Laughter and shouts abounded. There was a group climbing on the playground equipment, others kicking around a soccer ball, a few taking swings at a baseball with a bat, some sitting in bunches on the grass. No injuries. No fighting. That was just the way he wanted it when he was assigned playground duty.

"Look out!"

He turned at the same moment the baseball went zipping past his head. He took a quick step backward. Not that it mattered. By that time, the ball was past him and bouncing across the blacktop.

Lyssa Sampson jogged toward him. "Sorry, Mr. Bedford. You okay?"

"Yeah." He touched his temple, as if checking to see if he'd been hit. "Better watch those wild pitches."

"I didn't throw it." She jerked a thumb behind her. "It was a foul ball. Blame Vince. He hit it."

As if he'd heard what Lyssa said, Vince Johnson shouted, "Sorry, Mr. Bedford."

Al waved at the boy to let him know all was well.

Lyssa hurried after the baseball, obviously eager to return to the game.

Al chuckled. Moments like this, there was no doubt in his heart that he was born to be a teacher. He loved working with kids, shaping young minds, challenging them to achieve great things. He had to love it. Nobody entered public education—especially in a small town school district—because they want to get rich.

*Rich isn't necessary, but more would be nice.*

The thought brought a frown to his brow. He hated that money—or the lack thereof—was constantly on his mind. It made him feel petty and complaining. Shouldn't he have an attitude of gratitude instead? Shouldn't his first thoughts be about how much God had blessed him?

He turned, preparing to walk to the opposite end of the schoolyard. That's when he saw Cassandra heading toward him. She smiled, and there was a jaunty spring in her step that made her seem not a whole lot older than some of the kids on the playground.

"Did you hear?" she asked as she drew near.

"Hear what?"

"Our field trip to Craters of the Moon is a definite go."

"That's great."

"I know. I can think of at least a dozen projects my class can work on in relation to it."

Cassandra's excitement was palpable. Would she one day find herself worried about paying the mortgage and car payment and grocery bill from her teacher's salary?

"Al? What's troubling you?"

It bothered him that she could read him so well. It felt … wrong. Why was that?

He shook his head. "Nothing."

"If you ever need to talk, you know I'm only a classroom away."

"Sure. Thanks." He was saved from saying more by the ringing of the school bell, calling kids back to class.

GRETCHEN LIVINGSTON, AN ATTRACTIVE WOMAN IN HER MID-thirties, took a sip of vanilla chai tea and smiled. "Patti, this is so good. Thanks for making me a cup."

"I'm glad you like it."

Patti's neighbor ran her fingers through her short hair. "Oh, my. It's good to have a weekday off. It's so much easier to accomplish things around the house when I'm the only one at home."

"Sometimes I don't think I'll catch up until the twins are in high school."

Gretchen laughed. "I remember feeling that way when Amy was a baby. I can only imagine what it's like for you with two babies."

"Speaking of Amy." Patti sat down opposite Gretchen and motioned with her head toward the family room where the girl sat with the twins. "She's been such a help to me."

"Well, don't let her become a pest. You send her home anytime you don't want her here."

"She's never a pest, believe me. I hope my two will be as well-mannered when they're thirteen."

Gretchen smiled again. "That's a great compliment. Thanks."

"It's the truth." Patti lowered her gaze to the cup on the table. "Gretchen, when Amy was a newborn, were you ever ... did you ever—" She stopped and drew in a deep breath. "I'm so moody lately. Mom thinks maybe I should see a counselor. She wonders if I might have postpartum depression or something." As soon as she said it, she was sorry. She liked Gretchen and all, but they weren't close friends. Did she want her neighbors knowing her deep dark secrets? No!

Gretchen gave her shoulders a slight shrug as she shook her head. "I didn't get depressed after Amy was born, but I was really tired, so everything seemed twice as hard as it really was." She took another sip of tea. "But if you decide you need a counselor, I can recommend someone to you. Hayley Young. Do you know her?"

Patti shook her head.

"She has an office on Idaho south of Main Street. Very soft spoken and gentle. I went to see her a couple of years ago for a few months when I was struggling with something. She was a great help to me."

Gretchen couldn't know it, but just hearing she'd sought the help of a counselor herself made Patti feel less of a failure as a wife and mom. And as a woman.

"Now, I'd better get home so I can accomplish a few more of those nagging to-do items." Gretchen finished the last of her tea, then rose and carried her cup to the kitchen sink. As she headed for the back door, she called, "Amy, don't forget Mrs. Hargrove is picking you up at five o'clock."

"I won't, Mom. See you in a while."

Patti followed Gretchen to the door. "Thanks for coming over. And for telling me about Hayley Young."

"Glad to help, Patti. Have a nice evening."

"We will."

As she closed the back door, she breathed a silent prayer. *Please, let it be a nice evening.*

## CHAPTER 8

Delicious odors greeted Al as he entered the kitchen. Patti stood at the counter, holding the lid of the electric frying pan in one hand and a large pronged fork in the other.

"Smells good." It was one of his favorite meals, a juicy roast cooked with onions, carrots, and potatoes. When they were first married, Patti had asked his mother to show her how to prepare the dinner the way he liked it.

She turned her head and smiled. "Hi, honey. You're home just in time." She set the lid on the pan. "Dinner should be ready soon."

"The twins asleep?" He stepped forward and kissed her on the lips.

"Mmm."

He drew back. "Does that mean yes or no?"

She cocked her head toward the family room. "Have a look."

Lately, he and Patti had been careful what they said and how they said it. It was exhausting. A little like the proverbial walking on eggshells. But their methods seemed to be working.

He moved toward the family room. There, seated in the rocking chair, was Amy Livingston, Sunni in the crook of one arm, a bottle of milk in her opposite hand. Weston lay on a blanket on the floor, staring at a portable mobile.

"Amy came over after school again." Patti stepped to his side. "She already fed Wes, and now she's taking care of Sunni. I never would have gotten dinner ready on time without her help."

The girl glanced over her shoulder. "Hi, Mr. Bedford."

"Hey, Amy."

Patti touched his arm. "They've taken to the bottles of breast milk without complaint." Her voice lowered. "I thought maybe we could ask Amy and Miss Hart to watch the babies for a few hours next weekend or the one after so you and I could go out to eat and maybe see a movie."

"Amy *and* Miss Hart?"

"Yes. I'm afraid the twins would be too much for Miss Hart alone. She is seventy-six, after all. Amy's a great help, but she's still kind of young to be in charge. So I thought the two of them …" She let the explanation drift into silence, unfinished.

He cupped the side of her face with his right hand. "Sounds like a good idea to me. I'll check the paper and see what's playing at the Apollo."

The local weekly newspaper, the *Mountain View Press*, listed movie schedules for four weeks out. Although the Apollo Theater—which showed movies Friday through Sunday—rarely got first-run movies, most of the good films found their way to Hart's Crossing eventually. There should be something worth seeing in the next couple of weeks.

Patti's smile made her brown eyes sparkle. "Great." She kissed him on the cheek. "I'd better check on the roast. I don't want it to dry out."

Al watched her go, then entered the family room and lifted

his son into his arms. "Amy, would you like to ask your mom if you can stay for dinner? I'm sure there's plenty."

"No, thanks. I'm gonna spend the night at a friend's house. I'll have to leave pretty soon." She set the empty bottle aside and lifted Sunni to her cloth-covered shoulder, softly patting her back.

"You're getting to be a pro at that."

"Thanks. I took a child-care class at the school this summer. I like helping Mrs. Bedford with the babies. They're sweet." She laughed. "Most of the time."

Al chuckled as he settled onto the sofa. "Most of the time." He pressed his nose into the curve of Weston's shoulder and breathed in the baby softness. It was like a breath of joy, a reminder of how blessed he was, and how often he let the cares of the world make him forget it.

*Thank you, Father, for trusting me with this family.*

"Mr. Bedford?"

He opened his eyes to find Amy standing near the sofa.

"Do you want to hold Sunni too, or should I put her on the blanket? I gotta go now."

"I'll take her, Amy. Thanks."

The girl placed Sunni in the crook of Al's free arm, the two babies forming a *V* against his chest. "Did Mrs. Bedford tell you I'm writing for the school newspaper this year?"

"No, she didn't."

"She's helping me with some of my stories. You know. With the grammar and stuff. I'm thinking maybe someday I'll write a book and Mrs. Bedford could be my editor. Wouldn't that be cool?"

"Sure would."

She gave him a half wave, turned on her heel, and left, calling to Patti as she passed through the kitchen, "See you later, Mrs. Bedford."

"Bye, Amy," Patti returned. "Thanks for everything."

Al glanced from one twin to the other and felt the joy of fatherhood well up in him again. "Either one of you planning to be a writer when you grow up?"

Weston blew bubbles from his mouth and wriggled in Al's arm.

"Guess that means no." He leaned his head against the back of the sofa. *I wonder what you will be.*

His thoughts drifted to scenes from his own childhood. Warm summer days spent playing ball with friends or camping out in his backyard with his younger brother. Picnics with his mom's famous fried chicken, baked beans, coleslaw, and corn on the cob. Helping his dad feed the livestock and the way hay got into his hair and clothes, making him itch. Learning to drive the old, beat-up, two-ton farm truck the summer he was twelve. Knowing just about everybody in town, neighbor helping neighbor. Strict but loving parents.

It was a good life that he remembered. He wanted his children to have a similar childhood—safe, happy, without want for anything they needed. He would do anything to make that happen.

"Al? Dinner's ready." Patti stepped into view. "Are they awake?"

"Sunni's getting a little drowsy. Wes is wide awake, but I don't think he'll fuss if I put him down."

"Maybe they'll sleep while we eat."

"Hope so."

He rose from the sofa and carried the babies to the large blanket spread on the family room carpet, knelt, and laid them down. He waited to see if either would protest. They didn't.

After washing his hands in the kitchen sink, he went to the table, where Patti stood beside her chair, waiting for him. He kissed her cheek. "Everything looks great."

She gave him a tentative smile. "Sit down before it gets cold."

Something about her manner had changed since he first got home. She seemed nervous or tense. He decided not to say anything though. Better not to make waves. He could tell she was trying hard to please him. He didn't want to upset her by saying the wrong thing.

He held the back of her chair while she sat. Then he took his own place. He reached for her hand and bowed his head, and together they thanked God for all he provided.

∽

Several times during the meal, Al said how good it was, but Patti tasted little of what she put in her mouth. Her stomach was tied in too many knots to enjoy the dinner she'd labored over.

When should she tell him? When was the right time? While they were still eating? Or should she wait until they relaxed on the sofa? Maybe after a little television. Was one of his favorite shows on tonight? Perhaps she should let him watch it first.

No. She needed to do it now. She'd waited long enough. Another few minutes and she would explode from the tension she felt inside.

"Al." She set her fork on her plate. "I need to tell you something."

"What's that?"

*Just say it. Just get it out and over with.* "There's going to be a charge on the next credit card bill. It's from a store called Sweet Baby Things. The amount's pretty big, but I don't want you to be upset when you see it." She folded her hands in her lap, trying to hide her nerves. "My mom's paying for it. She's already sent the check. So you don't have to worry about it."

"What did you buy?"

"Remember when we had that discussion about adding formula to the twins' diet? Well, I decided you were right, that we didn't want to do that. The babies should stay on breast milk." She drew a quick breath and hurried on. "Mom thinks it would do us both good to get out, but we need babysitters, and the babysitters need to be able to feed the babies if they get hungry. So that's when I placed the order."

She was prevaricating, telling the truth and yet not quite. Why should it matter, she asked herself, that these things happened in a slightly different order?

"I still don't know what you bought."

She told him about the pump, explaining why it was absolutely top of the line and how terrific it was and why it would make her life as a nursing mother of twins so much easier. "It's what I used for those bottles Amy was feeding the babies when you got home." She couldn't tell from his expression what he was thinking.

"How much did it cost, Patti?"

"Three hundred and twenty dollars."

He echoed her in a soft voice. "Three hundred and twenty dollars. That's a lot."

"Mom's paying for it. Well, most of it. Three hundred is what she sent."

"She shouldn't have to pay for any of it." He placed his napkin on the table beside the plate and rose from his chair. With three strides, he arrived at the window, his hands shoved into the pockets of his trousers. "I should be able to buy the things you need."

Guilt twisted her insides.

"I should provide for my family."

"You *do* provide for us."

"Not well enough." He turned to face her, defeat in his eyes. "Maybe it's time I look for a position in a bigger school district.

If I start now, I might have another job by the start of the next school year."

Strange, she'd nagged him about that very thing for a number of months. But when he said it, it sounded awful.

"We don't have to decide that tonight," she said.

She wanted to go to him, put her arms around him, hold him tight, and tell him she loved him. Guilt kept her from doing so.

## CHAPTER 9

"Hey, hon." Al stood in the doorway to the garage, wiping greasy hands on a rag. "When I'm done changing the oil in the cars, how about we drive out to the farm."

Patti looked at her husband. The distance between them felt much farther than the width of the kitchen. "Sure. If you'd like."

"My folks haven't seen the twins in a week or so."

"I know. Your mom's got that charity event coming up soon, and your dad's getting ready for harvest."

They were talking but saying nothing that needed to be said. It was like being in a line dance and not knowing the steps, afraid to move, afraid to stand still.

He nodded. "Okay then. I'll give them a call and tell them we're coming after lunch." He looked as if he might say something more, then turned and stepped out of sight.

Seconds later, Patti heard the garage door close. The sound made her chest hurt. She went into the living room and sat on the sofa, closing her eyes, letting the temporary silence of the house envelop her.

She wanted things to be right between them. She wanted

things to be the way they used to be. She wanted to tell him all of her thoughts and feelings without hesitation. But how could she make that happen?

*Perhaps with God's help?*

She smiled sadly. She was no better at being honest with God than she was with Al. When was the last time she prayed, really prayed? When was the last time she tried to hear his voice?

Months. Many months. Long before she could blame it on the busyness of motherhood.

"I've made such a mess of things, Father. I've hurt Al, and I don't know how to undo the things I've done. Can you help me find my way? I don't even know how to start."

∼

AL'S GREAT-GRANDFATHER HAD MOVED TO SOUTH-CENTRAL IDAHO in 1915, soon after a canal system brought irrigation to the area. He started with 160 acres, and as his circumstances improved, he acquired more land, as did his son and his grandson, Al's dad. The Bedford farm today was nearly a thousand acres of apple orchards, corn fields, and row upon row of onions.

Within moments of Al bringing the minivan to a stop in front of the house, his mom appeared on the porch. "We're so glad you came," she called as she descended the steps.

Al got out of the van and hugged his mom. "Hope we're not intruding."

"Don't be silly. Seeing you and your family is the best part of any day." She kissed his cheek. "Now, let's get those babies into the house before they catch a chill."

"A chill? It's seventy-five degrees out."

She batted at his shoulder. "Don't argue with your mother."

"Yes, ma'am," he said with a laugh.

His mom rounded the minivan and hugged Patti. "How are you, dear?"

"I'm fine, Carolyne. Thanks."

"What can I do to help you?"

"If you'll carry Wes inside, I can handle Sunni and the diaper bag."

Al knew better than to get between grandmother and grandchildren. "Where's Dad?"

"Behind the barn. He's working on that old tractor he found at the auction last week."

"I'll see if I can give him a hand. Looks like you've got things under control here."

"Tell him there's pie when the two of you are ready to come in."

"What kind of pie?"

"Strawberry rhubarb."

"Mmm." Nobody made a better pie than his mom, and strawberry rhubarb was his favorite. "I think I'll tell him to hurry." He waited a moment, watching as the two women removed the infant seats from the back of the minivan. Then, seeing they wouldn't need his help, he strode toward the barn.

Mark Bedford farmed with modern equipment, but he had a penchant for antique tractors. He loved to buy, refurbish, and display them at the county fair. Tinkering with his collection brought him pleasure and relaxation.

Al found his dad lying on his back beneath a faded green John Deere. He stopped beside the large rear tire and leaned down. "Got yourself a new toy, I see."

"Hey, son. You here already? I thought I had another hour." His dad slid from under the tractor. "She's a beauty, isn't she? A 1953 Model 50. Runs pretty good. Won't take much to restore her." He stood and gave the machine an affectionate pat. "I got a good deal on her too."

"What does Mom think?"

His dad laughed. "Carolyne's just glad I've got a hobby that keeps me out from underfoot."

"But she might prefer model tractors to the real thing. They'd be cheaper and take up less space."

"True enough." He patted the antique tractor a second time before saying, "I imagine your mother's commandeered the grandkids. Suppose I ought to try to wrestle one of those babies away from her?"

"Not unless you want a broken arm. But she did say to tell you there's strawberry rhubarb pie ready for the eating."

"Well, what're we standing out here for?"

"My thoughts exactly."

"Help me put these tools away, will you?"

"Sure thing."

Within a matter of minutes, the tools were back in the toolbox and the toolbox was back in the barn. Then the two men started toward the house.

"Dad, I've been thinking about looking for a teaching position in one of the larger school districts. Maybe over in Boise."

His dad stopped walking. "You're not serious."

"Afraid so." He turned to face his father.

"But why?"

Al sighed. "Money." He shrugged. "My paycheck doesn't stretch far enough these days. Not with four of us."

"Do you need a loan? If you do, I can—"

"No, Dad. Thanks, but this is something I've got to work out for myself."

"When would you move?"

"Probably not until the next school year. I'll have to see what's out there. I guess it could be sooner than next fall, if a position opened up somewhere midterm, but that's not likely."

His dad raked his fingers through graying hair. "It'll break your mother's heart if you move away. Especially now that she's got grandchildren."

"Let's not say anything to her. It hasn't happened yet. It's just something I'm thinking about."

And the thinking weighed heavy on his heart.

∼

STANDING AT THE OPEN BACK DOOR, PATTI OBSERVED HER husband and father-in-law as they talked outside the large weathered barn. After a few moments, Mark placed a hand on Al's right shoulder. A gesture of comfort? Of sympathy?

Tears stung her eyes.

Al was unhappy, and it was her fault. She'd nagged at him. She'd lied to him. Worst of all, she'd made him feel like a failure as a husband and provider. What if she'd gone too far? What if he fell out of love with her?

"Is something wrong, Patti?"

Her mother-in-law's gentle voice drew her around. She opened her mouth to say nothing was wrong, but instead said, "Do you remember my dad?"

"Yes, I remember Grant. I never knew him well, of course. We didn't move in the same social circles."

"Do you think he ever loved my mom?"

Her mother-in-law rinsed the mixing bowl in her hand and set it in the dish drainer. Then she dried her hands on a towel before turning toward Patti. "That's a question you should ask your mother."

"She doesn't like to talk about him. Even after all these years. I remember how hurt she was when he left us. And then she got angry and stayed that way for a long time."

Carolyne leaned a hip against the counter, arms crossed over her chest. "What's this about, dear? Why are you asking about your dad?"

The unwelcome tears fell from Patti's eyes, tracing her cheeks. "Sometimes I think Al must be sorry he married me."

"Gracious. What a thing to say!"

"I've made him miserable lately."

Carolyne hurried to her side. "Come into the living room and sit down." With an arm around Patti's back, her mother-in-law steered her toward the sofa. "Now, tell me what's troubling you."

She wanted to comply. She wanted to pour out her heart, but doing so would feel like another betrayal of her husband. She'd done too much of that already. She'd hurt Al in too many ways.

"Patti." Carolyne's voice was gentle and low. "Are you afraid Al might do what your father did?"

There it was—her greatest fear, out in the open. What if he left her because of the things she'd said and done? What if he decided he couldn't live with her tears, her moods, her spending?

*What if I've made him so unhappy he turns to someone else?* She drew a shallow breath. *Someone like Cassandra Coble.*

She closed her eyes, wanting to shut out the pain in her heart.

"Al is nothing like Grant Sinclair." Carolyne placed the palm of her hand against Patti's cheek. "He isn't the type to walk out on his family. He loves you, and he loves those two precious babies. He isn't going anywhere without the three of you. I can promise you that. No matter what the trouble is, he'll go through it with you."

Patti looked at her mother-in-law, hoping she was right, wanting desperately to believe it.

Carolyne gave her an encouraging smile. "Every marriage goes through rough patches. Living with another person, no matter how much you love them, can be hard at times. And when you throw young kids into the mix..." She rolled her eyes. "When we were newlyweds, Mark and I used to fight like cats and dogs."

"You did?"

"Gracious, yes. That man was as stubborn as the day is long, and I was every bit as bad. My, we could butt heads. We still do, every now and then. And over the silliest things too."

Patti couldn't imagine her in-laws speaking a cross word to each other.

"Our biggest problem in the early years of marriage was I thought he should know what I felt, and he thought I should be able to read his mind. I've never known a single couple that worked for. It takes words to communicate."

Footsteps announced the arrival of the men on the back porch.

Carolyne stood. "Why don't you go wash away those tears? Then you and I can get ourselves a piece of that pie before those two eat it all." She smiled again. "And Patti, put away those worries. It'll turn out right. You'll see."

~

AL SLID THE EMPTY PLATE INTO THE CENTER OF THE TABLE.

"Would you like another slice?" his mom asked.

"Better not. Two was more than I needed." He pushed his chair back from the table and patted his stomach. "I should've stopped at one."

His dad rocked Weston on his thighs. "When you get to be my age, you'll have to stop at one. If I didn't limit myself, I'd weigh three hundred pounds by now."

Al smiled as he tried to picture an overweight Mark Bedford. Impossible to do. His father, now in his mid-fifties, still wore the same size trousers as when he'd graduated from college. Al knew this because his parents had renewed their wedding vows on their thirtieth anniversary, and his dad had been able to wear the suit he got married in.

His gaze traveled around the table as he remembered the Saturday he brought Patti home to meet his parents for the first time. After dating a couple of months, he knew Patti was destined to be more than just another girlfriend, and he wanted his family to know she was special to him. He remembered the way Patti laughed at his dad's jokes—even the lame ones—and raved over his mom's cooking.

More memories of other good times in this old farmhouse kitchen drifted into his mind. Christmases and Thanksgivings when his grandparents were still living. Birthday parties, both his and Eric's. The day he and Patti told his parents they were engaged. The day they announced they were expecting. Another day when they informed his folks they were having twins.

If he and Patti moved away from Hart's Crossing, would their kids have the same sort of rich memories as he had? How often would they get to see his parents? Would Wes have the opportunity to tinker with Grandpa Mark on some old tractor? Would Sunni learn to bake pies with Grandma Carolyne in this big old kitchen? Or even vice versa.

But maybe he was idealizing everything. Maybe they would make even better memories in a new home in a new town. Maybe if he wasn't so stressed over finances, he would be a better husband and dad.

*It's about more than money.*

He looked across the kitchen table at his wife who was listening to something his mom said. Love surged in his chest, a feeling so strong it was almost painful. Had she any idea how much he loved her?

*"And you husbands,"* Paul said in Ephesians, *"must love your wives with the same love Christ showed the church."*

Had he loved her that much? When he replayed the events of the past couple of weeks in his mind, he had to answer no. Even when he finally agreed that he would look into finding a better paying position, he'd done it with reluctance and an attitude that told her this was all her fault.

Pride. He'd let pride get in his way of doing the right things, of saying the right things.

*God, I'm sorry. Show me how to make it up to her.*

∼

Patti glanced across the table at her husband and found him watching her.

*I don't want us to leave Hart's Crossing. This is our home.*

She hoped her mother-in-law was wrong. She hoped Al could read her mind. At least this once.

*I'm sorry, Al.*

Somewhere in the New Testament, wives were instructed to respect their husbands. There hadn't been much respect going on when she was insisting on her own way, when she was buying things their budget couldn't handle, when she was asking for money from her mother behind his back. Or when she let fears surface, fears that he might one day walk out, the same way her father had. What sort of faith did that show? It didn't show faith. It said she didn't trust him. And perhaps he felt that lack of trust.

But she could change all that. She *must* change it. She needed to share her uncertainties and fears. She'd held back parts of herself from him since the day they met, and that was wrong of her. He was her husband. She needed to trust him with her full self, her full heart.

This morning, she'd told God she needed to know how to start setting things right. Well, now she had her answer. She would begin with trust. Trusting Al. Trusting God.

# CHAPTER 10

After putting the twins to bed for the night, Patti went in search of her husband. She found him in the family room with his laptop open, his fingers tapping on the keys.

"Are you working?" she asked as she sat on the sofa nearby.

He looked up. "I'm updating my resume."

"You don't need to do that."

"Yes, I do. It may take some time to find a better-paying position, but I think my qualifications are—"

"Al, I don't want you to find another job. I don't want us to move away from Hart's Crossing."

"You don't?" He closed the laptop. "What changed your mind?"

"I love you, Al, but I haven't shown it the way that I should. I … I've made things, possessions, this house, more important than they should be. I guess that's how I wanted you to prove your love for me. By providing all these things." She drew in a shuddery breath. "I was afraid, and the more afraid I was and the more we fought, the more wrong choices I made and the farther away you seemed."

Al set the laptop on the coffee table and reached for Patti's hand. "I'm not far away. I'm right here. I'll always be right here."

"I've been afraid that you wouldn't be. Always here with me, I mean."

"You have?"

"Yes."

"But—"

She reached up with her free hand and touched her index finger to his lips. "Let me finish."

He nodded, his gaze not leaving hers.

"My parents used to fight all the time before my dad walked out on us. When you and I started fighting, it brought up all of those unhappy memories. And then when I saw Cassandra flirting with you …"

Al's eyes widened.

"I was afraid I might be driving you to her."

"Patti, I would never be unfaithful, and I don't have any interest in Cassandra Coble."

She lowered her eyes to their clasped hands. "I know. Deep down inside, I know. But fear isn't very rational, is it?" When he didn't answer, she looked up again. "I think we should call Betty Frazier and put the house on the market. We can find a home with a smaller mortgage that is more suited to us."

"But you love this house."

"For the wrong reasons." Tears flooded her eyes. "And besides, I love you more."

With a tug on her hand, he drew her from the sofa and onto his lap, holding her close, her face nestled in the curve of his neck and shoulder.

"I'm sorry, Al. I'm sorry for not being honest, for not trusting you, for making you feel as if you've failed me. You haven't."

"I'm sorry, too." His breath brushed her ear as he spoke. "I could've done a lot of things differently. I love you, Patti."

She felt her body relax in his embrace. There was more that needed to be said between the two of them. It would take effort and patience and understanding to get their relationship back on track. But for now, it was enough to know they loved each other.

# EPILOGUE

December

"Merry Christmas, Mr. Bedford!" Lyssa Sampson called on her way out of the classroom.

"Merry Christmas, Lyssa. Enjoy the holidays."

"I will." The door swung closed behind her.

Ah, the sudden and very welcome silence.

Al made a quick sweep of the classroom, looking for anything that shouldn't be left behind until school resumed after the New Year. Finding nothing out of place, he returned to the front of the classroom. As he bent to retrieve his briefcase, his gaze alighted on the new photograph sitting on his desktop. There they were, the happy Bedford family—Al, Patti, Weston, and Sunni—all of them wearing red and white sweaters. Looking at the photograph made him grin every time.

"Knock, knock."

He turned. "Hey, beautiful."

Patti held the door open wide. "Are you ready to go?"

"I'm ready." He picked up his briefcase.

Twice a month, on the advice of their counselor, Al and Patti left the twins for a few hours with his parents or Miss Hart and Amy Livingston, and they did something fun, just the two of them. Dinner out, a movie, a walk in the park—it didn't matter what they did as long as both considered it fun and they did it together.

This afternoon they were decorating their new home for Christmas. The fifty-year-old house was surrounded by tall trees and mature shrubs, perfect for trimming with strings of lights. There were many couples he knew who wouldn't think hanging Christmas lights a fun activity, but he and Patti were both so glad to be moved into their new home before Christmas, they'd thought it a great idea.

Betty Frazier, their Realtor, said that closing on the sale of their old house and closing on the purchase of their new one so quickly had been nothing short of a miracle. Al agreed, especially since they were now debt free, except for their quite reasonable mortgage.

Arriving at the door, he set his briefcase on the floor so he could wrap his wife in his embrace and kiss her soundly. When they're lips parted, he said, "I love you."

Three simple words, but they spoke of trust and healing, determination and forgiveness, hopes and dreams. Thanks to wise counsel and a shared faith, they'd weathered the storm that had battered their marriage earlier in the year and come out stronger on the other side. Now he knew that when more trials came, as they did in every life, they would face them together.

With an arm still around Patti's shoulders, Al picked up his briefcase a second time and said, "Honey, let's go home."

ABOUT THE AUTHOR

Robin Lee Hatcher is the best-selling author of over eighty books. Her well-drawn characters and heartwarming stories of faith, courage, and love have earned her both critical acclaim and the devotion of readers. Her numerous awards include the Christy Award for Excellence in Christian Fiction, the RITA® Award for Best Inspirational Romance, Romantic Times Career Achievement Awards for Americana Romance and for Inspirational Fiction, the Carol Award, the 2011 Idahope Writer of the Year, and Lifetime Achievement Awards from both Romance Writers of America® (2001) and American Christian Fiction Writers (2014). *Catching Katie* was named one of the Best Books of 2004 by the Library Journal.

When not writing, Robin enjoys being with her family, spending time in the beautiful Idaho outdoors, Bible art journaling, reading books that make her cry, watching romantic movies, and decorative planning. A mother and grandmother, Robin makes her home on the outskirts of Boise, sharing it with a demanding Papillon dog and a persnickety tuxedo cat.

Learn more about Robin and her books by visiting her website at www.robinleehatcher.com

You can also find out more by joining her in the following ways:

Goodreads | Bookbub | Newsletter sign-up

ALSO BY ROBIN LEE HATCHER

**Stand Alone Titles**
*Make You Feel My Love*
*Even Forever*
*An Idaho Christmas*
*Here in Hart's Crossing*
*The Victory Club*
*Beyond the Shadows*
*Catching Katie*
*Whispers From Yesterday*
*The Shepherd's Voice*
*Ribbon of Years*
*Firstborn*
*The Forgiving Hour*
*Heart Rings*
*A Wish and a Prayer*
*When Love Blooms*
*A Carol for Christmas*
*Return to Me*
*Loving Libby*
*Wagered Heart*
*The Perfect Life*
*Speak to Me of Love*
*Trouble in Paradise*
*Another Chance to Love You*

*Bundle of Joy*

**The Coming to America Series**
*Dear Lady*
*Patterns of Love*
*In His Arms*
*Promised to Me*

**Where the Heart Lives Series**
*Belonging*
*Betrayal*
*Beloved*

**Books set in Kings Meadow**
*A Promise Kept*
*Love Without End*
*Whenever You Come Around*
*I Hope You Dance*
*Keeper of the Stars*

**Books set in Thunder Creek**
*You'll Think of Me*
*You're Gonna Love Me*

**The Sisters of Bethlehem Springs Series**
*A Vote of Confidence*
*Fit to Be Tied*
*A Matter of Character*

**Legacy of Faith series**
*Who I am With You*

*Cross My Heart*

*How Sweet It Is*

For a full list of books, visit www.robinleehatcher.com